Hare Today

Gone

Tomorrow

Other Titles by Author Pat Pratt

Old Jewels *A Tricycle Girls Mystery*

70-year-old self-proclaimed curmudgeon, Helen Boyer-Patterson, has been forced to reduce a life of independence to apartment-sized living at Golden Harvest Retirement Village. After a disgruntled settling in, sudden disappearances at the place pique her interest.

With lifelong friend, Maggie Taylor, and former fan-dancer, LeeAnne Warner, Helen forms HML—Healthy, Mature Ladies—Investigations—AKA the Tricycle Girls—to solve the crimes. There is no lack of suspects, but will the Tricycle Girls catch the jewel thieves or peddle into more trouble than they can ride out of?

No Stone Unturned *A Tricycle Girls Mystery*

Helen Patterson and her fellow Tricycle Girls, Maggie Taylor and LeeAnne Warner, embark on a week-long excursion to Stone Mountain, Georgia with other members of Golden Harvest, where they all reside. Along the way they encounter unwanted guests, unsavory characters, murder, and mayhem.

Helen and the girls have one week to catch the killer. The list of suspects is long, and Helen is right at the top because of her 60-year-old history with the deceased. They must solve the crime because all agree Helen would not look good in horizontal stripes.

Hare Today Gone Tomorrow

Pat Pratt

Pat Pratt Publishing

Publisher: Pat Pratt Publishing
Cover Design: Mystic Circle Books & Designs, LLC
Images: Courtesy of Pixabay

ISBN: 978-0-9980790-4-2 (Paperback)
978-0-9980790-5-9 (eBook)

Acknowledgments

There are many people to thank for the book you are holding. Top of the list are my local writers groups, Write On and Write Way, whose members all encouraged me when I was down and pushed me when I procrastinated.

A BIG thank you goes to Anita Dickason, friend, fellow writer, and former police person, who taught me the difference between a captain, a detective, and an officer. And, if that wasn't difficult enough, Anita took my random ideas for a book jacket design and turned them into a wonderful finished product. She also formatted the book, and did all the computer stuff that I am totally incapable of doing. Without her, this book would still be languishing in a dusty corner somewhere.

Last, but definitely not least, thanks to you, my readers. You kept asking when the next Tricycle Girls mystery would be available. Here it is. Hope you enjoy the reading as much as I enjoyed the writing.

Blessings

Pat Pratt

Table of Contents

HML

Healthy, Mature Ladies

Tricycle Girls

Investigation/Consultation

No Job Too Small

Chapter 1

The Halls Are Alive

I was in the middle of a tense scene in my latest nursery rhyme murder, 'Who killed Doc Robyn?'. Right at the moment where the heroine has devised a plan to apprehend the antagonist, her cell phone rings, alerts him, and he escapes again.

I jumped. Oh, wait, that was *my* cell phone. Drat! I pulled myself awake and fumbled for the wretched instrument on the table beside my recliner. Who dared call and disturb my reading – and my nap?

My name is Helen Boyer-Patterson, and I am a resident at Golden Harvest Retirement Village, in my home town of Loblolly, Georgia. Touted as "Upscale Apartments for Seniors", it's where your kids send you when your family home becomes more of a burden than a safe haven, and they don't want you underfoot and meddling in their lives. Not that I'd do that. I don't consider myself the meddling type. It's not so bad here; there's no upkeep to worry about. And, besides, my lifelong friend, Maggie Taylor, lives here. Maggie and I, along with our new-found friend, LeeAnne Warner, had formed a casual investigating business. We call ourselves The Tricycle Girls, and I am the Big Wheel of the operation. The activity keeps our minds alert, and we have been instrumental in helping solve some crimes in the last few months.

I tried to shake myself awake as the phone continued to ring. I had been doing a lot of napping since our senior group had returned from our vacation – and I use that term lightly – to Stone Mountain Park outside Atlanta, Georgia. That trip involved the death of Stanley Crowell, an old school acquaintance, and perennial bully and con man. His demise nearly landed me and my not-friend, Janine, The Snow Queen, Hopgood, in jail for his murder.

Neither of us had done it, of course, but it took the Tricycle Girls and all our gentlemen friends to clear up the mess. The man in charge of the case, Captain Rachett, might tell a different story of the outcome, but we all knew the truth.

Since our return home to Golden Harvest, I'd given my friends strict orders to keep their distance for a while. I was not ready or willing to be sucked into another of Maggie's grand schemes anytime soon.

The still blaring cell phone brought me out of my reverie. Caller ID announced it to be none other than dear, sweet Maggie. I flicked the phone on. "What?"

"And good afternoon to you, too," Maggie cheerily replied. "Come on down to the dining room for refreshments. LeeAnne and I saved you a seat."

"Oh, yay! What are we celebrating today? National Cinch Bug Day? Or maybe Nutty Squirrel Day? Sorry. Not interested!"

"Don't be that way, Helen," Maggie said. "And, actually, it's 'Month Without a Holiday' celebration, since August has no national holidays. Please join us. You've been holed up in your apartment for days. Emile made peach cobbler and homemade peach ice cream for the occasion."

"Well-l-l. Homemade ice cream? Not the store-bought stuff?"

"Yes," she said. "Bernie, El, and several other of the men, have been keeping an eye on it for hours, and it's being dished up right now. You'd better hurry, before it's gone!"

I groaned and dragged myself out of my comfy recliner to go be sociable. National Month Without a Holiday? Was that a real thing, or an excuse to congregate for no apparent reason? Well, there *was* homemade peach ice cream to consider!

I looked in the mirror, ran a comb through my short, white hair, and headed out the door. Maggie would probably say a few words about my wrinkled attire; but how dressed up does one need to get for a National Month Without a Holiday celebration, anyway?

I arrived at the dining room ready to enjoy the homemade ice cream and peach cobbler. My eyes and ears were assaulted by the sights and sounds of little people screaming and running rampant around the room. In my absence from activities around here had our quiet senior facility been converted into a daycare?

Maggie and LeeAnne waved from a table across the room, and I stomped over and plopped down in a vacant chair. "Where are the parents of these rowdy small people? My kids were never allowed to run wild in public. What's the world coming to?" I shook my head sadly. "There's absolutely no discipline anymore."

Maggie patted my arm as Elsworth Lumley strolled over. He placed two bowls of ice cream on the table, sat down beside her and pulled two spoons from his steel-gray shirt pocket.

She smiled lovingly into his gray eyes. "Thank you, El."

I glared at him. "Yes, thank you El. I guess I'll have to beat my

3

way through the hordes of ill-mannered children if I want ice cream."

"Or you could take this one."

I looked over my shoulder at the smiling face of Bernie Cox, the man who wanted to be more than my friend. Even seated, my 245-pound bulk seemed gargantuan to his compact 5'7" stature. "Hello, Bernie. That's sweet of you. But I don't want to take your dessert."

"You're not." He set two bowls in front of me and grinned.

That goofy grin always managed to churn up my stomach and render me speechless – not an easy thing to do. And it was beginning to annoy me!

George Hardestee, the administrator of our little "Over-the-Hill-ton", materialized beside Bernie with two more ice cream bowls and sat down beside LeeAnne.

Maggie and Lumley had been 'keeping company', as my dear, departed mother would say, for several months. He swears Elsworth Lumley is his real name, but I'm not convinced. I think he's a spy. The one thing I AM sure of is, he'd better not break my best friend's heart, or he will have to answer to me!

The new blooming romance at our table was LeeAnne. She and George Hardestee had recently developed a close friendship. Right now they were engrossed in their own conversation. I looked across at Maggie. She laughed at something Lumley whispered in her ear.

I shrugged and turned to Bernie. If I wanted to converse, I guess it would have to be with my short, myopic, would-be suitor. I scooped a bite of my ice cream-covered cobbler and waved my spoon around the room. "What do you know about this herd of children? Has the place been turned into an after-school drop-off for kids?"

He chuckled. "No, we've not become home-away-from-home for latch-key kids. They are actually from a city children's choir. Their director asked George and Carolyn if they could come sing for us. They need to practice for a big state-wide competition."

"And I guess we're kind of a captive audience, since we don't tend to run very fast or very far."

"Well, Helen, I wouldn't put it that way. They came to entertain us."

"Huh! And whose idea was it to bring them here, give them ice cream, and let them run off the sugar high for our entertainment?"

At that moment, a young man stepped forward and blew on a whistle. All little feet came to a halt. The giggling and screeching immediately stopped. This apparent leader of the screaming group, who didn't look much older than his charges, wore faded jeans, sneakers with no socks, and a T-shirt with the caption "Make A Joyful Noise". His sandy hair fell below his collar in back, and into his eyes at the front. He reached up and shoved the offending locks out of his face.

He cleared his throat and clapped his hands once. "Alright, gang, front and center. It's time to sing for these kind folks. They didn't come here to watch you eat ice cream and play tag."

The group lined up in semi-straight formation behind the young man, pushing and jostling a bit as they pointed and whispered among themselves. The young man turned to them, strategically moved a few forward or back. He then turned once again to face the audience of semi-interested seniors, most still eating their ice cream.

"Good afternoon, everyone," he began. "Thank you for having us here today. My name is Jason Knight, and these beautiful faces behind me comprise the Loblolly Make a Joyful Noise Children's choir. Our only requirements for membership are you must be between the ages of 8 and 16 and you must ..." he looked over his shoulder at the children. "What is our other requirement, gang?"

"YOU MUST LOVE TO MAKE A JOYFUL NOISE!" shouted the group, before dissolving into giggles.

Most of the audience stopped eating long enough to applaud the youngsters' exuberance.

"As some of you may know," he continued, "we are preparing for a regional competition. If we do well there, we will go on to State, and perhaps even to Nationals."

Hearty, "YEAHS!" and many fist pumps resounded from behind him. The young man beamed. "As you can see, they're excited. This program is privately funded, and winning can bring much needed cash to help keep us singing."

"Now, without further ado, I invite you to sit back, relax, and enjoy the show."

Chapter 2

Princess Ariadne

The previously rowdy group became a well-oiled singing machine as they entertained us with highlights from such musicals as <u>Sound of Music</u> and <u>Mary Poppins</u>. Even the least amicable of our curmudgeonly group was not immune to the beautiful, heartfelt harmonies of their finale, "Let There Be Peace on Earth." Bernie patted my hand inconspicuously under the table and Maggie, always prepared, quietly handed me a tissue.

When the applause died down we all stood to leave. George, Bernie, and Lumley strode off to discuss their upcoming golf game. One of the youngsters came up behind me and tapped my arm. "Excuse me, ma'am. My name is Samantha. Is this your card?" She held out one of the Tricycle Girls business cards.

"Yes it is," I said with a smile. "Don't tell me you're in need of an investigator."

She shook her head. "Not me. ReeAnn wanted to know."

A small, redhead peeked from behind Samantha, her big blue eyes glistened with tears, and she wiped them away with a small, dingy scrap of fabric.

LeeAnne squatted down so she was at eye level with the little red-headed waif. "Hello, ReeAnn. My name rhymes with yours. My name is LeeAnne." She gently tucked the girl's tousled hair behind her ears. "We have the same color hair. We could be twins."

The child cocked her head, puzzled by the suggestion, hid behind the older girl, and stubbornly said, "I'm called Reesie."

Samantha took her shoulders and pulled her back to face us. "Sorry about that. She's a little shy. Everyone calls her Reesie because she really likes those chocolate peanut butter cups." She patted the smaller girl's head and said, "Go ahead, Reesie, tell them what's wrong."

She looked down at her dusty tennis shoes and mumbled, "Ariadne's lost."

"What!?" exclaimed Maggie. "One of the children is missing? Helen, go talk to the music director. LeeAnne and I will find George."

I saluted. "Yes, Sir!"

The little waif tugged on my sleeve as I headed across the room. "Ariadne's not a kid!"

We all stopped and stared down at her. Hands on hips, I growled, "Who is Ariadne then? And what kind of a name is Ariadne, anyway?"

She sniffled and swiped at her tears with the back of her hand. "Ariadne was a princess! *My Ariadne* is my stuffed bunny – and my best friend."

"STUFFED BUNNY!? You lost your toy and you want us to find it for you? Sorry, lost toys are not our responsibility." I pointed my finger at her. "Maybe you need to clean up your bedroom. It's probably under your bed."

She burst into tears, turned, and buried her head in LeeAnne's chest.

"Helen, you made the poor baby cry." She rocked the child

back and forth. "Miss Helen didn't mean to make you sad. She can be a little gruff sometimes," she told the sobbing child.

She glared at me. "Tell her you're sorry, Helen."

"Yeah. Sorry about that, ReeAnn." I patted her on the head.

She sniffled again. "It's Reesie!" She held the card up so I could see. "Your card says No Job Too Small. Ariadne is a small little bunny, and she's lost and all alone. She's probably scared all by herself." She swiped the back of her hand across her nose. Again!

"Maggie, for crying out loud, give the child one of your tissues before she wipes that stuff all over me!"

Maggie handed her a tissue and sat down. "Come tell us about Ariadne." She patted the chair beside her.

"She's about this tall." Reesie spread her hands apart eight or ten inches.

"She's bunny color and has on her blue sweater with big white buttons. One of her ears stands up and the other one kinda of flops into her eyes."

"Wait a minute," I said. "What is bunny color? I don't remember that shade in my crayon box."

The child's lips quivered, and she looked at her friend.

"Ariadne is tan," supplied Samantha.

"Okay, tan bunny, blue sweater, floppy ears. Got it."

"Are you going to write that down on your legal pad, Helen?" Maggie joked.

"No," I huffed. "I think I can remember it."

"Where did you last see Ariadne?" LeeAnne asked.

She plopped down between LeeAnne and Maggie, but kept her eyes on her friend, Samantha. "Two days ago. We were at the park across from the shelter." She held up the soiled piece of cloth. "This is her blankie. I wrapped her in it and sat her on the ground beside the monkey bars. I wanted to climb and she's afraid of high places. She likes to watch me so I don't fall. Then Samantha said we had to hurry back home to eat. I thought I picked Ariadne up with her blankie, but when we got home she wasn't there."

LeeAnne looked at Samantha. "You live close to the shelter?"

She shook her head. "We live *in* the shelter. Reesie's mom works evenings at the hospital and I make sure Reesie gets home alright. Ariadne really is her best friend. She usually won't go anywhere without her."

"Have you checked the park?" asked Maggie.

"Yes. A group of us kids from the shelter looked all over for Ariadne that night, until it got dark and we had to get back. They lock the doors at nine."

Maggie and LeeAnne both looked at me. "What do you think, Helen? Our card does say No Job Too Small. We could give it a try."

I sighed. "Oh, alright. At least it's not a jewel heist or a murder. No one is likely to get hurt, unless we fall off the swings at the park."

Maggie stood. "There you go, Reesie. We'll help look for Ariadne. Now you and Samantha had better go catch up with your group before the bus goes off without you. Oh, before you go, what is your last name? We need to know how to find you to bring Ariadne home."

"Walberg. Reesie and Ariadne Walberg. And my mom's Cynthia Walberg." The girl stood and gave Maggie and LeeAnne a hug. When she held out her grimy little hands to me, I reached down and patted her head. "Alrighty then, The Tricycle Girls have another case to solve." I pointed toward the choir director, who was counting noses and lining up the once-again-noisy group. "You go along now. We'll let you know if we find your toy."

She stomped her worn tennis shoe on the floor, barely missing my toes. "Ariadne's not a toy, she's my friend!"

"Stubborn little brat," I mused as the two girls walked hand-in-hand back to their friends.

Maggie chuckled. "Yes, she's very determined. Kind of reminds me of you."

Humph!" I groused. "Not likely." Yet there was something familiar about the unkempt little waif.

I smiled. "She is tenacious, I'll give her that."

Leeanne jangled her car keys in my face. "Anybody up for a road trip?"

"Right now?" I whined.

"Why not," Maggie nodded. "I'm game. We've got some time until dinner..."

"Supper," I corrected her.

"Whatever," she shrugged. "We have plenty of time before the *evening meal* to go check out the park. Maybe we'll have better luck than the kids did. Besides, we're full of cobbler and ice cream. We probably won't even be hungry at dinner – supper – time."

"Speak for yourself," I growled as I headed for the door. "Alright, come on. Let's get this over with."

LeeAnne led the way. She was the only one of us three who still had a working vehicle. Maggie's car bit the dust shortly after she moved in, and my kids, bless their hearts, said the world was a much safer place if I used public transportation. I had given my old car to my granddaughter, Ellyn, since she was the one person in my family who visited me on a regular basis.

Golden Harvest had a van and driver for our use, and the city bus had a stop just outside of our 'gated community'. It was easy enough to get around – if you could remember the blasted code to exit and enter the place.

We trudged around the park, checking swings, seesaws and slides, and garnered a few stares. The adults accompanying the children kept us in their sights as if we might be escapees from a nuthouse. The children ran to cut ahead of us at their favorite playground apparatus, as if we might wrestle a swing from them, or push them away from the monkey bars.

Maggie shook her head. "There's obviously nothing here. Maybe someone else found Ariadne and took her home."

I looked around one more time. Several large birds glided over the stand of trees adjacent to the park. I nudged Maggie and pointed. "Aren't those vultures? They've found something in the woods."

Maggie followed my gaze. "Probably a dead animal."

I headed in that direction. "Come on. Let's go check it out."

As they plodded behind me, LeeAnne said, "You realize Ariadne is a stuffed bunny, right? Vultures don't eat fake rabbits."

"Just a hunch," I said. "Humor me."

"Don't we always," Maggie sighed.

A broken-down fence separated the wooded area from the park. We stepped across the fence and into the brush. "I didn't come prepared to take a walk on the wild side," LeeAnne groused. "These briars are really scratchy!"

I patted her arm. "Quit complaining, City Girl. You're in the country now."

"And now I vividly remember why I remained a city girl!"

We crunched a bit further into the underbrush. I walked ahead to make a path for the others to follow, and suddenly heard the buzz of what sounded like a million flies ahead. I spotted a dark jacket lying behind a tree and stopped my friends from going any further. "Stay right there. We need to call the police. I just found Ariadne."

"Uh, Helen," she said, "I don't think the police will be interested in a stuffed rabbit."

I turned to face them. "No, but they might be interested in the body that has it clutched in his hands."

Chapter 3

We Were Rabbit Hunting, Officer

I swatted at one of the pesky flies that had left the swarm in search of private dining, pulled out my cell phone, and attempted to flick it on. "Darn! Guess I forgot to charge this blasted thing again." I turned to my friends, who were rooted to a spot behind me. "Can one of you call 9-1-1, please?"

LeeAnne stepped back a few paces, dialed, and gave the information. She called to me in a shaky voice, "Helen, the dispatcher wants to know if I'm sure he's dead."

I looked over my shoulder and scowled. "I'm not going to go check for a pulse, but the blank staring eyes and the number of flies dive-bombing the body are a pretty good indication that he's not just lying around napping in the woods."

She gagged and staggered back a few more paces to finish the call.

Maggie, behind me on my other side, touched my arm, and I jumped. "Helen, are you okay?"

I felt a bit dizzy, lifted my hand to my chest and realized I was taking short, shallow breaths. I turned to her and nodded. She peeked around me. "Who is he?"

I found my voice and shouted, "How should I know? Do you

think I'm intimately acquainted with every dead body that turns up around me?"

I could feel her shaking as she grabbed my arm. "No, of course not. It was a dumb question. I guess it's the shock." She tugged on my arm. "Let's get out of here, I don't feel very good, and you look pale."

I nodded again. "Yeah. Sorry I yelled. I'm a bit stressed, too."

LeeAnne stepped up beside us and glanced at the body. Her hand flew to her mouth and she gasped. "I think I know him – at least I've met him. He came by Golden Harvest a few days ago to talk to George. He interrupted our game of Gin Rummy."

Maggie and I looked at each other and raised our eyebrows. Gin Rummy equated to the senior citizen version of getting to first base.

"Why are you gawking at me?" she asked.

I shrugged. "Oh, nothing. What did he want?"

"I'm not exactly sure. George told him to make an appointment, but he said he wasn't interested in moving in. He asked some strange questions – What we knew about the neighborhood - If the people at the shelter caused any problems – Did we know any of them or anything about them. George told him those weren't questions he would or could answer."

"That's odd," Maggie said.

"Yes, George thought so, too. Oh, he gave us his card, in case," she air-quoted, "there any questions we *could* answer."

She dug around in her purse, pulled out a card, and read: "Ivan Maurice Reddy, Private Investigator. 555-4321." She handed me the card.

I looked it over, and, in spite of the gruesome situation,

chuckled. "His initials are – were – I. M." I shook my head sadly. "Well, Mr. I. M. Reddy, I'll bet you weren't ready for this!"

Approaching sirens caused a stir among the folks milling around the park. Adults pulled their children in close. "Come on, girls, let's go talk to the police and get back home in time for supper – hopefully."

LeeAnne grabbed my arm. With Maggie on my left and LeeAnne tugging on my right, I felt like the wishbone of the Thanksgiving turkey. I pulled away from them before they decided to make a wish using my appendages, and stomped ahead.

"Helen, aren't you going to get Ariadne?" LeeAnne asked.

I stopped short. I'd forgotten all about the reason for our trek to the park. I turned to go back for the thing, but Maggie stopped me. "Uh, Helen, I think you should leave it there. It's part of a crime scene."

Having recently been accused of messing with a body at a crime, I hesitated. That incident nearly landed me in jail. "You're right, Mags. We'll have to tell the little redhead the cops have her rabbit."

"Her name is ReeAnn," said Maggie.

"Or Reesie," added LeeAnne.

"Right. And the rabbit in question is Ariadne. It's still a weird name for a toy," I said as I stepped across the broken-down fence line.

We waited as the police strolled toward us. A cocky young patrol officer, with all the swagger of a high school jock who is used to getting his way, sauntered up first. "Are you the bunch who called in about the body? Where is it? How did you find it? Do you know who it is?"

I didn't like his attitude. "Is your father around? This must be take-your-cocky-kid-to-work day."

He huffed up. "I'll have you know I graduated from the academy – top 10% of my class!"

I stood toe-to-toe and eye-to-eye with him. "Oh Yeah? When? Last week?"

Maggie grabbed my arm – again - as a man, attired in a neat dark suit, walked up, and said, "That will do, Justin."

I looked up into the light blue eyes of the one who shut Justin up – or down, as the case may be.

He smiled and extended his hand. "Detective Dale Metcalf. Sorry about that. He's new to the force and very gung ho. He'll settle down eventually. They all do.

"I realize this has been a shock for you, but can you point us in the direction of the body, please? No sense in you having to tromp back into the brush. I assume that's where you stumbled across it."

After shaking his hand, I pointed. "Straight in, behind that first tree."

He called to Justin and another officer. "Charlie, you two go check it out. I'll ask these ladies a few questions and join you." He turned to us. "Are you alright to speak to me right now?"

We nodded.

He pulled a small notebook from his pocket. "Can I get your names for the record?"

He wrote down our names and pertinent information, then slid the pen and notepad back into his pocket. "How did you happen across the body?"

Maggie and LeeAnne both looked at me. "We were looking for a rabbit," I said.

He ran his long fingers through his light brown hair graying at the temples and pinched the bridge of his nose. "You were rabbit hunting?" He looked us up and down. "You're not dressed for hunting. And, might I remind you, this is a city park – no hunting allowed." He smiled to let us know he was joking – sort of.

"A stuffed rabbit," LeeAnne blurted out.

He furrowed his brow, and she filled him in on Reesie, Ariadne and all that had happened that day. She finally stopped to take a breath.

Maggie spoke up. "The dead guy had the bunny clutched in his hand when we found him. Please take good care of it. We promised Reesie we'd find her friend. Can we tell her Ariadne is in protective custody for a while?"

He chuckled. "Sure. I've got a granddaughter who carries a little elephant everywhere she goes. Calls it Ellie. I know how kids get attached to things."

Maggie took his hand. "Thank you. That bunny is her security. I'm sure living at the shelter must be upsetting."

He rubbed his chin. "Yes, you're right. I wonder who this guy was."

"Oh," I said. "His name is – was – Ivan Maurice Reddy."

"And how do you know that, Mrs. Patterson?"

I handed him the card. "He came by our place of residence the other day and asked our director, George Hardestee, a lot of questions about the shelter and its occupants."

He looked at the card. "Hmm, a P.I. That's odd. No address listed."

"I noticed that, too," LeeAnne said. "That's pretty unusual. It looks as though he printed them out on his computer, like Helen did our business cards. He's probably not even a real private investigator."

"He's *probably* not anything anymore – except dead," I scoffed.

"Well, ladies, I'll let you get back to Golden Harvest. I'll come by to speak with Mr. Hardestee. And I might have some more questions for you, too."

LeeAnne spoke up. "Could I ask a favor, Detective?"

"What is it, Mrs. Warner?"

"Could we go with you if you have to speak with Reesie? I think she will be less frightened if there's a familiar face with you."

"Yes," added Maggie. "And we can reassure her that Ariadne is fine."

"That's actually a good idea, ladies. I'll let you know when I'm going to the shelter."

"Hey, Metcalf," a voice shouted from the brush. "We need a couple more officers out here. This guy's been shot!"

Maggie, LeeAnne, and I all gasped, and I watched my friends pale. My blasted luck! Another murder. Why couldn't the guy have dropped dead from a heart attack? Or attacked by killer flies?

And what was he doing with the little redhead's stuffed bunny?

Chapter 4

I Didn't Even Know the Guy

We barely made it back home in time for supper. Lumley and George waved as we entered the dining room. Bernie stood and pulled out a chair for me. The meal was disappointing and consisted of way too many greens and vegetables, only one small slice of turkey breast, and no potatoes. Emile had obviously over-extended himself on the mid-afternoon snacks of cobbler and ice cream, because the pitiful excuse for dessert was one lonely sugar cookie.

I bit into mine. "It's a good thing I have some fig bars in my apartment. A body could starve around here on only one cookie." I munched on it. "Tastes store-bought, too."

Maggie sipped her tea. "When did you get so picky about your food, Helen? This was a wonderfully refreshing meal for a warm summer evening."

"Too much salad," I harrumphed. "Reminds me of all that kudzu weed the restaurants tried to pass off on us on that *vacation* you made me go on last month."

"It's actually pretty ingenious all the ways people have figured out to use kudzu," LeeAnne said. "Looks like it's here to stay. Might as well get some good out of it."

"Right," George concurred. "Like they say, 'If you can't beat 'em, join 'em'. And it looks like kudzu can't be beat."

Lumley draped his arm over the back of Maggie's chair. "Where did you ladies go today that caused you to nearly be late for dinner?"

"Supper," I muttered under my breath.

Maggie and LeeAnne looked at me with raised eyebrows.

"What?" I sputtered. "Why are you both gawking at me? It wasn't my idea to go traipsing around searching for some child's lost toy. You two dragged me to the park!"

"Yes," said Maggie. "But you're the one who found the body."

George and Lumley both slammed their iced tea glasses on the table. "What?!" they said in near-perfect unison.

Maggie began to fill them in on our little escapade of tromping around in the woods in search of a stuffed rabbit, and me nearly tripping over a body.

Lumley looked at me, shook his head, and ran his hands through his steel-gray hair.

LeeAnne continued the gruesome tale, ending with, "…and Detective Metcalf will be by here tomorrow to ask you a few questions, George."

"Why me? I didn't stumble over the body." He glared at me. "That seems to be Helen's specialty."

"No," I glared back at him, "but, unlike me, you knew the guy."

"What? It was someone I know? Perhaps you should have started with that bit of information!" He reached for his iced tea with a shaking hand. "Who was he?"

LeeAnne laid her hand on his free arm. "He wasn't a friend,

George. Remember that strange guy who came by a few days ago asking about the shelter and the people there? He said he was a private investigator, and gave us a card."

"Oh yes, I remember. He interrupted our Gin Rummy game."

George smiled at her. "And I was ahead of you for once."

"That's great, guys. Very romantic. But can we finish this up so I can go back to my apartment for some real dessert?"

LeeAnne shrugged. "That's about it," she said, "except the police said he'd been shot."

"And," Maggie added, "he had Ariadne clutched in his hand."

Lumley rubbed his face with his free hand. "Please tell me Ariadne is the aforementioned toy and not some poor child."

"Of course it was the toy," I huffed. "Jeez, do you think we'd leave that kind of pertinent information as an after-thought if a child was involved?"

"No offense, Helen, but I've yet to discover what, to you, is pertinent. You have a single-minded ability to block out logic at times, and walk into things willy-nilly."

I stood up, hands on hips. "Is that so? Well, let me tell you something, *Mr. Lumley...*"

"Helen, sit down!" Maggie demanded.

I sat.

"You two go to your corners for a time-out."

She turned to Lumley. "El, I know Helen can be single-minded and stubborn sometimes..."

"Sometimes?" he huffed.

She continued. "But she does have good detection skills, and a logical mind. She's always liked puzzles and mysteries. She almost always knows the perpetrators in the books she reads before the protagonist figures it out."

I beamed and sat straighter in my chair.

Lumley crossed his arms over his chest and growled, "She should stick to reading, then."

She frowned at him, then at me. "However, Helen, El has a point. You don't always think before you act, which has put you in danger in the past. You know I love you like the sister I never had but, face it, you don't always use common sense. You're too old to be Nancy Drew, and Miss Marple almost never got directly involved in the murders she helped solve."

It was Lumley's turn to sit straighter. I slumped.

She took my hand across the table. "All I'm asking is that you be more careful."

I nodded. "Point noted."

Bernie, who had remained quiet up to now, merely smiled sweetly at me and asked, "What are you going to do about this murdered guy?"

"Me? Why me? I didn't even know the guy. I'm not likely to be accused of killing him. I have no reason to get involved."

He nodded. "I know, but aren't you the least bit curious? I kind of enjoyed all the sleuthing last time. And," he added, winking at Maggie, "I thought you played a good Nancy Drew-Marple."

I smiled into his myopic blue eyes. "Thanks, Bernie."

"Don't encourage her," Maggie said. "She'll have us all out chasing around looking for clues. I don't know about the rest of you but, after that last fiasco, I'm ready to hang up my Tricycle Girls credentials."

"Aw, c'mon, Mags," I said, "It wasn't that bad."

She marched around the table and grabbed my shoulders. "Not that bad?! Helen, have you forgotten – you almost got shot!"

I brushed my hand in the air as if to swat away the thought –

like the flies buzzing around Mr. I. M. Reddy. "It was an accident. And the bullet missed me."

Lumley fumed, stood and came to stand by Maggie. I could almost see smoke spewing out his ears. "Do you know the statistics on the number of homicides that are listed as accidents?"

To push his anger-meter button I smiled and said, "No, but I'm pretty sure I could find the information on the internet, if you really want to know."

He sighed and put his arm around Maggie's slim waist. "I give up, Helen. But please don't do anything that might get Maggie hurt."

I glared at him. "Right back at you, Big Guy."

The following day began with indigestion. The thought of Detective Metcalf's impending visit hovered over our breakfast table like a bad odor everyone noticed but no one wanted to acknowledge. I munched on my pancakes and eggs with less enthusiasm than usual, and watched as Maggie and LeeAnne nibbled on their fruit and yogurt. I sopped a forkful of pancake into the pool of syrup on my plate, popped it into my mouth, and pointed my fork at them. "You two won't last until lunch on that little bit of food."

Maggie pointed her spoon back at me. "All that sugary syrup isn't good for you, Helen. I'm surprised you don't have diabetes! I prefer a healthy diet."

"I know you do. But you know what the great philosopher 'They' says – '*Eat healthy, exercise, die anyway.*' I'll take my chances."

"How could I forget, when you keep reminding me," Maggie

sighed. "Your two favorite people to quote are 'They' and 'Anonymous'. Did you ever consider that perhaps the reason we don't know their names is because they didn't want to accept responsibility for some of the things they said?"

"Nah. The truth will always find a way."

Maggie grinned. "Who said that, *They* or *Anonymous*?"

I shrugged. "Not sure." I finished my last bite and wiped my mouth with my napkin. "Maybe I just coined a phrase."

Maggie shook her head as Lumley muttered, "That's doubtful."

A voice came over the intercom: "Mr. Hardestee, there's someone here to see you."

George stood and interrupted our little debate. "That must be the police detective. Are you ladies finished here?"

Maggie stood and smiled at me. "Truce?"

I pushed my chair back and linked my arm in hers as we followed George. "Always," I grinned. "We haven't been best friends all these years by holding back. That's one of the things I love about you, Mags, you try to keep me in line."

She squeezed my arm. "Yes, with *try* being the key word. Reining you in is a full-time job!"

"Gotta keep you on your toes."

Bernie and Lumley excused themselves from our little parade as we neared George's office. Lumley and Maggie made plans to meet later, Bernie nodded and gave me a wink as the two turned and walked away discussing options of chess or golf after their morning exercise in the workout room.

Detective Metcalf met us outside George's office. He nodded and smiled. "Good morning, ladies."

LeeAnne introduced him to George and the two shook hands.

25

He addressed us, "I don't have any questions for you ladies at this time. I'd like to speak with Mr. Hardestee privately. I have arranged to visit ReeAnn and her mother this morning. If any or all of you would be willing to come along, I'd appreciate it. As you pointed out yesterday, it might be less intimidating for the child if you were present."

We all agreed to go with him. LeeAnne told George to give her a call when the detective was ready to leave, and invited Maggie and me to her apartment to await his summons.

When we got to LeeAnne's I paced back and forth until Maggie shouted, "For crying out loud, Helen, sit down. What's wrong with you?"

I stopped and wrung my hands. "Do you think Detective Metcalf will make us ride to the shelter in his squad car? After the ordeal with Captain Rachett on that trip to Stone Mountain, I'm not overly fond of being chauffeured around by policemen."

I had spent way too much time under the scrutiny of the bulldog of a man in charge of solving the murder of an old acquaintance of ours on that trip. I wasn't anxious for a repeat performance.

"Relax," said LeeAnne. "Like you said earlier, you've got no connection to this guy. No one's likely to accuse you of his murder."

I nodded, sat down, and pulled my ever-present yellow legal pad out of my bag. "That's true."

I jotted down some questions. Putting words to paper always helped me sort through problems.

Number 1: Why was Reddy asking about the shelter?

Number 2. Did he have a connection to someone there?

Number 3. Why did he take the little redhead's stuffed toy?

LeeAnne looked over my shoulder and read the questions out loud.

Maggie groaned. "You're going to get us mixed up in the middle of another mystery, aren't you, Helen?"

"Hey," I reminded her, pointing my pen at her and LeeAnne, "you two are the ones who were all gung ho to find the kid's toy. No Job Too Small, huh? Well, we found it! Now, like it or not, we are mixed up in this mess."

I tapped my pen to my chin. "A couple of other questions keep rattling around in my brain. First, are the little redhead and her mother in danger from whoever killed that P.I.? And second, is the mother somehow involved in his death?"

Chapter 5

You're Dismissed

I jumped at the chirping of LeeAnne's cell phone and stuffed my legal pad into my bag.

"Okay, girls," she announced. "Detective Metcalf is waiting for us at the front door."

We headed that way, Maggie and LeeAnne in spirited conversation, me trudging along behind like a prisoner to the gallows. They slowed for me to catch up and Maggie crooked her arm in mine.

"What's wrong, Helen? You know you don't have to come with us if you'd rather not."

"It's nothing," I said. "I want to meet ReeAnn's mother. But," a shiver worked its way through me and raised goosebumps on the arm Maggie had latched onto, "I have a bad feeling about this whole situation."

LeeAnne took my other arm. "I think the guys may be right. You read so many mysteries you see a mystery in everything."

We had reached the door and the detective stood ready to escort us out of the building. LeeAnne pulled her car keys from her purse and dangled them in front of the detective. "We can follow you and save you a trip to bring us back here, if it's alright."

"Yes. That will be fine." He held the door for us and followed behind. He even opened LeeAnne's door after she unlocked her car.

Maggie whispered, "His mother must have raised him right."

"Either that or he's after something from us," I groused.

As we settled into the car, me in my usual position of shotgun, Maggie asked, "What could he possibly want from us?"

I turned to face her. "Information."

"What information?" asked LeeAnne. "We don't know anything."

"Yeah, but he doesn't know that. He probably thinks we're mixed up in that P.I.'s murder somehow."

We pulled up to the shelter and, as we exited the car, Maggie said, "We've been over this before, Helen. Detective Metcalf has no reason to suspect any of us. I've never seen you so worked up."

She grabbed my shoulders. "You know I say this with love. You've never cared before what anyone thought about anything you may or may not have said or done. I don't know how to deal with you when you are second-guessing everything. I want my friend back who doesn't give a fat rat's fanny about what people think!"

I took a deep breath and smiled. "You're right, Mags. Thanks for the pep talk."

Detective Metcalf approached hesitantly. "Am I interrupting something?"

"No, no," I said as I brushed Maggie's hands off my shoulders.

"I asked Helen if she remembered to bring her legal pad," Maggie stammered, "to take notes."

I patted my bag. "Yup. Got it right here. Shall we get on with it?"

Detective Metcalf shrugged and we followed him up the steps to the porch of the women's shelter.

A brassy, gum-chewing bleach-blond answered our knock. She wore skin-tight hot pink capris and a flowered crop top. The hot pink color carried over to her long manicured fingers and pedicured toes. The detective introduced himself and showed his badge. "We're here to see Cynthia Walberg and her daughter, ReeAnn."

The woman leaned against the door. "I'm Cynthia, but you can call me Cindy. My kid's around here somewhere, probably sittin' in our room crying about that danged stuffed rabbit of hers."

She pointed to her left. "Go on in there to what they call the sitting room. Sounds like they're trying to fancy up this dump, or somethin'. I'll go find my kid." She turned and hollered down the hall, "ReeAnn, get on out here. The cops want to talk to you."

The little redhead peaked out of one of the doors and headed our way, head down.

Cynthia – Cindy – popped her gum and frowned at LeeAnne, Maggie, and me. "You old ladies aren't cops, too, are you?"

I opened my mouth but Maggie grabbed my arm and spoke up before I could utter a word. "No, we're from Golden Harvest Retirement Village." She introduced us and went on. "ReeAnn's singing group gave a performance at our place. They did a wonderful job. I'm sure you are very proud."

We sat down on worn but functional furniture. The detective, Maggie, and I chose lumpy, overstuffed chairs. LeeAnne opted for the sagging couch.

Cindy Walberg yawned. "Oh yeah, the music stuff gives her

something to do – keeps her out of trouble and out of my hair. I work nights, ya know, so I sleep during the day."

"That must be very difficult for you both, Mrs. Walberg," Maggie said.

Cindy held up her hands. "*Miss* Walberg. I wasn't married to ReeAnn's old man – or any other worthless jerk," she spat out.

Maggie pursed her lips and LeeAnne put her arm around ReeAnn, who had sat down beside her.

Detective Metcalf spoke up. "Ms. Walberg, I hate to take up your time, but I have a few questions I need to ask. You may have heard that a man was found dead at the park where the children play."

"Yeah, I heard about it. What's it got to do with me and my kid? You don't think she killed him, do you?" She let out a raucous laugh. Maggie, LeeAnne, and I cringed.

"No, we don't believe that at all. But the man was found with your child's toy clutched in his hand."

ReeAnn shouted, "You found Ariadne?" She hugged LeeAnne. "Where is she? Can I have her back now?"

Maggie moved to the couch, sat on the other side of the child, and took her hand. "We made Detective Metcalf promise to take very good care of Ariadne, but he needs to keep her with him right now."

ReeAnn looked at the detective. "Is Ariadne helping with your 'vestigation?"

He smiled. "Yes, she's been a big help. And she may have some very valuable information for us. These ladies and I," he pointed to Maggie, LeeAnne, and me, "will bring Ariadne back home soon, okay?"

She nodded. "She's very smart, but I bet she misses me. Tell her I miss her, too."

"I will."

Cindy huffed. "Her old man gave that stupid rabbit to her a few years ago. I've tried to get rid of it, but she throws a fit when I mention it. She needs to grow up and get over it!"

Detective Metcalf looked from me to LeeAnne and Maggie. "ReeAnn, would you show the ladies your room while I have a word with your mother?"

I pulled the legal pad and gel pen from my bag and laid it on my lap. "I'll just sit here, if you don't mind. My old knees are acting up."

He scowled at me and said under his breath, "Fine. But don't interrupt my questioning."

ReeAnn nodded, stood, took Maggie's and LeeAnne's hands, and led them away. I sat there poised with my legal pad, sketching bubble-gum-blowing skulls, and fingers with talons. The detective turned his attention to the mother, who was quickly making my short list of murder suspects.

"Ms. Walberg," Detective Metcalf began, "what can you tell us about your... about ReeAnn's father?"

"Vinnie? Why? What do you want to know?"

"For starters, what is his full name?"

"It's Vincent. Vincent Armitage. His family has a jewelry store somewhere."

"Armitage?" I gasped. "As in Armitage Fine Jewelers, in Savannah? *That* Armitage?"

She shrugged and popped her gum. "I guess."

I glanced at the detective and he raised his eyebrows. "Is Mr. Armitage a violent man?" he asked.

Cindy laughed. "Vinnie? Violent? Nah, he's a pussycat."

"He never hit you or threatened you?"

"No way. Wait. You think Vinnie might have killed that guy?" She laughed so hard I was afraid she'd swallow her wad of gum.

"We're checking out all possibilities," Metcalf said.

She choked back her laugh and pounded her chest. "Well, you can check Vinnie off your list. He's no killer."

I pointed my pen in her direction. "Ms. Walberg...Cindy...might I ask why you seem to be running away from a seemingly good situation with Mr. Armitage? Were there extenuating circumstances?"

She frowned and wrinkled her nose. "Exten...extenu – what?"

"Extenuating circumstances," I repeated. "You said he isn't violent. Is he perhaps married? Is that why you referred to him as," I checked my notes, 'a worthless jerk'?"

"Ha! All men are worthless jerks. Sooner or later they're all the same. I just never hang around until that happens. I gotta protect myself an' my kid, ya know?"

"Protect yourself from what, Ms. Walberg?" Metcalf asked, taking back the questioning.

"Nothin' I can't handle, officer."

She squared her shoulders and faced me. "To answer your question, lady, since you seem to be his secretary," she cocked her head in the detective's direction, "No, Vinnie isn't married. But on a scale of 1 to 10, he's a zero. The only way he could kill anybody would be to bore them to death. Everything all buttoned up and proper. Suit and tie, black Italian loafers. But absolutely no fun! You know the type, right?"

An old, hurtful memory flashed through my mind, and I caught my breath. The thought of this woman hobnobbing with the Armitage's would never work. When I didn't answer, she continued. "He didn't want to go dancing, or to the bars where all the good times are. He never could slip away for an afternoon picnic or to go wading in the pond. I didn't have the right clothes to go to the black-tie dinners he talked about. I always turned him down. He didn't want to do any fun stuff with me. A real dud."

It didn't take a psychologist to see she was mentally pushing him away.

She leaned forward and laughed. "Then you know what he did?"

I shook my head and kept my pen poised above my writing pad.

She slapped her knees. "He came to me and wanted to do the right thing – those were his words – *the right thing* – when I got knocked up. I couldn't see myself as the buttoned-up wife of a no-personality bore, so I skipped out."

I looked over at Detective Metcalf. "Have you seen Mr. Armitage lately?" he asked.

She scratched her head with one of her talons. "Not for seven or eight months. Not long before I moved here. He keeps popping up like that, trying to get me to change my mind about becoming Mrs. Boring-Armitage."

"It sounds as though he cares about your child's welfare," Detective Metcalf said.

"Whatever," she shrugged again. "He'd end up like my old man, the original worthless jerk. Pop took off when I was nine and left me and my ma with nothin'. She finally drank herself to death when I was fourteen, an' I've taken care of myself ever since."

I got the sudden impression Cindy didn't think as badly of Vincent Armitage as she let on.

"What about ReeAnn?" I asked. "Maybe she'd like…"

Detective Metcalf interrupted me. "Ms. Walberg, you mentioned earlier that you'd had no threats you couldn't handle. Could you elaborate...uh, could you give me a little more detail about that statement?"

"You know how it is, officer."

He leaned forward and rested his forearms on his knees. "It's Detective. And, no, I'm afraid I don't know how it is. Why don't you explain it to me."

"Guys get pushy and territorial. Like, there's this place I go to after work sometimes – to unwind, you know – before I head home after my shift." She paused and chewed on her lip.

"Go on, Ms. Walberg."

"Well, this one guy, Gus, I think they call him, he's a big, burly oaf with an attitude. I went in the place one night and he started bragging, showing off, like, and challenged me to a game of pool. I beat the pants off him, and he got sore. Now, every time I stop by there, he wants to challenge me to a rematch, and won't take no for an answer. Not only that, but another guy bought me a drink last week and Gus broke a pool cue over his head.

"Charlie called the cops and banned him from the place for fighting. Gus was really mad about it, and told me it was all my fault."

"That sounds pretty violent to me," I said to no one in particular.

The detective nodded. "I have to agree with Mrs. Patterson, Ms. Walberg." He handed her a note pad and pen. "Would you write down the name and location of the bar for me, please? And also write down Mr. Armitage's information, if you have it. I'd like to speak with this Charlie – and Gus – and ReeAnn's father."

She jotted down the information and handed the note pad back to the detective

He stood to leave. "Thank you for your time. Could you go tell Mrs. Warner and Mrs. Taylor we're ready to leave? If I have any more questions I'll come back to see you. I want you and ReeAnn to be very careful until we figure out what this is all about." He handed her one of his cards. "And, if you have any questions, or think of something else, please give me a call."

Cindy hollered down the hall for her daughter, and Maggie and LeeAnne walked toward us guided by ReeAnn, each with one of her hands in theirs.

LeeAnne squatted down to give the girl a hug. "Thank you for showing us your room. May we come back to visit again?"

ReeAnn nodded, then ran over and hugged Maggie. "Thank you all for finding Ariadne." She smiled up at Detective Metcalf. "Bring her home soon, please."

He tousled her curly red locks. "You bet, Sweetie."

I stuffed the legal pad in my bag and followed the three of them out to the parking area. "What's our next move, Detective?"

"My next move is to find a killer and solve this crime. Your move is to go back to Golden Harvest. I appreciate you coming with me today – I'm sure ReeAnn did too – but I don't need you three interfering in my investigation. Thank you for your help."

As he turned to leave, I sputtered, "Wait a minute..." before Maggie grabbed my arm and ushered me to LeeAnne's car. "You're very welcome, Detective," she called over her shoulder. "If there's anything else you need from us, you know where to find us."

She opened the passenger side door and practically shoved

me inside. "Hey, what're you doing?" I shouted as she gave me her 'look'.

"Helen, please get in the car and don't upset Detective Metcalf any further," she half-whispered through clenched teeth.

She slammed my door as I maneuvered into my seat belt. LeeAnne started the car, Maggie situated herself in the backseat and said, "OK LeeAnne, get us home. We've got some detective work to do!"

Chapter 6

He Whose Name Shall Never Be Spoken

I asked, "Why the rush to get me in the car, Maggie?"

"Well, LeeAnne and I had an interesting visit with Reesie." She leaned forward from the backseat and patted my shoulder. "I'll fill you in when we get home."

"What's wrong with right now? You shoved me in this car like we're escaping from some crazed maniac!"

"All in good time, Helen. All in good time."

The rest of the short ride remained a silent one. LeeAnne pulled up to Golden Harvest and punched in the code to open the gate. "Did you learn anything during your interrogation of Reesie's mother, Helen?" she asked as she maneuvered easily into a parking spot.

Maggie laughed as we exited the car. "You've been reading too many of Helen's mysteries, LeeAnne. You make it sound as if they were in a locked room with metal chairs, a single lightbulb, and Helen and the detective playing good cop-bad cop."

I nodded. "As a matter of fact, I did learn some things. For one, Ms. Walberg thinks I'm Detective Metcalf's secretary."

They both laughed. Then Maggie said, "That may come in

handy if we need to talk to her later. It might give us some leverage."

"Hmmm. I like having leverage. Leverage for what, exactly?" I asked.

Maggie shrugged. "I don't know. That's the thing about leverage – it's good to have around in case you need it."

I took her arm. "Why, Maggie, you're getting downright devious. I like it!"

"Okay girls," LeeAnne said. "It's almost lunchtime. I'm going to freshen up. We can plan our strategy while we eat."

"How about after we eat? I don't want to spoil my lunch with strategy sessions." I suggested. "We can meet at my place."

"Good idea," said Maggie. "Besides, I'm sure El will meet us for lunch – and possibly George, too. I'd like to talk this over with you two before we mention it to the guys."

"Wow! More and more devious! And I thought you shared everything with Lumley."

"Helen, when are you going to start calling him Elsworth?" Maggie asked. "And I *will* share the information – when the time is right."

LeeAnne headed down the hall to her apartment. "Sounds like a plan. But let's meet at my place. I've got some sparkling grape juice and cheese and crackers."

"Yea, fake champagne and cheese. I'm in. I'll bring my fig bars for something sweet."

Maggie groaned. "You and your fig bars. I'm surprised you don't carry a supply in that oversized bag of yours."

I smiled, reached in my tote and pulled out a zip lock bag of my favorite snacks. "Actually, I do."

Lumley was already seated when we got to the dining room. He stood, pulled out chairs on either side of him for Maggie and LeeAnne. Bernie materialized from some hidden place, and made a big to-do about helping me into my chair. He sat beside me and looked across at LeeAnne. "George sends his apologies. He's running late, but he'll try to be here shortly."

"Thanks, Bernie. So, what did you fellows do this beautiful morning."

Lumley chuckled. "Bernie gave me a lesson in humility. We bet on our golf game and he trounced me. I may have to take out a loan." He grinned at Maggie. "Got any money I can borrow?"

Maggie gasped. "You bet on the game? How much did you lose?"

Here it comes, I thought. *The man is going to take advantage of my friend. I knew it! I was right about him!*

I stood up, pointed my finger at him. "Lumley, you are NOT..."

Bernie stood, grabbed the hand I was pointing at Lumley, and burst out laughing.

I forgot about Lumley, turned, and hollered, "Bernie Cox, what part of this is funny to you? That man," I pointed again at Lumley, "is about to take my best friend for perhaps every cent she's got, because of your stupid bet. How dare you laugh!"

As I turned to stomp away, my chair crashed over. I tripped, and suddenly both Lumley and Bernie grabbed me so I didn't follow the chair to the floor. I shook them both off and glanced around the room. Every bifocaled eye in the place was fixed on me.

"Helen," Lumley whispered, "the bet was for a dollar."

"A dollar? ONE dollar?" I stuttered.

He righted my chair. "Yes, One dollar. I would never ask

Maggie to cover any bet I lost – and I would *never* bet more than I could afford to lose."

I sagged back into my chair. "One dollar. Guess I kind of made a fool of myself."

Maggie grinned. "Yeah, you did. But the look on your face was priceless!"

Lumley draped his arm over the back of Maggie's chair. "Helen, Maggie is truly blessed to have such a loyal friend as you."

"Thank you… Elsworth," I choked out.

Maggie beamed.

"So," Bernie asked, "how did the visit to our little missing bunny girl go?"

"Uh, well…" I stammered.

"She was definitely glad to know Ariadne is safe," LeeAnne said.

"Yes, and Detective Metcalf assured her he would get her friend home to her soon," Maggie added.

Bernie rubbed his hands together in anticipation. "When are we going to begin our investigation?"

I crossed my arms over my chest. "The detective made it clear we are to stay out of his way. He doesn't need our assistance."

"Uh huh, right. Like I said, when and where do we start?"

"As a matter of fact," Maggie said, "we're having a strategy session at LeeAnne's apartment about 1:30. You men are welcome to stop by."

"Strategy session, huh? That sounds like fun. I'll be there," Bernie said.

"Yes, me too," Elsworth added. "I want to see what you gals are getting yourselves into this time." I figured after his comment about my being a loyal friend, I was going to have to quit calling him Lumley.

I glared at Maggie. "As much as I hate to agree with you, Lum... uh, Elsworth, I'd like to know that, myself."

"All in good time, Helen," Maggie said.

"Yeah, yeah. You said that in the car. My patience is running a little thin, here!"

"Patience?" she laughed. "You have no patience! You don't plan, you act! You don't develop ideas, you dive in! You don't think, you..."

I leaned toward her, waved my hands, and said, "Okay, okay. I hear you. But could you keep it down? You're causing a commotion."

She glanced around the room. All heads had turned in our direction, and most nodded in agreement with her.

She smiled and waved at the bobbing heads. "Can we discuss this later, please? I'd like to finish my lunch," she said under her breath. She bent her head and focused on her food with a concentration she usually reserved only for Lumley.

I wasn't going to get any more out of her. Instead, I stabbed the dang infernal greens and finished my lunch in silence.

When we rose to leave, LeeAnne said she was going to go call George to see if he could make it to our 'strategy meeting'. Lumley and Maggie walked away hand-in-hand, which left me standing beside a grinning Bernie Cox.

"May I escort you to your apartment, Helen? Or we could sit in the garden on this beautiful day."

"Uh, no thanks, Bernie. I need to go, uh, freshen up before the meeting later." I stumbled away and waved back at him. "See you at 1:30 at LeeAnne's."

My cell phone rang as I entered my apartment and I fished it out of my bag. "What's up, Mags? I left you not ten minutes ago. What earth-shattering news has transpired since then that couldn't wait until we meet at 1:30?"

"I think you, LeeAnne, and I should get together a little earlier than that – say 1:00 – and discuss some things before the guys arrive," she said breathlessly.

"What's the big secret, Maggie? Oh wait, I know - 'All in good time'."

At a little past one o'clock we had settled in at LeeAnne's, sparkling grape juice in hand. I tossed my bag of fig bars beside the cheese and crackers precisely arranged on a cut glass platter.

LeeAnne jumped up and grabbed the bag. "Here, let me get a plate for these, Helen."

I grabbed it back. "Why bother? They'll eat just fine this way. Sit! I want you and Maggie to tell me exactly what's going on. I don't like all this secrecy!"

"Ha! What you mean is you don't like being the one not knowing the secret," Maggie scoffed.

"Maybe so," I huffed. "You two have been acting strange ever since we left the little redhead's place, and I want to know why!" I glared from one to the other. "Oh, my word. Do you think her mom is mixed up in the murder?"

Maggie picked up a cracker and some cheese and placed them on a napkin in front of her. "The little redhead has a name, Helen – it's Reesie. And no, I don't think her mom had anything to do with your dead guy."

"Why is it always MY dead guy?" I whined. "You sound like I

deliberately go out looking for dead people aimlessly lying around."

"Well," LeeAnne laughed, "bodies have tended to turn up a lot around you lately. What are the odds of a civilian stumbling across three corpses in less than a year?" She smiled at Maggie. "Elsworth might be able to give us those statistics."

"I don't care about any stupid statistics!" I hollered.

I closed my eyes, folded my hands on the table, took a deep breath, and continued. "I guess I have seen more than my share of strange deaths in the last few months."

I looked from LeeAnne to Maggie. "But if this isn't about the dead guy, what's it about?"

"We're going to help get Reesie's mom and dad together!" they said in unison.

"What?! You're going to play matchmaker between that brassy woman and one of Georgia's Bluebloods?" I shook my head. "That sounds like a disaster in the making! What could possibly go wrong?" I popped a cracker in my mouth, followed it with a swig of juice, and stared at my well-meaning friends. "Oh, wait – I know what could go wrong – EVERYTHING!"

"Might I remind you this is not some re-enactment of <u>Grease, the Musical</u> or <u>Pygmalion</u>. And I don't foresee any happy endings! Cindy Walberg and Vincent Armitage are like oil and water – they won't mix – they are too different!" I rubbed my face with my hands and swallowed hard.

Maggie leaned toward me. "How can you be sure of that, Helen? You don't even know Vincent Armitage."

"No, but I know the type! Uptight, wrapped in a cocoon of wealth and privilege, sheltered from the real world. He doesn't have a clue what it's like to have to scrimp and save and make do.

He's never had to work to put food on the table, or find money to repair a leaky roof, or…"

Maggie came around to my side of the table and gave me a hug. "Okay. We're not talking about Vincent Armitage anymore, are we?"

I swiped my hands across my face and stared at the table.

"I get it! Ambi broke your heart. But that was a lifetime ago."

"Ambi? Who's Ambi?" LeeAnne asked.

"Ambrose Pennington the Third," Maggie answered.

I stiffened and shook Maggie's arm off my shoulders. "I told you that name was never again to be mentioned in my presence. And today is part of that NEVER!"

"Sorry I asked," LeeAnne muttered.

I sat there in silence for a few moments and let Maggie rub my neck and shoulders. Finally I sighed. "It's alright. Sorry I overreacted." I looked at my friend, who had seen me through all the ups and downs of my seventy-odd years. "You have my permission to tell LeeAnne the sad story of me and He-whose-name-shall-never-be-spoken."

"Are you sure?" she asked. "I don't want to be the cause of one of your meltdowns. I'm not sure either one of us is up to that."

I nodded.

She turned to LeeAnne. "Like I said, this all happened a lifetime ago, while Helen was working on her MBA."

"I assume this was before her ex, the infamous Harry," LeeAnne said.

"Yes," Maggie nodded. "But Harry was one of the hangers-on – you know – always riding in the wake of the rich and famous – a rich guy wannabe."

"That's how Harry and I met," I sighed. "He followed

Ambrose around like a faithful minion, doing Ambi's bidding." I chuckled. "It was kind of funny, actually, watching him wallow in the attention."

"Right," agreed Maggie. "And when Ambi moved on..."

"When he dumped me," I said.

"Yes, that. After he *dumped you*, Harry hung around and let you cry on his shoulder."

"Ah," said LeeAnne, "Harry became your rebound love. But what happened with the rich guy?"

"I guess I was kind of like Harry, flattered by the fact Ambi showed an interest in me. In case you haven't noticed, I'm not the debutante type."

LeeAnne patted my arm. "Don't put yourself down, Helen. You have a lot to offer."

"Yeah. About 245 pounds! Although not quite that much back then."

"Well," said Maggie, steering the conversation back to the subject, "I think Ambrose was attracted to you because you were a challenge. He was used to having women fall all over themselves to get his attention. He had to work to make you like him."

Love him," I sighed. "I really loved him. When I fell, I fell hard – and fast."

"Uh oh," said LeeAnne. "I know this story has a sad ending. What did he do?"

I found it impossible to speak, so Maggie continued. "Spring Break came, and Helen invited Ambrose to come here to Loblolly with her to meet her friends and family, and maybe go to the beach in Savanna for the week."

"He laughed at me," I choked out. "He said, 'You're kidding, right? The beach at Savannah? I'm off to the Riviera.' Then he kissed me on the cheek – *on the cheek* - and said, 'Have a nice life, Kiddo.' I was devastated!"

"Wow! That was cold," LeeAnne said. "So you think Vincent Armitage is another Ambrose Pennington?"

I shrugged. "Stands to reason, doesn't it? Cindy Walberg is Vincent's challenge. She's probably right. Once he makes the conquest, he'll be off to the Riviera - or wherever the Armitage's go – and she'll be crushed."

"You don't know that, Helen. Not every rich guy is Ambrose Pennington," Maggie said.

"And you've forgotten that Vincent Armitage has a daughter. Doesn't he have a right to be in her life?" added LeeAnne. "Reesie wants to get to know her father. And she told us her mom would like that too, but she's scared."

"Ah, now I get it. The little scamp wants you two to play matchmaker. Well, good luck with that!" I sat back, suddenly tired, and not the least bit tempted to eat another fig bar.

Chapter 7

A Chance For Romance?

A knock on the door broke up our pre-meeting meeting. LeeAnne ushered Elsworth and Bernie into the apartment and offered them refreshments. "George said he'd try to stop by, but couldn't make any promises," she announced.

We pulled some chairs from around the table and formed a haphazard circle in the living area. Elsworth and Maggie settled on the small sofa and LeeAnne took one of the overstuffed chairs. I opted for the other comfy seat and Bernie scooted a dining room chair closer to me and plopped down.

Elsworth scanned the room and our faces. "It looks as though you ladies got a head start on our meeting. Were you planning something clandestine in our absence?"

I blushed and LeeAnne shook her head. Maggie looked pleadingly at me.

"Fine!" I hissed. "Tell them all about He-whose-name-shall-never-be spoken. Run my sad, pathetic heart through broken glass – *again*." I glared at her and Elsworth, sitting there so lovey-dovey.

Maggie came over and gave me a hug. "I'm sorry, Helen. I didn't realize this idea LeeAnne and I had would affect you this severely. But don't you think it's worth a try?"

"Yeah, so is building a habitable colony on Mars. But I don't see that happening any time soon, either."

Elsworth took Maggie's hand as she sat back down beside him. "Hold up a minute. You've lost me."

"Yeah, me too," nodded Bernie. He placed his hand on mine that had a death grip on the arm of my chair. "Did someone hurt you, Helen?" He puffed up. "When and where and why?"

I loosened my choke-hold on the chair arm. "It was a long time ago." I sighed. "I didn't realize until today it still bothered me."

Bernie squeezed my hand. "I thought this meeting was to discuss the little redhead and the case of the lost bunny. What does that have to do with you getting your heart broken?"

"It has nothing – and everything – to do with what Maggie and LeeAnne have in mind. Go ahead and run your brilliant idea past them, Maggie."

Another knock on the door caused LeeAnne to jump to her feet. "That must be George. Hold that thought, Maggie. He'll want to hear the whole story."

LeeAnne beamed as she and George walked back in hand-in-hand.

"Hi everyone. Sorry I'm late, and I won't be able to stay long. I have a board meeting at 2:15. Did I miss anything?"

Elsworth shook his head. "No, I don't think so. Maggie was about to tell us something concerning Helen's broken heart and how it applies to murder, colonies on Mars, and stuffed rabbits."

"Okay," George laughed, "it's pretty much business as usual where these three wonderful ladies are concerned."

Elsworth crossed his arms over his chest and stared at me. "Pretty much."

Maggie filled them in on our earlier discussion, including the details of my encounter with Ambrose Pennington the Third.

Elsworth leaned forward. "Let me get this straight – you're not out to solve the murder?"

"No!" said Maggie and LeeAnne at the same time I mumbled, "Maybe."

"Are you trying to get a happily-ever-after for Reesie? I think it's a wonderful idea," said Bernie.

I harrumphed and pointed at my friends. "That's their plan. Odds are not in their favor on that happening." I looked at Bernie. "You haven't met Cindy Walberg. She's a steady worker, and I'm sure a good mother. But her brassy, gum-chewing, loud personality would never be able to fit into the high-society of a Vincent Armitage. She could never measure up, and she knows it."

"Do you really think it's impossible for Vincent Armitage and Cindy Walberg to fall in love?" asked LeeAnne.

I turned to her. "No, not impossible – but highly improbable. The world's not full of fairy tale stories with happily-ever-afters."

Bernie patted my arm. "That's sad and cynical."

"Ha! I've always been cynical. Ask Maggie. In fact, it's what makes me angry with myself about the Ambrose fiasco. How did I ever fall for him in the first place? Where was my good sense and cynicism when I needed it most?"

"It sounds as though Cindy Walberg has a fair amount of cynicism, too," Bernie said.

I shook my head. "Realism, not cynicism. I've got to give her credit, though. She's smarter than I was. She recognizes the differences between her and some rich guy are bigger hurdles than she wants to tackle."

"Are you saying we should stay in our places and not try to better ourselves? What about reaching for the stars? What about following your dreams?" LeeAnne stopped to take a breath. "Frankly, Helen, your attitude sounds defeatist. And I'm still a believer in love! I know you were hurt. But you didn't see the look in Reesie's eyes when she told us about her dad giving her that bunny."

I pointed my pen in her direction. "And about that bunny. Why did the dead guy have it? There's something not right about this whole mess. And even though I'm opposed to all this matchmaking stuff of yours, I would like to have a word or two with Mr. Armitage."

"But Detective Metcalf asked – no, *ordered* – us to stay out of the investigation," said LeeAnne.

Maggie laughed. "I know you haven't known Helen long but, in the time you have known her, can you remember her obeying an order? Especially when it interfered with what she was determined to do?"

"So true," LeeAnne agreed. "Ordering Helen not to do something is a sure way to insure she does do it!"

"Hello. Excuse me. I'm right here. Don't talk about me as if I've crossed the Great Divide and can't hear you."

Bernie rubbed his hands together. "Now we get to the good stuff. We *are* going to investigate the murder?"

Elsworth ran his hands through his steel-gray hair. "I knew it. Helen, you're a murder-mystery junkie." He looked at the men. "Guys, I guess that means we're on guard duty again."

"Great!" said Bernie. "When do we start?"

LeeAnne said, "Does this mean the Tricycle Girls are back in business?"

Maggie groaned.

"C'mon Mags. We'll check Vincent Armitage out to see if your matchmaking idea is plausible. No harm in that. And, in the process, we can ask some discreet questions to see if he knows why the dead guy was spying on Reesie and her mom."

"Discreet? You don't know how to be discreet! And we don't know Mr. Reddy had anything to do with Reesie or Ms. Walberg."

LeeAnne spoke up. "He did have her bunny when we found him. That's got to mean something."

Maggie sagged and looked at LeeAnne. "You're both jumping to conclusions. But I guess I'll have to join you to try to keep you out of trouble."

Elsworth stood and took Maggie's hand. "And I'll try to keep you safe."

I stuffed my legal pad into my bag. "That's the spirit, guys. I'm headed back to my apartment to organize my notes."

I pointed my gel pen at Elsworth. "El, can you ask your 'friends' about our dead guy? Oh, and there's some guy named Gus and a bartender called Charlie. I didn't get their full names.

"George, maybe you can work on the Armitage angle. As an accountant you have more credibility with the snooty crowd."

Bernie helped me up from the chair. It had been much easier getting into than out of the comfy seat. "What about me? What's my job?"

"I don't know right now, but I'll think of something."

"Bernie, will you try to keep Helen from doing anything dangerous or stupid," Elsworth growled.

Before I could respond, he added, "Maggie would never forgive me if anything happened to her. And," he added, grinning at me, "she's kind of growing on me, too."

Bernie's enthusiasm wormed its way into my dark mood on

our stroll to my apartment. He flitted about like a bee in a field of new clover as we walked down the hallway.

"You know, Helen, you get a glow about you and a sparkle in your eyes when you're working on a problem. It makes you even more beautiful."

"Ha!" I scoffed. "You're so full of it, Bernie Cox. You only want to get mixed up in this murder investigation. I'm not the one you need to flatter to manage that! Detective Metcalf is the person you need to follow around."

Bernie crooked his arm through mine. "If I didn't know you better, I'd be insulted. I'm not Ambrose Whatever-his-name-was, the Third. Sure, I'd like to get involved in this investigation. But do you know why?"

"Not really," I shrugged.

"Because you want it so badly. I see you come to life when you're working out a problem. I love your big yellow legal pad. I love the concentration on your face. I even love the annoying way you have of tapping your pen against your notes when you're concentrating."

He jumped in front of me and grabbed my arms. I stopped short to keep from plowing him over.

"And," he said, his voice husky, "Mr. Ambrose the Third got it wrong. I would have gone to the beach at Savannah – or to that colony on Mars you mentioned – to spend a week in your company!" He let go of me and crossed his arms in a determined stance. "So there!"

I could feel my cheeks – and maybe even my toes – turning pink. "Wow," I stammered. "That was probably the nicest thing anyone has ever said to me."

He smiled. "Well, it's true. Where do we start?"

I laughed, took his arm and we headed back down the hall. "My friend, you are incorrigible. You're almost as tenacious and single-minded as me."

He beamed. "And that, sweet lady, is probably the nicest thing anyone has ever said to me."

His compliment flustered me and I nearly walked past my apartment door. He tapped my arm and I jerked away, startled by the tingling sensation that ran up to my shoulder. I stared at him, confused by the reaction, and rubbed my forearm. The tingling surely wasn't from his touch – I must be having a heart attack. Yeah, that was more logical.

"What?" I asked, more abruptly than I intended.

He pointed to his left. "Uh, this is your apartment." He tilted his head, concern showing through his bifocals in those deep blue eyes. "Are you okay, Helen? Your face is flushed." I fumbled for my key. "Yes, I'm fine."

He took the key from my shaking hand and unlocked my door. "Come sit down, let me get you a glass of water or something."

He led me in and made me sit in my recliner. "Should I call 9-1-1?"

I shook my head.

"How about Maggie? I could ask her to come over."

"No, Bernie. Sit down and quit hovering. I'm fine – or I will be. Dredging up all those old memories must have affected me more than I realized."

He handed me a glass of water, sat down across from me and rested his forearms on his knees. "Remembering our past can do that – especially when we thought those things were dead and buried. It's startling when they show back up to taunt us."

I sipped my water, a bit calmer now, and raised my eyebrows.

"You sound as though you speak from experience."

He reached out and took my hand. "Look at us, Helen. We're in our 70's. If we haven't had some heartaches in all those years, we haven't lived. I'm not one to kiss and tell, but I've lived! Having your heart broken a time or two is part of that living." He squeezed my hand before letting it go.

"I've never asked if you were married, Bernie. I guess old married people assume everyone else has also tied the knot at some point."

He leaned back and closed his eyes. "Tied and untied." He opened his eyes and smiled. "She was a lounge singer in one of the places I played. Her name was Lorelei," he sighed.

"Lorelei. Huh? Wasn't Lorelei a siren in Greek or Roman mythology who lured sailors to their deaths?"

"Actually it was German mythology. Lorelei was the name of a group of sirens on the River Rhine. The name means alluring, and she was that! She had a haunting, smoky voice that reeled me in. But, unfortunately, I wasn't the only one."

"Oh, oh. Don't tell me she had a whole creel of other fish she had reeled in."

He laughed and relaxed in his chair. "Good analogy."

"What happened after she had you in her creel?"

"The usual. Whirlwind romance. We got married six weeks after we met."

I gasped. "Six weeks? That's not even enough time to learn each other's names, let alone make a lifetime commitment!"

"Tell me about it," he sighed. "I was totally smitten. What was it you said about Ambrose the Third? When you fell, you fell hard and fast. That was me with Lorelei. Some of the guys tried to warn me, but people in love don't listen to reason."

"I'm so sorry, Bernie. I never should have brought it up."

He leaned forward and took my hand again. "It's okay, Helen. I hadn't thought about Lorelei in nearly forty years, but the conversation about your ordeal brought it back to mind. It's just a memory – part of that living we talked about."

"Can I ask how long you were together?"

"The marriage lasted one week longer than the courtship. Seven weeks after the I Do's I got a 'Dear Tall Boy' note saying she had a better offer. She ran off to New York with Sam Fogarty, who promised to help her become a Broadway star. The divorce papers reached me the next day. Tied and untied – done and undone. And life goes on."

"And you never remarried?"

"Nah. My job kept me on the road too much to settle down. And I could always find gigs, or sit in with a band any place I happened to be. People like Chow Down Duncan, Dog Ear Barker, and Mama Jo Roberts became my family. I still keep in touch with the ones who are still around. Unfortunately, the family gets smaller every year."

"Do they still call you Tall Boy?" I teased.

"Yup," he said. "I wear that name like a badge of honor. It's gotten me into – and out of – a lot of bars over the years!"

He snapped his fingers. "Say, that's something I could do with you."

"What's that? Go to a bar? Bars aren't really my thing – unless it's a dessert bar. Then I'm all in!"

"No, no," he said, "although we could do that sometime, if you'd like. Bars are my thing! I know bars and bar people. You mentioned a place Cindy Walberg frequented. I could go with you to question the proprietor. What did you say his name was?"

I grabbed my legal pad and checked. "She called him Charlie, but I don't know if he's a bartender, a bouncer, or simply a bystander."

"Okay, Charlie. We've got a name, we can get his credentials."

I skimmed through my notes. "The guy who bothered her she thinks was Gus."

He nodded. "Another thing we can check when we find this Charlie fellow. What is the name of the bar?"

"I think she wrote Pickled Onion on the detective's note pad." I wrinkled my nose. "Does that sound right? I had to read it upside down."

He laughed. "Pickled Onion, huh? Sounds like the kind of place Tall boy, Dog Ear, and Chow Down would meet back in the day."

He pulled out his cell phone and punched a few buttons. "I found it!"

He stood up and held out his hand. "Miss Helen, would you care to go bar-hopping with me this evening?"

I reached out and took his hand. "Why, Mr. Tall Boy, I'd be delighted."

Chapter 8

Bar-Hopping

Maggie and LeeAnne acted appropriately pleased and stunned when Bernie announced at supped he and I would be going out for the evening – to a bar, no less. "I thought we'd check out the local nightlife," he explained.

"Local nightlife?" Maggie questioned. "Helen, your idea of nightlife is fig bars and a cozy mystery, not frequenting smoky bars."

"We're not *frequenting,*" I scoffed. "It's a one-time foray into the darker side of Loblolly. And Bernie has a long history with bars. I'll be perfectly safe."

"I'm sure this foray, as you call it, has something to do with Cindy Walberg and the murder investigation you have been requested to stay out of," said Elsworth. "I'm glad you're going along, Bernie, but what do you hope to learn?"

"Well," Bernie said. "Maybe the proprietor, Charlie, will have some useful information about that Gus fellow Ms. Walberg said bothered her."

"Bothered her!" Maggie shouted. "She said he broke a pool

cue over someone's head. That sounds like a lot more than being bothered. That's assault!"

"Right," I agreed. "He might be responsible for that P.I.'s murder."

"Exactly," she said. "Here you go again, getting mixed up with unstable people. Have you forgotten the gun-wielding Artie Stoltz? Or getting hit in the head with a golf club?" She threw her hands in the air. "What's the use? Why do I waste my time attempting to get you to listen to reason?"

I smiled and patted her hand. "Because you care about me? Don't worry so much, Mags. Look at this as an educational adventure. I could add a new column to my newsletter – 'Interesting Places to Visit in Loblolly'. I could feature a different establishment in the *Harvester* each week. No one should care – it would be free advertising for their businesses. Call it a fact-finding mission."

Maggie pushed her salad around on her plate. "If it was just that, it would be fine." She pointed her fork at me. "But with you it's never *just* anything! You have a knack for picking at people's secrets like a kid picking at a bloody scab. I'm afraid you will be the one who ends up bloodied one of these days."

I shoved a forkful of roast into my mouth, chewed, and swallowed. "And thank you for that analogy. A lesser person may have lost their appetite at hearing that little tidbit. But as you all can see, I'm not, nor have I ever been, a lesser person."

Everyone laughed, and the tension was broken.

George spoke up. "I could come along if you'd like, Bernie." He smiled at his dinner companion. "Perhaps LeeAnne would care to accompany me."

I glanced at her in time to see the color rise in her cheeks. I really wanted to do this alone, but I hated to deny LeeAnne a night out with George.

"Okay," I relented. "You can come. But I think Bernie should take the lead on questioning this Charlie, since he's more familiar with…" I fumbled for the right words.

He took my hand. "I'm more familiar with rowdy drinkers?"

I nodded and pulled my hand away. "Yeah, that."

We decided to take George's car, settled on 8 o'clock as a meeting time, and casual dress as our attire. I knew Bernie's casual dress would include one of his ever-present bow ties. My granddaughter, Ellyn, had deemed it 'retro cute'.

I had to agree. Bernie in a bow tie was pretty cute.

Bernie knocked on my door at 7:45. "Good evening, Helen," he said as I opened the door. "You look lovely, as always."

I stammered my thanks, even though all I had done since supper was wash my face and run a comb through my hair.

Bernie sported a bow tie with musical notes and saxophones in gold on a royal blue background. The blue accentuated the blue in his eyes. "You look nice too, Bernie. Is that a new tie?"

He straightened it and smiled. "This used to be my signature tie back in my musical days. I decided to wear it tonight for luck."

"What kind of luck? Do you plan on asking about a sax-playing gig?" I teased.

He shrugged. "Hey, you never know. Although this Pickled Onion place doesn't sound like the right kind of venue for a jazz band. No, I was thinking more along the line of getting answers to our questions. In fact," he added, "I came by early to see if you had any thoughts on what we might ask this Charlie person."

"Good idea," I said as I pulled out my legal pad. "First, I guess we – or you – could ask him about that Gus character, and if he had any bad dealings with him other than with Cindy Walberg. Oh, and we could ask some discreet questions about her, too."

"Discreet questions, like what?" Bernie asked. "I'm not sure I'd be comfortable asking personal questions about a lady."

I nodded and tapped my pen on my pad. "Okay, I'll ask the questions about Cindy- after you loosen up Charlie's tongue about Gus and the riot he caused."

Bernie laughed. "It wasn't exactly a riot. I've seen plenty of riots and bar brawls in my day! From what you said, it sounded as though this Charlie fellow got the situation under control pretty quickly."

"Maybe. Or perhaps Cindy played down the whole thing." I pointed my pen at him. "You could also ask who else was there. Other witnesses might give us some clues."

"Good idea." He checked his watch. "Are you ready? George said he and LeeAnne would meet us out front at eight."

My phone rang as I stuffed my legal pad back in my bag. I checked the caller ID. "Hold up. It's Maggie." I pushed the speaker button. "Hello, Mags. What's up? Did you decide to tag along with us? Bernie and I are walking out the door."

"No, I'll pass. I wanted to remind you to be careful tonight. Don't ruffle anyone's feathers. Men who hit people with pool cues could be capable of worse things."

"Yes, Mother."

Bernie spoke up. "Hello, Maggie. Helen has you on speaker phone. I promise to keep her safe. And George will be present, too. Between the two of us, we should be able to keep her out of trouble."

"Alright, Bernie. I'm going to hold you to it. Go have fun. And,

Helen, call me the minute you get home. Otherwise, I'll worry all night!"

I sighed. "Yes, Mother. But I don't know why you're so worried. Most people socialize in bars all the time without incident."

"Right. But you aren't most people. Incidents seem to follow you around."

I glanced at Bernie, raised my eyebrows, and smiled. "Bernie is wearing his lucky tie. I'll be fine."

He tugged on my arm and pointed to his watch. "Gotta go, Mags. George and LeeAnne are waiting. I promise to call you later." I pushed the End Call button before she could proffer any more warnings.

George and LeeAnne were deep in conversation when we walked up, oblivious to our approach. They turned, startled, when I spoke. "Sorry we're late. Maggie called with some motherly advice as we were leaving."

"That's sweet," said LeeAnne. She smiled at George, who held the door for her. "Kind of like having a sister to worry about you."

"Yeah, sweet," I grumbled. "She hovers and worries too much! She acts like I can't take care of myself, or I'll fall off a cliff or something if she's not around to protect me."

George laughed as he opened the car door for LeeAnne, "You've got to admit, Helen, she's pulled you back from some precarious precipices over the years. She's always been the voice of caution to your unbounded curiosity."

"I guess," I mumbled as Bernie helped me into the back seat, walked to the other side and seated himself beside me. "We are like sisters," I had to admit. "We sure squabble like siblings at times, but we've always been there for each other." The thought of my childhood friend calmed me once again.

Bernie gave George the address of the Pickled Onion and we were off on our night of raucous bar-hopping.

George pulled into the parking lot of the non-descript building. A few cars were scattered about, but it didn't appear to be a local hot spot of entertainment.

"Looks pretty quiet," George noted as he helped LeeAnne from the car.

I extracted myself from the back seat without Bernie's help, grabbed my bag and slung it over my shoulder. We tentatively walked up to the battered door which was plastered with signs: No shirt-No Service, No smoking, and, the most ominous, No Guns.

Our decision to play it cool and nonchalant was disrupted the minute we opened the door and walked in. All eyes turned to glare at us, and we realized our idea of casual dress was way overdone for this establishment.

Two burly men in wife-beater tanks paused in their pool game, a semi-comatose, greasy-haired guy in a booth lifted his head and eyed us, took a swig of his beer, and laid his head back on the table.

LeeAnne grabbed George's arm and whispered, "Maybe this wasn't such a good idea."

Only Bernie appeared unaffected by the atmosphere. He took my arm, sauntered up to the bar and held out his hand to the gray-haired man wiping down the counter. "Charlie Markham? Is that really you?"

A spark of recognition crossed the man's face.

Bernie continued. "The last time I saw you was at the Ostrich Club. That had to have been at least twenty years ago."

"Tall Boy Cox?" the man said as he reached over the counter

and grabbed Bernie's shoulders. "Wow. Small world, as they say. Still wearing the lucky tie, I see. What brings you to this dump? You used to frequent classier joints."

Bernie laughed. "I could say the same for you, Charlie." He touched my shoulder. "This is my lady friend, Helen Patterson." He turned and gestured behind him, "and these two are our friends, George and LeeAnne." He motioned for them to sit on two adjacent bar stools. "Don't be shy, Charlie's an old friend."

At my urging, Charlie launched into stories of Bernie in his heyday, playing to crowds up and down the Eastern Seaboard. He looked at me as if to give validation to Bernie's talent. "Tall Boy was good – no, he was one of the best sax players I ever heard. He could have made the big-time. One of the recording giants even approached him to cut a record deal, but he turned them down!"

I stared at Bernie. "Is that true?"

He blushed and shrugged. "That was all part of another time – another world, actually."

Charlie slapped the bar. "Hey, Tall Boy. I've been saving something in case I ever saw you again. Although I really never expected you to walk into this place." He dug around in a box under the bar and came up with a tall, thin glass. He made a big to do of rinsing it out, wiped it and set it on the bar. Etched on the side was 'Tall Boy'.

"Wow!" said Bernie as he turned the glass in his hands. "Never thought I'd see this again. Mama Jo had it made for my birthday one year. How did you come by it?"

Charlie laughed as he poured beer from the tap into Bernie's glass. "I was still at the Ostrich Club when it closed down. I grabbed a couple of mementoes when I left. I've carried this thing around to every bar I've worked in since, figuring you might show up someday. It's yours, if you want it."

"Thanks, Charlie. I'd be honored."

"Guess that lucky tie still works," he said as he wiped his hands on the towel. "Now, what can I get for the rest of you folks? My treat. This is a family reunion."

LeeAnne and I opted for white wine and George said, "Club soda for me, Charlie. I'm the designated driver."

"So, Tall Boy," Charlie said as he set our drinks in front of us, "what's the occasion? I know you're not here for the atmosphere."

Bernie filled him in on the reason for our visit, and said we were seeking some answers for Cindy Walberg and her daughter.

"Are you another Private Eye?"

"*Another* private eye?" I echoed. "Has someone else been in here asking about Ms. Walberg?"

"Yeah," he said. "Some guy came in here a week or so ago asking questions about Cindy. I told her about it and she got real nervous." He held up his hand. "He gave me his card. It's around here someplace."

He walked to the end of the bar, scanned a corkboard full of notes and cards, came back and laid one in front of us. It was exactly like the card George had received. I. M. Reddy definitely had something to do with Cindy Walberg! But what?

"What did you tell him?" I asked.

"Told him I didn't know her. I figure she's entitled to her privacy. When I told her someone had been in here asking about her, she kind of freaked out. In fact, she hasn't been back since."

"What about the altercation with this fellow, Gus? She mentioned him to Helen," Bernie said.

65

Charlie raked his hand through his hair. "Gus is a trouble-maker. I kicked him out permanently after he assaulted another customer. I don't need the aggravation!"

"What about Ms. Walberg?" I asked. "Do you think Gus might retaliate somehow because she snubbed him? Maybe he felt she was leading him on."

"Cindy? Nah. She's a great gal. A little rough around the edges, maybe, but a hard worker. And she thinks the sun rises and sets around that little girl of hers. She's always bragging and showing pictures of Reesie to anyone who'll listen. Cutest little redhead ever! Cindy says she's got that red-headed spunkiness, too." He scratched his chin. "Actually, that P.I. mentioned her. He called her ReeAnn. I played dumb, like I had no idea what he was talking about."

"That was a good call on your part," said Bernie.

"You don't think Cindy's in danger, do you? I'd hate for something to happen to her. She's kind of like a daughter to me."

Bernie shook his head. "I don't know, Charlie, but it's possible. The P.I. who asked about her is dead."

He combed his fingers through his hair. "Oh, my word!"

Bernie turned to me. "Helen, give Charlie one of your cards."

I dug in my bag and handed over one of the Tricycle Girls business cards. "Will you call if you think of or hear anything, please?"

Charlie read the card. "So you *are* P.I.s?"

"Not really. Amateur sleuths at best. We've been asked by Reesie to help her and her mom in another matter."

"But," added George, "this dead P.I. seems to pop up at every turn. We can't rule out the possibility that Ms. Walberg and her daughter might be in some danger."

LeeAnne spoke for the first time. "You'll probably be getting a visit from Detective Metcalf of the police department. He's keeping an eye on Ms. Walberg and Reesie."

"Right," I added. "It might be wise to not mention our visit here. He kind of told me to keep my nose out of police business."

We visited for a few more minutes, finished our drinks, and decided to head back home. Charlie didn't know where Gus lived, but promised to let us know if he found out. He rinsed Bernie's Tall Boy glass, wrapped it in a towel and handed it to him. We promised to come back and reminisce again sometime. I, for one, wanted to hear more about Bernie "Tall Boy" Cox.

Chapter 9

Old Friends and New Places

LeeAnne said as we headed back home, "This has been an interesting outing." She turned to face Bernie. "Your friend, Charlie, seems like a nice guy."

He nodded. "It proves once again the adage about six degrees of separation. It really is a small world."

"What did we learn?" I asked.

"Not much," George groused.

LeeAnne slapped him playfully on the arm. "That's not true. We learned Cindy Walberg isn't as brash and hard as she tries to let on. We learned she thinks the world of Reesie."

"And," I added, "according to Charlie, she's not the type of person to lead someone on. Any feelings that Gus fellow may have had were all one-sided."

"But," added George, "Charlie may be biased. After all, he did say he thought of her like a daughter."

"Yeah," Bernie laughed. "That's Charlie. He always did take in strays – people and animals. He has a big heart. But he has good instincts, too. I don't think he'd feel protective of Cindy if she wasn't basically a good person."

"That's not much, but it's a start," I sighed. "All we found out is Cindy's put a protective shell around herself that may be hard to crack."

"So we don't crack it," said LeeAnne. "We warm it up and melt it like rich chocolate. And what better way to do that than to help her find love?"

"UGH! You and Maggie and your happily-ever-afters." I slumped back in my seat.

George peered at us through the rearview mirror. "We learned one other thing."

"What's that?" questioned LeeAnne.

"We found out there's an almost-celebrity in our midst. Someday, Bernie, you've got to fill us in on why you turned down that record deal."

Bernie squirmed in the seat and held tight to his newly rescued Tall Boy.

It was after ten when we got back to Golden Harvest. George offered to walk LeeAnne to her apartment, and Bernie followed along beside me to my door.

"Thank you for a wonderful evening, Helen. We need to do this more often. Perhaps next time we can check out that dessert bar you mentioned."

I laughed. "I'm not sure there is such a thing, but I'd be willing to find out."

"It's a date, then." He stretched up and gave me a peck on the cheek. "Sweet dreams."

I watched, flustered yet again, as Tall Boy Bernie Cox sauntered down the hall.

I hesitated to call Maggie at this late hour, but decided she'd be up pacing anyway. I hit her number on my speed dial and she answered on the first ring.

"Oh, Helen, you're back. Was it awful? What did you find out?"

"Slow down, Maggie. It was an interesting evening." I filled her in on our visit and ended with the bit about Bernie and Charlie being acquaintances from years ago.

"That's interesting," she said. "Bernie's a star and Cindy Walberg isn't as hard as she wants everyone to think."

"Seems that way. I think Reesie is right. Cindy is afraid to let her guard down because she might get hurt."

"Right," agreed Maggie. "And the worry is doubled because if she gets hurt, so does Reesie."

"Exactly."

"Our next step is to talk to Vincent Armitage."

"I don't know, Mags. I'm still not sure trying to get them together is a good thing."

"I understand your concerns. But don't we at least need to try?" she pleaded. "If George can get us in to see Mr. Armitage, we will have a better feel about his intentions."

"Oh, alright. But I checked our business cards, and nowhere on them does it mention anything about match-making!"

Maggie laughed. "But they do say 'No Job Too Small.'"

"Ha! Making a match between Cindy Walberg and Vincent Armitage will not be a small job!"

Questions flew around our breakfast table the next morning. I had transcribed my notes the night before after talking to Maggie, and had my legal pad beside me on the table. Between bites we discussed our next move.

Bernie added cream to his coffee and sipped it. "El, have you found any information on the dead guy?"

"Not much. He was licensed and ran his business out of his apartment in Savannah. Small operation, not very lucrative. Advertised locally and appears to have spent most of his time digging up dirt on cheating husbands and wives."

I added that information to my notes. "Maybe Mr. Armitage hired him to spy on Cindy Walberg."

"Why would he do that?" asked LeeAnne. "Cindy said he kept trying to get her to marry him."

I shrugged. "Maybe he was tired of waiting, or wanted to pressure her into a commitment. Who knows how those people think," I sputtered.

LeeAnne patted my hand. "You're basing your comments on your experience with Ambrose again."

"Of course I am," I huffed. "What other frame of reference do I have in dealing with the self-appointed entitled of the world?"

"Helen may have a point," Elsworth interjected. "Perhaps Mr. Armitage thought if he could find some dirt to incriminate Ms. Walberg, he could take the child away from her."

Maggie gasped. "That's cruel!"

He draped his arm over her shoulders. "Yes, it is. But people do cruel things all the time. If Mr. Armitage felt entitled, as Helen pointed out, he might try any means available to obtain what he felt was rightfully his."

"That settles it, then," I said. "Our next interview has to be with Vincent Armitage. George, can you try to arrange that for us?"

He nodded. "I've called some acquaintances in the business, and hopefully will hear back from one of them by lunchtime. I heard Vincent Armitage has been scouting around this area to expand the Armitage family holdings. He's supposed to be in Loblolly today or tomorrow checking out sites for a new mid-line store."

"Oh," I said, "taking the business to the masses, huh? What's the world coming to, when just any old body can buy an Armitage diamond?"

"Maybe they'll sell cubic zirconia to us lesser folks," Bernie joked.

Never one to let a grammatical error slip by me, I asked, "Shouldn't that be cubic *zirconias?* Or do you think they will only have one in stock?"

Bernie patted my arm. "Sorry, Helen, but in this case, the word zirconia is both singular and plural."

Maggie applauded. "Someone finally caught Helen in an English error!" She high-fived Bernie across the table. "Way to go!"

"Are you sure?" I huffed.

He grinned. "Yup."

We left the table without a clear plan. I was distracted, still flummoxed about the zirconia episode, and checked the word in my dictionary as soon as I got home. Of course he was correct. If I was wrong about that, what else might I be wrong about?

George called me the next day and said he had arranged to meet Vincent Armitage at a new strip mall at 1:15. He invited me along as he assumed, rightfully so, that I'd demand to be included.

"How did you manage this interview?" I asked as I settled into George's Lexus.

"As I said, Mr. Armitage is scouting out storefronts for an expansion here. I'm on Loblolly's board that represents the company developing the property, and volunteered to come show him around."

I popped him on the arm. "Look at you, big man in city planning."

He shrugged. "No big deal. If you would show up at city council meetings you could get voted onto some board or another, too."

"Ha! The city wouldn't want me jumping in and stirring up the waters. Nope, not interested. There are lots of people better qualified – and more interested in city politics."

George laughed. "Not as many as you might think. It's actually a very small pool to jump into."

"All the more reason to stay away."

We pulled into the new mall. Several stores were already open for business. I spotted a sporting goods store, a beauty shop, and, my personal favorite, a 99-cent store. What's not to love about being able to purchase all the necessities of life for under a dollar! They even carried my fig bars. Perhaps we'd have time after talking with Vincent Armitage to go replenish my supply.

Two well-dressed men, who looked to be in their thirties, stood in front of the vacant building. One had dark hair and a surely look as he flailed his arms and appeared to be arguing with the other. I only caught a few words of the heated conversation – something about "…your slumming will be the downfall of the Armitage name!"

The argument stopped abruptly as we neared. The quiet one of the pair turned and held out his hand. I knew before his introduction this had to be the little redhead's father – same blue eyes, same red hair.

George shook his outstretched hand. "Mr. Armitage, nice to

meet you. I'm George Hardestee, and this is my friend, Helen Patterson."

Vincent's smile as he took my hand was strained, his eyes clouded, his hands clammy. Mr. Armitage was not a happy man. Through clenched teeth he introduced us to the source of his anger. "This is my cousin, David Armitage. He and I have some creative differences about the direction the business should go. I'm attempting to get him to see a bigger vision..."

"And I am attempting to get Vinnie to listen to reason," David growled.

Vincent smiled. "Ah yes. David has always been the voice of reason to my wild, passionate ideas."

George dangled the keys. "Well, then, shall we go inside? Perhaps your vision will become clearer if you show him around."

The tension between the cousins was as thick as the stale air in the empty building. George found a light switch, but even that didn't erase the dark coldness emanating from those two. Vincent talked about recessed lighting, glass cases, tile floors, while David grumbled and scowled.

When Vincent mentioned the back could be used for offices, George said to David, "Perhaps you'd like to see that area." He nodded to Vincent, "I'll leave you in Mrs. Patterson's good company, if you'll excuse us for a moment."

Vincent looked confused and attempted small-talk.

"Mr. Armitage," I said, "we don't have time for chit-chat. I'm here on behalf of your daughter."

"My daughter?" he stammered.

"ReeAnn," I said.

He sighed. "What about her? And why are you here on her behalf? Is this an extortion attempt?"

I laughed and handed him one of the Tricycle Girls business cards. "Goodness no! But ReeAnn asked for our help."

He glanced at the card. "What are you? A private investigator?" And why does ReeAnn need your help? Are she and Cynthia in some kind of trouble?"

I heard George's voice heading our way. "It's a long story. Would you be willing to come talk with my friends and me? We live at Golden Harvest Retirement Village." I pointed to the approaching Cousin Armitage. "I'd like to discuss this without your 'voice of reason' overhearing."

"I agree. You have piqued my curiosity. David and I have another appointment at three. I will see him to the hotel afterward and can be at your residence," he glanced at the card, "Golden Harvest, around 4:30. Will that work for you?"

"Perfect. Call the number on the card and I'll open the gate for you."

David Armitage still looked surly as he and George returned.

"What do you think, now, David? Can you envision the possibilities?" Vincent asked.

He posed a confrontational stance, arms crossed over his chest. "I can envision the *impossibilities*, nothing more."

Vincent threw his arm over David's shoulder. "Ah, David. Nothing is impossible for the person who can dream."

David shook him off. "You go ahead and dream. And, while your head is in the clouds, I'll have my feet here on the ground to keep you from dreaming the Armitage good name into oblivion!"

Vincent shook his head. "Thank you for your time, Mr.

Hardestee. I'll be in touch." As we left he held up the card I had given him and nodded to me. "Mrs. Patterson, I hope to see you again soon."

"I do believe there are some conflicting dynamics in the Armitage family," George said as he opened the car door for me.

"I believe you're right, George. The Old Guard versus the New. And change always comes at a price. I wonder who holds the purse strings to the Armitage fortune?"

"Ah," said George, "Nadine Witherspoon, who represents this building's owners, filled me in on the Armitage background." He reached into his briefcase, pulled out a chart of the Armitage family tree, and handed it to me.

"Wow. This Nadine, whoever she is, did a thorough job. It's actually kind of creepy that she knows so much about the Armitage's."

George laughed. "She's the leader of the local genealogical society, and she put this together at my request. You did ask me to check into the family."

"That I did."

I looked over the chart as George pointed to the name at the top of the tree. "Great-grandpa, John Clarke Armitage, dealt in banking and land development." He tapped the next name. "His fortune passed to his only child, Jeremiah, who expanded the wealth into investments – those investments being gold and diamonds."

I followed along on the chart. "It shows Jeremiah had two sons, Nathaniel and Nicholas. Do they share equally in the family fortune?"

"No, not according to Nadine. As you can see by the chart, Nathaniel, the older son, was Vincent's father. His first wife,"

Vincent's mother, Alice, died several years ago. He had recently remarried a woman called Constance, a trophy wife, if Nadine is correct – and she's seldom wrong about these matters. Nathaniel gave Vincent controlling shares in the company and all assets before he passed away last year."

"I'll bet Nicholas didn't like that!"

"Nadine said brother Nick was the prodigal son and lived by the James Dean code: Live fast, love hard, die young, and leave a beautiful memory. He died in a car crash a few years ago. She said his son, David, seems to have inherited his father's wild ways."

"Nadine again? Do I need to warn LeeAnne about this Nadine person? Don't you dare break her heart!"

He laughed. "No chance of that. Nadine is just a friend, tough as nails, and devoted to her husband of fifty years."

"Good. Okay, back to the Armitages, from what I caught of the argument between the cousins, David isn't happy about Vincent playing fast and loose with the family fortune."

"You could be right. But it doesn't explain the murder."

I tucked the family history in my bag. "I'll have to talk this over with Maggie and LeeAnne. We need to hurry, though. Vincent is coming by at four thirty."

Chapter 10

Fake Wine and Squeeze Cheese

George agreed to my side trip to the 99-cent store to purchase fig bars. I also found some of the fake wine Maggie and LeeAnne were so fond of serving. Perhaps we could ply Vincent Armitage with fake liquor to loosen his tongue. I was sure getting Cindy Walberg to change her mind toward him would require the real thing, though – and lots of it!

The store featured no little cheese cubes, but I picked up crackers and that cheese in a can my kids had always liked. My skills didn't run toward fancy dinner parties – I'd always been more of a squeeze-cheese and little weenies kind of entertainer. I was sure Maggie would roll her eyes and shake her head, but this was my party, and squeeze cheese and fig bars were on the menu.

I called Maggie as soon as I got home, and she and LeeAnne were at my door in minutes.

"What was Mr. Armitage like?" Maggie asked as they sat down at my table. "Did he make you feel uncomfortable?"

I sat down with them. "I actually met two Mr. Armitages."

They both stared at me.

"Like two actual people, or does Vincent Armitage have Dr. Jekyll and Mr. Hyde personalities?" LeeAnne joked.

Maggie laughed. "LeeAnne, you've got to quit reading those mysteries Helen gives you. Try some nice romance novels for a change."

I smiled at my friend. "I must say, those romances bring color to your cheeks, Mags. But I like my entertainment to have some guns thrown in, and my touchy-feely stuff to include fists and rabbit kicks."

She held out her hands. "Chalk that up as another point of disagreement. Tell us your tale of the two Armitage's."

I clasped my hands on the table and began. "When George and I got to the storefront, there were two men standing out front arguing. One of them said to the other something about him ruining the Armitage name. "

I stopped for a breath, and my friends leaned toward me in anticipation. Then Maggie looked a LeeAnne. "Helen takes these dramatic pauses for effect. She wants to see how curious her listeners are, and if they'll ask questions she has no intention of answering until she's good and ready. It's driven me crazy for years!"

Leeanne leaned toward Maggie and smiled. "Dr. Jekyll and Mr. Hyde crazy?"

"Not that bad – at least so far," she said. "But it's getting close!" Her voice became a growl and she reached her hands across the table, claw-like, toward me. "I feel I could turn at any time."

"Okay, okay," I said. "The one doing the threatening was David Armitage, the other was the little redhead's father."

"LeeAnne clasped her hands to her chest. "Is he handsome?"

"Are you sure you're not reading Maggie's romance novels?" I asked. "But, to answer your question, both men were nice-

79

looking, with that raised-with-the-best air about them. Both wore custom-made clothes, looked to be in their thirties. David, who is an Armitage cousin, is dark – dark hair, dark brown eyes, dark, brooding posture. Evidently he's not happy with Vincent's expansion plans. Typical, elite-rich attitude."

Maggie glanced at me. "Another Ambrose, I assume?"

I nodded. "Seemed like it to me."

"What about Reesie's father?" LeeAnne asked. "Was he snooty, too?"

I scratched my head with my pen. "He was very down-to-earth. In fact, if I hadn't known better, I wouldn't have guessed he was one of *them*. Except for being a bit formal and uptight, he seemed like a nice guy. He has red hair, like Reesie, and she inherited his blue eyes. There's no mistaking her parentage."

"What else did you find out?" Maggie asked.

I filled them in on the family background George had provided.

"That's about it." I checked the time. "But he'll be here in about thirty minutes to talk with us if you have any questions."

"What?" My friends shouted.

"Why didn't you tell us sooner?" Maggie whined. "I've got to go change!"

"Me too," said LeeAnne. "And we have no snacks to serve. I haven't replenished our supply!"

I patted her hand. "You two go do whatever you need to do. I've got everything under control. I had George make a stop on our way home."

My friends breathed a sigh of relief. "I'm impressed, Helen," Maggie said, as the two of them got to the door. "Who knew you'd ever get the hang of entertaining? LeeAnne must be rubbing off on you. Goodness knows you've not taken any of my advice over the years."

I laughed and shooed them out the door with the assurance I did know how to throw a party, I just usually chose not to.

My friends returned in record time, freshly pressed and lipsticked. I had run a comb through my hair and splashed water on my face. I smiled at Maggie as she eyed my appearance and shook her head.

Vincent Armitage phoned at precisely 4:30. I had to give him points for punctuality. I told him I'd open the gate and meet him at the front door.

I handed my phone to LeeAnne. "Punch in the code, will you? I never can remember it. Without you two, I'd be a prisoner in this place."

They laughed and I headed to the front to greet the little redhead's pater.

I shook his hand. "Thank you for coming, Mr. Armitage."

He nodded. "I must say, I am still puzzled by the request, but also curious. Your mention of ReeAnn did raise some red flags. I would do anything to protect her."

I cocked my head in his direction as we made the short walk to my apartment. "Anything?"

"Yes. Well, anything within reason."

"Ah. Now that leaves a lot of options on the table, doesn't it?"

I opened my door. "Here we are, Mr. Armitage. Welcome to my humble abode."

I introduced him to my friends and directed him to sit at the small table.

"Please, call me Vincent." He held up our business card. "Now, tell me about the Tricycle Girls and exactly what you all have to do with Cynthia and my daughter!"

I stood and made my way the few steps to the kitchen area. "Straight to the point. I like that. Maggie, why don't you and LeeAnne fill Vincent in on some of our escapades while I prepare the snacks."

"Do you need any help?" asked LeeAnne.

"No, there's not enough room over here for me and another person – even a light-weight like you."

I managed to locate four almost-matching glasses in the cupboard and serviceable plates for my fig bars and crackers. When I pulled the cheese out and began decorating my canapes, Maggie asked, "What in the world are you doing, Helen?"

I held up my can of squeeze cheese. "Fixing hors d'oeuvres – my way."

I handed her the plate of fig bars and held out the bottle of fake wine to our guest. "Vincent, would you do the honors of opening the wine, please?"

He smiled. "I would be delighted, Mrs. Patterson."

I smiled back. "Please call me Helen."

"Alright, Helen it is."

Maggie stepped over to retrieve the glasses and said under her breath, "Helen, I never thought you'd serve our guest cheese from a can."

Vincent heard the exchange and laughed. "Helen, the cheese is wonderful. Cynthia introduced me to the wonder of squeeze cheese."

"Really?" LeeAnne asked. "Tell us about it."

"Yes, really," he sighed. "One day she came to my office at

lunchtime with a basket and said she had prepared a picnic lunch for us. I told her I was terribly busy. She insisted there were park benches and a beautiful view only a block away, and, besides, everyone had to eat, so I relented."

I could see romantic stars in my friends' eyes, and rolled mine in return.

Vincent continued. "We sat down and she pulled crackers and a bottle of wine from her basket. When I protested it was too early in the day to drink, she held out the bottle. 'No alcohol,' she said. Then out came this can of stuff and she squirted it onto a cracker and handed it to me. 'Eat up,' she said. I asked what, exactly, it was she wanted me to eat, and she said, 'It's cheese, Silly'."

He stared at the cheese cracker in his hand while Maggie and LeeAnne held their breath as they waited for him to continue.

I poured our wine and tapped my glass with a spoon. "What happened? Tell us before my friends pass out from lack of oxygen."

He blinked and accepted the paper towel I tore from the roll in the center of the table.

"Oh, right." He set the cracker on the makeshift napkin and swiped his hand across his face as though awaking from a dream. "It was absolutely delightful. I had never had anything like it. Who knew cheese could come from a can?" His eyes took on a faraway look. "Yes, delightful." He sighed. "But I spoiled the moment. I told her I really must get back to work. The light seemed to leave her eyes. I could tell I had hurt her deeply. Cynthia is the most wonderful, unique, passionate person I've ever met. But I lost her that day."

"How sad! You never saw her again?" LeeAnne asked.

He shook his head. "Let's say there were no more surprise picnics on park benches."

He cleared his throat and sat straighter in his chair. "What is all this mysterious innuendo about Cynthia and my daughter? You said it isn't an attempt to extort money from me. But, as my cousin would say, it has all the earmarks of one."

Maggie and LeeAnne both gasped. I slapped my hands on the table. "Now, hold on, *Mr. Armitage*. Just because you happen to have a little more money than other people doesn't mean they are all out to prey on your wealth and privilege. My friends and I have no desire to extort anything from you. Neither, by the way, do Cindy Walberg and her daughter!"

Maggie patted my arm. "Take a breath, Helen."

She directed her eyes toward our guest/accuser. "Mr. Armitage – Vincent – let me explain. Your daughter, ReeAnn – she likes to be called Reesie, by the way – came to Golden Harvest with her singing group to entertain us. She saw one of our business cards and asked if we would help find her best friend, Ariadne."

"A friend of hers went missing? How awful," Vincent said.

LeeAnne spoke up. "Her friend, Ariadne, is the stuffed rabbit you gave her."

Between the two of them, my friends filled him in on Ariadne's disappearance, us finding I. M. Reddy's body, and our trip to the Pickled Onion. They conveniently left out any information on their idea to get Cindy Walberg and him together.

He appeared shaken by the announcement. "Do the police believe Cynthia and ReeAnn might be in danger?"

"Detective Metcalf has cars patrolling the area. He told Cindy to be careful, and warned them against going out alone," Maggie assured him.

"The detective will be coming to interview you, too," LeeAnne added.

84

He nodded. "Yes, Detective Metcalf has already contacted me. I have an appointment with him tomorrow. He was very vague about his visit. He only stated that my name came up in a case he was working on."

I leaned forward. "Mr. Armitage – Vincent - what do you know about this dead guy, I. M. Reddy? Did you hire a private detective to find Cindy and ReeAnn?"

There was a collective gasp from my friends and our guest. "Helen, that was a bit blunt," Maggie scolded. She glanced at Vincent. "I apologize for Helen. She's not always tactful. In fact, she thinks the word 'tact' means to hammer small nails in the wall."

"Ha ha," I said. "When I have a question, I ask. What's wrong with that?"

Vincent spoke up. "No need to apologize, Mrs. Taylor. To answer your question, Helen, no, I did not have to hire a detective to find Cynthia and my daughter. I always know where they are."

"How is that?" I asked.

"Cynthia tells me."

Chapter 11

Do the Right Thing

Now it was our turn to gasp. "What!?" I stammered.

He nodded and a sad smile played on his lips. "It's part of an agreement Cynthia and I have. She keeps me informed of where she and ReeAnn are living, and if she is ever in need of anything she promised to let me know."

He sighed. "Cynthia is very independent. She's also very distrustful. She must have been badly hurt by someone.

"I lost her that day on the park bench. She no longer wanted me in her life. I walked away without realizing at the time how great the loss really was."

He stared at the floor and wrung his hands. "I couldn't concentrate at work. I kept seeing her eyes sparkling when she handed me that little cracker, and the profound sadness in them when I got up and walked away."

Maggie touched his hands. "I'm so sorry."

He glanced at her, rubbed his face with his hands, and choked out, "I went back to that bench at noon every day for a week, hoping she would be there. I wanted to apologize. She never returned."

LeeAnne and Maggie sat there enthralled by his pitiful story. Vincent sat silent after his confession and stared ahead again, reliving, no doubt, the day he dumped Cindy Walberg.

To break the morbid silence I asked, "If you never saw Cindy again, when did the two of you make this alleged agreement?"

"Helen!" Maggie shouted.

Vincent sighed – again.

This whole conversation had begun to get annoying. All these sighs and pitiful gazes were reminiscent of a 19th century drawing room melodrama. "What's the big deal, Maggie? I told you when I have a question, I ask. What good does it do to sugar-coat things?"

Vincent looked up. "Helen is correct. Being forthright is always best.

"And, to answer the question, Helen, although I said I lost her that day, I have, on numerous occasions, spoken with Cynthia. When my attempts to catch her at the park bench failed, I went to the hospital where she was employed."

"Yes," said LeeAnne, "she mentioned she works in a hospital. Is she a nurse?"

Vincent shook his head sadly. "No, although she confided in me that she desired go into that profession, she doesn't have the time or funds to pursue the education. She loves helping people and would be a wonderful nurse. Unfortunately, she won't allow me to help her. At this time she works in housekeeping."

"Okay, people, let's get back on point. You went to see her. Then what?"

"She told me she was carrying our child." His eyes again got that far-away gaze. "I told her I wanted to do the right thing, and we should get married immediately. For some reason she took offense. She said doing the right thing wasn't a good enough reason to get married. I argued my case, but she was adamant. The only compromise she made was to assure me she would always keep me informed as to where she and our child were living. And if she ever needed anything she would let me know."

He ran his hands through his red hair. "It's not much, but," he smiled sadly, "Cynthia is a wonderfully exasperating, independent woman. I fell in love with that independence. Now, it seems, I'm reaping the rewards of that very independence I admired."

Maggie touched his arm. "That's sadly beautiful. Have you ever told her that?"

He shook his head. "Not in those words."

"Yeah, yeah. That's sad. If you didn't set a P. I. onto Cindy, do you have any idea who might want to spy on her?"

His head jerked in my direction, a sudden flash of insight in his eyes, and then gone.

"No, none," he said, a bit too quickly. "Why would anyone follow Cynthia? What could they possibly hope to gain? Perhaps it is someone from her past. Are you sure she and ReeAnn are sufficiently protected? Perhaps I should hire someone to discreetly keep an eye on the situation."

"That's up to you," Maggie said. "But how do you think Cynthia would feel if she found out you had someone secretly watching her?"

He laughed. "She would be furious! Her independence does not allow for any type of weakness or lack of self-sufficiency. She thinks she must fight the world all on her own."

"That's the impression we got, too," LeeAnne gestured to Maggie. "How about this? After you speak with Detective Metcalf, go have a talk with her. Voice your concerns and let her know you want to be assured of hers and ReeAnn's safety."

"She will turn down the offer."

LeeAnne nodded. "Most likely. But the gesture will register

with her. She'll know you really care about their welfare – and there are no strings attached."

"Yes," agreed Maggie. "And that way everything will be out in the open. No secret spying. And Detective Metcalf assured us he's keeping an eye on Cindy and ReeAnn."

Vincent nodded. "That would probably be best. And it would give me an excuse to meet with Cynthia – and possibly see ReeAnn."

He glanced at his watch – a Rolex, if I wasn't mistaken. "If there is nothing else you ladies need, I really should get back to the hotel. David made reservations for dinner. And we must discuss ideas gleaned from our meetings today."

He pulled a business card from his wallet, scribbled a number on the back and handed it to me. "This is my personal number. If you ladies discover any information concerning Cynthia and ReeAnn please call me. When I speak with your detective I will give him the number also. But I am confident," he smiled around the table at us, "you ladies will be much more forthcoming than he about any developments."

He stood, shook our hands, and headed toward the door.

"I've coded in the number to the gate," Maggie said. "It should open when you drive up."

"Thank you." His eyes twinkled. "I thought you might have me locked in here until I confessed to something."

We all laughed and assured him that was not our intent.

"It has been refreshing meeting all of you. I see the same determination in you that I find exceptional in my Cynthia." He waved his hand in parting. "I hope to see you all again, under more pleasant circumstances."

LeeAnne leaned against the door after his departure. "Wasn't that the sweetest thing?"

"Yes," Maggie agreed as she set about clearing away our snacks. "He really cares for Cindy and Reesie."

LeeAnne held her hands over her heart. "He called her 'My Cynthia' and thinks she's exceptional. He really does love her!"

Always Devil's advocate, I spoke up. "Either that or he believes she's a possession – another thing he can own!"

"Oh, Helen," LeeAnne sighed. "You saw the look in his eyes when he talked about her. That wasn't possession, that was love."

"I agree," said Maggie.

She picked up the can of cheese and added, "Helen, as much as I hate to admit it, your squeeze cheese turned out to be the perfect hors d'oeuvre. Who knew canned cheese would evoke such happy – and sad – memories. When he picked up that cracker I actually saw tears in his eyes!"

"Yeah," I said. "I saw something in his eyes, too. When I asked if he had any idea who might be spying on Cindy I caught a spark of recognition in those eyes. Despite his denial, I think he has some idea who might have hired I.M. Reddy!"

Maggie discontinued her puttering. "Oh, dear. You don't suppose he will put himself in any danger, do you?"

"Doubtful. In my experience with the privileged gentry, as slight as it is..."

"And as biased as it might be," added Maggie.

"Perhaps," I shrugged. "As I was saying, in my experience, the rich don't resort to physical violence. They appeal to a baser nature – greed. He will no doubt line the perpetrator's pockets and that will be the end of it."

"But, Helen," LeeAnne said, "a murder has been committed. That sounds like more than greed."

"I have to agree with LeeAnne, Helen. There's something more involved in this than simple greed. What would be the point of spying on Cindy and Reesie? They have no money."

"No. But Vincent Armitage does. And in my experience…"

"Here we go again. You mean in all your mystery novels?" Maggie asked.

I considered that. "Well, yes. But the scenario holds true. It usually boils down to love or money. Think about the cases we've been involved in. The first was a jewel theft – money. The second was both love and money. Stanley Crowell had taken money by false pretenses from people. And he had abused the affections of numerous naïve women. Love and Money. I rest my case."

Maggie threw her hands in the air. "I give up. What do you have in mind?"

We sat at my table and I pulled out my legal pad. "Okay, girls, let's start our murder list."

"I thought we were going to work on a love connection between Cindy and Vincent," LeeAnne said.

Maggie agreed. "It's obvious he has deep feelings for her."

"Maybe," I said. "But you heard Cindy. Having feelings doesn't translate to personality. She said he was boring – B-O-R-I-N-G! You saw him. He's like a cardboard cutout. He's so stiff and formal he doesn't even use contractions when he speaks. He's a walking 19th century elocution lesson, with no emotion."

"I disagree," said LeeAnne. "Your squeeze cheese and crackers brought tears to his eyes."

"Oh, goody! All we have to do is bring in a few cases of canned cheese and he'll steal Cindy's heart. Sounds like a perfect plan!"

Maggie sat back down beside me. "LeeAnne is right, Helen. When he spoke about Cindy he dropped some of that formality. He only needs a little push to loosen up a bit."

I threw my hands in the air. "I can picture it now." I panned the room with my arms. "The two of you playing Professor Higgins to Cindy. "The Rr-r-rain in Spain –" I rolled my R's in my best dramatic fashion. "And, telling Vincent Armitage he'd 'better shape up' will be a hoot. Good luck, ladies."

"Helen, you should have been on the stage. I'm signing you up for our next talent show," LeeAnne laughed.

"Not on your life, my friend!"

I could see my friends were not as convinced as I that Vincent Armitage might be holding something back. "You two are basing your argument on the assumption he's in love with Cindy."

"But Helen," Maggie began, "you heard him speak of her…"

I held up my hands to stop her gushing reminder of Vincent's supposed undying affection for his lost love. "Yeah, yeah. I heard it all. And I'm still not convinced he doesn't have some ulterior motive for his behavior. I'm sure he knows, or at least suspects, something or someone – if he's not, in fact, mixed up in the whole mess himself."

"Okay, if that's the case, let's make a list of people he might suspect," suggested LeeAnne.

I plopped my legal pad on the table. "Good idea. Where do we start?"

"How about that cousin, David?" asked Maggie. "You mentioned, Helen, that he wasn't very keen on the direction Vincent wants to go with the Armitage name."

I nodded. "True. David Armitage definitely didn't act like he was on board with the whole 'expansion to the masses' idea." I jotted his name at the top of the page and put a star beside it.

Maggie glanced at my note. "What's the star for?"

"It's a notation for people we need to talk to. Okay, who else?"

"What about Vincent's mother? She may not like Vincent's plans either," said LeeAnne.

"Step-mother," I reminded her. "She's a trophy wife. She's about Vincent's age, from what George said."

I shook my pen in her direction. "But she could have been upset if she found out Vincent has an illegitimate child who may, at some point, lay claim to the Armitage fortune. The rich don't easily let go of their riches. Sharing is a dirty word in their vocabulary. There may be other Armitage family members with a motive, too. We'll have to dig deeper into their insular bloodline to find out."

"I understand your cynicism, Helen," said Maggie, "and that might explain someone in the family hiring a PI. But why would they murder him?"

"Good question. Maybe the hirer and the murderer are two separate people."

LeeAnne groaned. "We're looking for two people?"

"Perhaps, but not necessarily," I said. "It seems to me that the acts have to be connected somehow. We have to figure out who had motives both to spy on Cindy Walberg and to kill Mr. Reddy."

I added the step-mother, Constance, under David's name and frowned. With only two names, it wasn't much of a list yet. Under those I jotted, *Various Armitage Family Members* with a question mark.

"Anyone else we might be able to talk to? Maggie, do you know if El has gotten any information on the tough guy in the bar?"

"Not as far as I know. I guess we should have another strategy meeting. We can ask the guys at dinner," she turned to me and smiled, "or, in your case, Helen, supper – if they are available this evening."

"We live in an old folks' home. We're always available!" I whined. "Our world is closing in on us. Before long, we'll all be confined to one room or one bed, and at the mercy of one nurse who will feed and change us as if we are over-sized infants!"

"Helen!" Maggie shouted. "That is SO not true." She stopped, took a breath, and slapped her hand on the table. "First, this is not – I repeat NOT – an old folks' home. And I, for one, do not intend to sit around and wait for the end you have pictured to catch up with me!"

"Hear! Hear!" LeeAnne raised her fist in agreement. "I'm not going into that 'good night' without a fight. What's gotten into you, Helen? You usually thumb your nose at such stereo-typing."

I sighed. "I don't know. All those young people who showed up to sing – the parents in the park who held onto their kids when we were there - the guys in that bar who stared at us like we were escapees from a home for decrepit old folks. And one of the characters in the book I'm reading quoted Shakespeare's soliloquy on the seven ages of man. It all reminds me I'm sliding down the back side of my life."

"Wow!" said LeeAnne. "With thoughts like that, it's no wonder you're depressed."

Maggie patted my hand. "Helen, think of all the positive things you've accomplished since you moved here. It was your newsletter that initiated our first investigation. It was at your insistence we followed through on your hunches and broke up that jewel theft ring."

"Yes," added LeeAnne, "and you kept us all on track to solve Stanley Crowell's murder."

Maggie shuddered. "Where you almost got shot!"

"That *was* a bit scary," LeeAnne nodded. "Those don't sound like the acts of someone sliding down the hill to senility."

She snapped her fingers. "You should start writing mysteries that feature Healthy Mature Ladies – like us," she said, fluffing her red hair. "The crime-fighting Tricycle Girls are a force to be reckoned with!"

Her enthusiasm made me laugh. "You're right. Like *they say*, age is only a number." I slapped my legal pad on the table. "Let's get together with the guys this evening and make some plans. But not here. I'm about hostessed out for the day." I held up the empty cheese can. "And I'm out of hors d'oeuvres."

Chapter 12

Two Couples Plus Two Singles Equals...

Our afternoon snacks had more than taken the edge off our appetites at suppertime. It's a good thing, because the meal consisted of nothing more than a salad. "What's this?" I groused. "Where's our meat? I need protein!"

"It's a cob salad, Helen," Maggie explained.

"What? I've never understood why it's called a cob salad. Does it have corn cobs in it?"

Maggie sighed. "You know it doesn't, Helen. But, look, it has baby corn."

"And grilled chicken breast," added LeeAnne.

"I don't like having to dig through a bunch of leaves to find my meat," I whined, as I picked my way through my salad.

Maggie pointed to the bowls the waitstaff set in front of us. "There's French onion soup, too."

"Oh joy. The chef must have had some stale bread he had to use up."

"You're in a mood tonight," said Bernie. "Have you had a bad day?"

I shrugged as I spotted another piece of chicken, popped it into my mouth, and chewed it slowly.

Maggie spoke up. "We met with Vincent Armitage today, and Helen is convinced he knows something about this case."

I swallowed and continued her thought. "Right. I got the distinct impression he either knows or suspects who hired the PI. He says it wasn't him because Cindy Walberg always lets him know where she and ReeAnn are staying."

"Hmm," said Elsworth, "that's odd."

"Evidently they made a deal," added LeeAnne. "She promised to keep him apprised of hers and Reesie's whereabouts and let him know if she needed anything."

"Interesting," said Bernie. "Rather a convoluted arrangement. But, from the way you ladies described her, Cindy Walberg does seem to be very headstrong and independent."

Maggie laughed. "You're right. She's very determined to face the world on her own terms. Given her background, that's understandable. Mr. Armitage said her determination is what drew him to her."

"Right," I added as I freed the last chicken bit from its leafy nest and stabbed it with my fork. "But it's also the very thing that makes this match-making idea of yours so absurd. Cindy Walberg's street-wise attitude will not blend with the Armitage elitism. People like us are fun playthings, but we don't get taken home to meet the parents!" I put the piece of elite chicken in my mouth and ground it between my molars.

"Oh oh," said George. I don't believe we're talking about Cindy and Vincent anymore."

Bernie laid his hand on my arm. "Nope. I believe we've circled back to What's-his-name the Third." He touched my chin with his free hand and turned my face toward his. "Helen, Maggie and LeeAnne only want to give Mr. Armitage and Ms. Walberg a chance to get to know one another. That's the only way they can determine if there's enough to build a relationship on."

Maggie reached across the table and took my hand. "That's right, Helen. We want them to have a chance. We don't want them to wake up forty years from now sad that they had missed out on love."

I removed my hand and arm from my touchy-feely friends' grasp and offered a sad smile. "That was kind of schmaltzy, Professor and Mrs. Higgins. Believe it or not, I'm not against love and happily-ever-after. But I don't want Cindy Walberg to wake up in forty years and find that the name Vincent Armitage leaves a bitter taste in her mouth."

I pushed the rest of my salad away and managed to take in an almost normal breath. No way would I allow Ambrose Pennington III to affect me ever again. I reached down into my bag to retrieve my legal pad and compose myself, and raised up, pen and pad in hand. "Okay, folks. Shall we have our discussion here, or adjourn to someone's apartment for our briefing?"

LeeAnne raised her eyebrows. "But, Helen, the dessert hasn't been served yet. I can't believe you're so anxious to leave the table."

"Ha! The way this meal is going, dessert is probably kale ice cream, or something just as disgusting!"

As if to prove me wrong, the waitstaff began passing out slices of cherry cheesecake with huge dollops of whipped cream on top. I wavered. "Okay, our meeting can wait until after dessert."

"Good plan," said Bernie as he dived into his cheesecake.

We finished our dessert in silence except for the scraping of forks across our plates. When we pushed our chairs back to leave the table, Elsworth took Maggie's hand and offered to host our meeting in his apartment. I had only been inside his stark living quarters once. That was when I interviewed him for my newsletter, the Harvester. At that time he was a suspect, at least in my mind, in the thefts that were occurring here. I remembered his place had few amenities – a glass-topped chrome table more fit for a boardroom than a dining room, a world map on the wall, and a bookcase – all cold and uninviting. But then, if it wasn't for Maggie and my granddaughter, Ellyn, with their penchant for brightening me up, my place wouldn't be much better. Ellyn had brought in fluffy throw pillows, obscure art prints, and added family pictures to my walls. "In case you forget who we are," she had half-joked.

Maggie had tried to brighten and update my wardrobe, brought in plants and flowers, and convinced me to switch from paper plates and cups to the 'real thing'. After the plants died, I replaced them with more durable, plastic ones.

My mouth fell open when El unlocked his door and ushered us in. I could immediately see Maggie's touch. The glass and chrome table was still the focal point, but a purple cyclamen plant perched in the center of it. The blue-gray recliner she had helped him pick out sat in front of the bookcase, and a floor-to-ceiling lamp completed the reading area. A small sofa – what my dear, departed mother would have called a settee – sat opposite, and angled to look out the patio doors.

El pulled two folding chairs from his closet and placed them at the table with the other four chairs. While he removed his world map from the cork board and carefully rolled it, I continued my gaze around the transformed space. Black and white pictures of ancient Greek and Roman architecture adorned the walls. Everything fit perfectly with his personality.

99

"Wow," I said, "Your place almost looks lived in."

He smiled and gave Maggie a hug. "I owe it all to this woman. She convinced me this wouldn't be home until I made it look homey."

I nodded. "Between Maggie and my granddaughter, my place got converted, too." I looked around. "The only things missing here are the throw pillows. Maybe I should send my granddaughter over to help you with that."

Everyone laughed.

I pointed to the cyclamen. "A little hint about that plant – it has to be watered. The good news is they make plastic ones that look almost real – and never need watering."

His deep, baritone laugh filled the room as he looked lovingly into my friend's eyes. "If it was left to me, the poor thing wouldn't make it. But Maggie has a magic touch. It's nearly doubled in size since we got it."

Maggie beamed at his compliment as he pulled out a chair for her. "Shall we sit and begin our meeting?" he asked. "I cleared the corkboard so we can tack notes to it. The visual sometimes helps me plan my steps."

We all sat – the two couples and Bernie and me. I looked at them. By default it seemed Bernie and I had become the third couple in our group. I reached for my legal pad and rummaged for my gel pen. In this search for a happy ending for Cindy and Vincent, I wasn't sure how I felt about being coupled with Bernie Cox. I slapped my notepad on the table. I didn't have time for any introspection, romantic or otherwise. I had a murder to solve!

George and I filled El and Bernie in on our visit with Vincent Armitage and his cousin, David. Then Maggie and LeeAnne built a very romantic story from Vincent's confession about Cindy and him and the squeeze cheese episode.

"That's kind of sweet," said Bernie. "Who would have thought cheese in a can could evoke such nice memories?"

El shook his head. "Squeeze cheese, huh? That's a new one. I must have missed out on that fad."

"It's not a fad!" I retorted. "It's a staple. Practically one of the four food groups – right along with crackers, and fig bars." I leaned back and tented my fingers under my chin. "Yup. Cheese for milk and protein, crackers for grain, and fig bars for fruit. Can't get more well-balanced than that!"

Everyone laughed, and Maggie asked, "Who wrote that food pyramid, the same person who declared catsup was a vegetable?"

"Of course catsup is a vegetable! It comes from tomatoes, doesn't it?" I tilted my head and grinned. "Or would that make it a fruit?"

She shrugged. "Whatever."

"If that's the case," added LeeAnne with a smile, "does that mean milk is meat because it comes from a cow?"

El stood up and loomed over us. "Ladies, I believe we're getting off point."

We giggled and tried to bring ourselves back to order.

"Squeeze cheese aside," he continued, "what was your general impression of Mr. Armitage? Did he seem aboveboard? Or was he evasive when you talked with him?"

Maggie and LeeAnne looked at me. I scowled and pointed my pen at them. "You two give your romantic interpretation of our interview first."

They proceeded to do just that. By the time they were done, Cindy Walberg and Vincent Armitage were candidates for the next

'*Pretty Woman*' movie, with Oscar nods going to Maggie and LeeAnne as co-writers of the script.

When they had wound down, El looked at me. "Helen, do you have anything to add?"

I cleared my throat. "I'm sure everyone is aware of my concerns and cautions. I believe Vincent Armitage knows more than he's telling. I think he's protecting someone."

"Or," said Bernie, "maybe he suspects more than one person and wants to verify his suspicions before he makes accusations."

"We considered that," said LeeAnne. "If that's the case, I hope he won't put himself in danger."

I scribbled a bullseye at the top of my page with a dollar sign dead-center. "Like I said, the rich don't resort to violence. Their weapon of choice is money."

"Unless," said George, "he suspects a family member. None of them could be bought off."

Elsworth nodded. "You may be right, George. Who do we have on our list?"

Maggie suggested David Armitage. LeeAnne added Constance Armitage, the step-mom, as well as the various Armitage family members. I kept Vincent's name on the list.

Elsworth said he would try to dig deeper into the family. He already had someone checking the PI's files for other possibilities.

It's nice to have a covert group on your side, I thought.

I snapped to attention when Elsworth said, "Helen, could you write the names down and we'll tack them on our board?" He produced a marker and a stack of three-by-five cards from somewhere and handed them to me. "Let's do it in bold lettering so we don't have to strain our eyes."

Rumbles of laughter and 'Good idea!' emanated around the

table, and five pairs of senior-citizen eyes stared at me. I stared back. We really were an unlikely crime-solving group. We'd been lucky so far. I prayed our luck would continue. I wrote the names and handed them to Elsworth, who tacked them neatly on our murder board.

With our pitiful list of suspects in front of us, we decided there wasn't much more we could do that evening. George offered LeeAnne his arm and asked if she'd like to take a stroll to take advantage of the balmy moonlit night.

Maggie busied herself straightening the chairs around Elsworth's table, no doubt waiting for Bernie and me to leave so she could be alone with 'her man'.

I started to ask if she'd like for me to wait and walk her back to her apartment, knowing it would fluster her. Bernie saved me from initiating my mean streak by taking my arm and suggesting we also take a walk to discuss our next move toward solving our mystery.

As he escorted me down the hall he looked up into my eyes and cocked an eyebrow. "You really intended to do it, didn't you?"

I stared back at him and feigned innocence. "Intended to do what?"

He laughed and squeezed my arm. "I could see your wheels turning back there in El's apartment. You had that look of attempted sabotage in your eye. You had in mind to embarrass Maggie somehow, didn't you?"

"I was merely going to ask if she wanted to walk together to our apartments."

"Uh huh. And?"

"And what?" I removed my arm from his and placed my hands

on my hips. "What are you implying, Bernie Cox? That I'd try to sabotage Maggie's relationship?"

He stepped in front of me, stopped and turned to face me. "No. Not intentionally, at least." He reached around me, unlocked the door to his apartment, and motioned for me to enter.

"Into your apartment?" I stammered.

One side of his mouth turned up in a slight smile. "Why, young lady, are you afraid I'll compromise your sensibilities by ushering you into my lair?"

"I – uh –no," I stuttered. "It's not that." I stood in the doorway and peered inside as if facing a precipice over which I might tumble at any second. This was virgin territory. I'd never before been in Bernie's apartment. And, unlike meeting in Elsworth's place, this was different. Venturing into Bernie's space indicated an intimacy I wasn't sure I was prepared for.

You're being ridiculous, I chided myself. I sucked in a deep breath and stepped across the threshold. One small step into a room – one giant step for an overweight, under-confident, senior citizen who dragged lots of bad choices in men as baggage behind her.

As the door clicked closed, I expelled the breath, confident that, if the need arose, I could sit on Bernie's lap and incapacitate him.

Chapter 13

High Hopes

Bernie picked up on my hesitancy and, without a word, took my hand. "If you'd be more comfortable, we could go sit on the patio – or go to the library."

I shook my head and stammered, "No, it's fine – I'm fine – your place is fine."

"Okay. Now that we've established that everything is fine, would you care to have a seat?" He ushered me to a worn, but comfortable-looking small couch upholstered in light beige faux suede. "Here, sit in my favorite place. It's where I do all my deep thinking."

I eased into the softness. "Deep thinking, huh?"

Bernie flopped down beside me. "There's a button on the arm rest. Push it."

As I did, the seat slowly angled back and a footrest popped up. "Whoa. That was a surprise! I would be doing more napping than thinking if I sat in this thing for long."

He chuckled. "I've found deep thinking requires intervals of rest, don't you agree? I read somewhere that Einstein only required about four hours of sleep a night. I've come to the conclusion it's because he had a comfy chair and took power naps during the day."

"I'm sure he would have if he'd had a 'deep-thinking chair' like this one."

I gazed around his apartment. Brightly colored posters of impressionistic jazz musicians, that bore striking resemblances to Mardi Gras scenes, adorned the walls. A shelf held black and white photos with his newly retrieved 'Tall Boy' glass centered in the mix. I nodded toward the photo grouping. "Are those pictures of some of your jazz friends?"

"Yeah, most of them. I think you would have liked them – and they would have loved you."

"Me? What would people like Dog-Ear or Chow Down see in someone like me? The only thing I can play is the radio."

Bernie patted my hand and I couldn't help pause and consider the familiarity of that slight touch. "Independence, Helen. You've got independence – and gumption!"

I had to laugh. "Gumption? Now that's a word I haven't heard in a while."

His blue eyes twinkled with excitement. "You're a fighter for what you believe in, Helen, the same way my friends fought for what they believed in. They didn't give up on their dreams when others told them they were wasting their time, and they always supported each other. They were – we were – family. One's ups and downs were everyone's ups and downs."

I nodded my head in understanding. "Like the Three Musketeers – All for one, and one for all."

"And like the Tricycle Girls," he added. "You work as a team. Not one of you stands up and takes all the credit. Your strength is in working together."

A light suddenly went on in my brain. I reached over, took Bernie's hand, and his eyes took on a glow at the surprised gesture. I looked into those deep blue eyes. "That's why you turned down the music contract. Your family wasn't included in the invitation, was it?"

He shrugged and stared at the photos on his shelf for a long while before he spoke. "That's part of it."

He stood up, cleared his throat, and held out his hand. "Come meet my family."

I pushed the button to bring myself back to an upright position. He helped me to my feet and held my hand as we crossed the room. He picked up the first photo and handed it to me. A dark-skinned man, who appeared to be seated at a child-sized piano, flashed a toothy grin at the camera. His large eyes sparkled as if he shared an inside joke with the cameraman. "That's got to be Chow Down Duncan," I said. "Is that a baby piano, or is he really so big he overshadows it?"

Bernie laughed. "It's a full-sized piano, but Chow Down was a super-sized fella." He got that far-away look in his eyes that's reserved for all our best-remembered people and places. "And he had a heart as big as his appetite. Chow Down never met a man or a meal he didn't like."

He placed the photo back in its place and handed me another. In this one, Chow Down sat in the background and a sultry and substantial dark-haired woman leaned against the piano. Also in the picture were a bass player, a drummer, and a very young Bernie, with his saxophone. I pointed to the woman. "Lorelei?"

"No, that's Mama Jo Roberts. She took us all under her wing - tried to keep us on the straight-and-narrow – for the most part. She and Chow Down came out of New Orleans and were together until he went to the Great Jazz Band in the sky."

He cleared his throat and pointed at the other players. "That's Dog-Ear Barkley on bass, and Salty Pepper on the skins – uh, drums."

I pointed. "And there's a very young you wearing your bow tie."

"Yeah, that was my signature – that and the Tall Boy glass. Hard to believe we were ever that young."

"I know what you mean," I said as I placed the photo back on the shelf. "But, as my friends keep reminding me, age is just a number." I punched his arm. "You still play a pretty mean sax."

He squeezed my hand. "Why, thank you, Darlin'."

I hurriedly pointed to another photo to avoid any further intimacy. "Who are these folks? That's definitely not Chow Down at the piano."

"No, that's Blind Willy and his band, 'The MisFits." Willy was born blind and taught himself to play the piano. He became a mentor to guys with disabilities or who were down on their luck." He pointed to the drummer. "That's Lefty Wright, the best one-armed drummer in the world – at least in our jazz world. Other members came and went as Willy helped them out and they moved on. I sat in on a lot of sessions with them. That's where I met Lorelei. She was their singer. That's her." His hand brushed across the face of a beautiful, petite woman who smiled defiantly back at the photographer – or someone else outside the picture.

"Hmm. Did Blind Willy mentor her, too?"

"In a way. She was out of New Orleans, too – the land of voodoo and witchy women. She was born Hazel Upton, but legally changed her name to Lorelei – no last name, just Lorelei. Said it created an 'air of mystery'. She had one green eye and one brown eye, and some folks thought she could put a hex on you if you crossed her." He laughed. "She never denied the story and, once she gained confidence in herself, used it to her advantage."

I put my arm through his. "That's it. She put a hex on you."

He smiled. "No, not a hex. But I was definitely spellbound for a short time."

He took the picture from me and placed it with the others. "Okay, enough reminiscing."

He led me to a small drop-leaf table, raised a leaf, centered its leg underneath, and pulled two wooden chairs up to it. "Alright, you woman of mystery, sit down and dig out that legal pad. It's time we started working on the Great Bunny Caper."

Bernie and I discussed reasons why the PI might be stalking Cindy Walberg and Reesie. All avenues seemed to lead back to the Armitage family.

I doodled exclamation points on either side of the Armitage name. "They've got to be mixed up in this mess. Hopefully, Elsworth and his 'friends'," - I air-quoted the word – "will have some luck digging into their backgrounds."

"From what little I know about El's friends, I don't believe they rely on luck in their investigations," he said.

"You're right. I'm just glad they're on our side."

"At least right now," Bernie added. "If you ever get on their radar, that could change in a hurry! Don't think for a minute that El's 'friends' have any family allegiances!"

"Humph. I guess we'll have to stay off their radar, then, won't we? Besides, I have connections - and a secret weapon."

"Sounds as though you've thought this thing through. Secret weapon, huh? What is it?"

I leaned close to his ear. "You're sure your place isn't bugged?"

As he sat back he cast eyes around the room before zeroing in on my face that was barely able to hold back my amusement. I burst out laughing.

"Good one, Helen. You had me going for a minute. What is this secret weapon of yours?"

"Maggie," I said with a grin.

"Maggie? She's your secret weapon? Does she know that?"

I shook my head. "Doesn't matter. The way I see it, if Elsworth is as smitten with her as she is with him, all I have to do is put a bug in her ear and she'll tell him to have his 'friends' back off."

"Devious," Bernie replied. "That's a weapon, alright. And it gives a whole new definition to the phrase, 'Love Connection'."

"Speaking of love connection," I said, "what do you think about Maggie's and LeeAnne's idea to get Cindy and Vincent together? I'm afraid it's a disaster waiting to happen."

Bernie placed his hand on mine. "Like the poet said, 'Better to have love and lost'. I have to agree with the gals on this one; Ms. Walberg and Mr. Armitage deserve a chance at love. And Reesie would really like to have her father in her life, don't you agree?"

I doodled pieces of hearts on my legal pad and looked into his eyes. "But what if he breaks her heart?"

He put his hands on my shoulders and turned me to face him. "That's a risk they'll have to decide whether or not they want to take. You know what they say," he squeezed my shoulders lightly, "The greater the risk, the greater the reward."

I felt that flushing, tingly, heart-attacky sensation in my arms again, and twisted out of his grasp. I had to regain control of this situation – and fast! "Ha!" I scoffed. "Sounds as though you've been reading the 'Clichés for Every Occasion' manual."

He put his hands up in defense. "Guilty as charged. But clichés are here for a reason – their truths have stood the test of time. Oops, there I go again. There's no escaping them – they're everywhere!"

"It's so true," I said. I placed my notes back in my bag and yawned. "It's been a long day. I'd better head home."

Bernie stood with me. "I'll walk you to your door, to make sure you're safe. After all," his eyes twinkled, "who knows what evil lurks in the hearts and minds of men?"

"The shadow knows," we said at the same time as we stepped out the door and literally ran into Janine the Snow Queen.

"Speaking of lurking," I grumbled, "why are you loitering outside Bernie's door, Janine?"

She ignored me and cooed, "Hi, Bernie. I was wondering if you'd like to come by my place and listen to a new jazz album I recently bought."

"Oh? What's the band's name, Ms. Hopgood?" he asked.

She touched his arm. "Now, Bernie, I told you to call me Janine."

I cleared my throat. "I'll leave you two to discuss jazz. I'm headed to my place."

I took off down the hall at my senior citizen sprint and, before I knew it, Bernie stepped up beside me and took my arm. "Slow down, girl. You're not running a race."

"That's what you think! I am definitely running a race away from that woman. She's been a thorn in my side all my life!"

He nudged me with his elbow. "I think I'm rubbing off on you; you're resorting to clichés."

I laughed in spite of the irrational irritation I felt at Janine's outrageous flirting with my man. *Whoa! Where did that thought come from? He is not my man – is he?*

I strode on down the hall, Bernie double-stepping to keep up. "Do you often go to Janine's to listen to jazz?" I asked, even though I was afraid I didn't want to hear the answer.

He stepped in front of me and stopped – again. I slammed to a halt, crossed my arms and said, "You need to quit doing that. One of these days my forward momentum is going to be too much and I'll plow you over!"

He laughed. "I'll take that chance."

I centered my gaze on a spot down the hall.

"Helen," he pleaded, "look at me."

I managed to slow my breathing and look into his blue eyes.

He continued. "I have never been to Ms. Hopgood's apartment to listen to jazz – or do anything else! Although, I have to say, she persistently makes requests. His eyes sparkled. "Helen..."

I cocked my head. "What?"

"This is not a cliché, Helen. I only have eyes for you."

My head spun, and I could feel my cheeks getting flushed. I could not – Would not – let myself become like a love-struck school girl. I had always countered intimacy with sarcasm. The only defense is a good offense, right? Or was that the other way around? Whatever. I'd have to go on the offensive to regain control – at least of my breathing.

A hand on my arm brought me out of my reverie and I looked into Bernie's concerned eyes.

"Are you okay, Helen?"

"Uh, yeah," I stammered. "I was - I was digging in my memory banks for a come-back cliché for that last comment you made."

His face fell. "I told you that wasn't a cliché. I meant it."

The sadness in his eyes tore into my heart. "I know," I whispered.

I took a deep breath. "In spite of all my internal arguments, I like you, too. I would rather be with you than with about anyone I know, except maybe Maggie and LeeAnne."

A slight smile returned to his lips. "I guess that's a start, if not high praise, since you admit you don't like most people."

"Yeah, and Janine Hopgood is at the top of that don't-like list," I hissed. "I must admit, she hasn't been quite as annoying since we got back from Stone Mountain. I thought she had latched onto Jonah Burkowitz. He's ga-ga about her. One hanger-on should be enough for her!"

He took my arm and we meandered on down the hall. "Do I detect a bit of the Green-eyed Monster in you, my dear?"

I bit the inside of my cheek to keep silent, and he continued. "Well, you needn't worry. She doesn't stand a chance against you."

I slid back closer to my comfort zone and laughed. "I guess she thinks all's fair in love and war."

"It's a lost cause for her," he added with a sigh.

"Personally, I think she's got bats in her belfry."

"She'd be mad as a wet hen to hear you say that, Helen."

By this time I was laughing so hard my sides hurt, and Bernie bent at the waist, hands on his knees, to catch his breath. "One more and I swear I'm done," he gasped. "I promise you, her flattery will get her nowhere."

"Okay, this will be my last effort, too." I thought for a moment before speaking my final cliché. "You may take Janine's advances with a grain of salt, but she's always been determined. She's not going to give up and run off with her tail between her legs."

"Enough!" he guffawed. "I trust you to keep that She-wolf from blowing my house down."

Our laughter had died down by the time we reached my apartment. As I pulled out my key and unlocked my door, Bernie took my free hand and kissed it. "Parting is such sweet sorrow," he quoted with a smile.

"I thought you said you were done," I chuckled.

"Sorry." He gave me a sheepish grin. "I couldn't help myself."

I stood in my doorway, rubbed the back of my just-kissed hand, and watched as Bernie waltzed down the hall whistling, 'High Hopes'.

Chapter 14

Road Trip

The next morning passed awkwardly. I found myself unable to enjoy breakfast with my usual gusto, and Bernie's incessant good humor didn't help my mood. Maggie commented on my ill-temper, but had sense enough to not ask for details.

Bernie sauntered in at lunchtime, again whistling 'High Hopes'. I turned and flashed him a glare that used to strike fear into the hearts of my children.

"That look doesn't scare me," he whispered in my ear as he pulled out a chair for me.

"It should!" I grumbled.

A smile played on his lips and I found it impossible to maintain my annoyance. "No more whistling that song, please," I begged under my breath. "It's embarrassing."

"Your wish is my command, fair lady." He scooted my chair to the table and plopped down beside me, still grinning.

As we left the dining room after a somewhat unsatisfying meal, Maggie hooked her arm in mine. "What's wrong, Helen? You seem to be off your feed today?"

"Humph! You make me sound like some 4-H project calf!

There's nothing wrong with me. I'm fine!"

Bernie smiled and waved as he walked by talking with George. LeeAnne ambled up on my other side and sing-songed, "Bernie asked me to tell you he was going to play a round of golf with George, but he had high hopes of seeing you later. He said you would understand."

I stiffened. "That man just won't let it go! He's determined to irritate me."

"He is determined, I'll give him that," said Maggie. "Most men would have given up and walked away by now."

"True," agreed LeeAnne. "You haven't given him a lot of encouragement to hang around."

"But there he still is, "I sighed. "I can't turn around without practically tripping over him. One of these days I'm liable to accidently plow him down."

I absent-mindedly rubbed the back of the hand Bernie had kissed the night before. "He kissed my hand!" I blurted out to my friends.

We were in front of LeeAnne's apartment. She dropped her keycard trying to open her door, quickly retrieved it, and she and Maggie practically shoved me inside.

"He kissed your hand?" LeeAnne oozed. "How romantic."

"Sit, sit," Maggie ordered. "Details. We want details. Was it your first kiss?"

I sat at the table, my friends on either side of me. "First of all, there will be no details. Second, technically *we* didn't kiss. He kissed my hand. That's it!"

"For it to have unnerved you this much, it must have been the first time he did that," Maggie surmised.

"Well, yes," I stammered. "He'd never kissed my hand before."

"Aha!" LeeAnne rubbed her hands together. "There have been other kisses, just not hand-kisses. Now we're getting somewhere. Tell us more."

"He kissed my cheek a couple of times," I mumbled. "But it was only a peck on the cheek – like you'd give a friend." I rubbed the back of my hand again. "This was different, somehow."

"Hmm," said LeeAnne. "If I might make an observation here, I don't think Bernie's intentions have changed. I think you're seeing them differently."

"I have to agree," added Maggie. "You do like Bernie, don't you?"

I shrugged. "I guess. No, I do. But I'm… I don't know."

I rubbed my hands together and folded them in front of me. "I'm too old. And I don't have time for this romantic stuff."

LeeAnne looked at Maggie. "She's got it bad."

Maggie nodded. "Oh, yeah."

She peeled my hands apart and held onto one. "Helen, aren't you the one who recently said," she raised her eyebrow to LeeAnne and they chimed together, "We're old. All we have is time."

I groaned. My words had come back to haunt me. I pulled my hand away. "I don't have time for *this*. We have a murder to solve. And, according to the two of you, a romance to instigate." I shook my finger in their direction. "And I don't mean mine!"

"You're right," agreed Maggie. "Any ideas on how we're going to accomplish either of those things?"

"Well," drawled LeeAnne, "this may be a longshot, but I read in the society pages the current Constance Armitage is sponsoring an open house next week at the Savannah Civic Center to raise money for a humane, no-kill animal shelter in Savannah."

I turned to her. "And how do you propose we wrangle an invite to this get-together?"

LeeAnne held up the paper. "No problem. It's open to the public. A twenty-five dollar donation gets us in."

"Twenty-five dollars?" I gasped and cupped my hand to my chest. "Each?!"

"Yes, Helen, each. But it's for a good cause. All the money goes to the foundation for the animal shelter – to save all those poor, unwanted pets," LeeAnne explained.

"That seems like an oxymoron. If nobody wants them, how can they be called 'pets'? And what are they being 'saved for'? So they can grow old in a cage somewhere? Maybe it should be called A Domestic Animal Zoo."

"That's pretty harsh, Helen," said LeeAnne. "Don't you like animals?"

"I love animals – as long as they belong to someone else! What I don't like are irresponsible animal owners, who dump pets when they decide they don't want them anymore."

I slapped my hands on the table. "For example, my boys brought home a mama guinea pig and her five babies one time that someone had obviously dumped in a ditch. My kids passed out the babies to all their friends, to give them homes. It was a nice gesture on their part – besides, I told them they couldn't keep all the furry little monsters. But I'm not sure what the parents thought about their kids becoming instant pet owners. I hope they didn't end up back in that ditch."

"That's what this shelter will do, Helen," said Maggie. "It will help find forever homes for animals whose owners, for some reason or another, can't keep them any longer."

"Hmm," I said, "It's actually not a bad idea. Okay, I'll throw in twenty-five dollars to meet the person who wants to save the world, one animal at a time. And perhaps we can determine if her love for animals extends to people – especially to people who might be able to put their hands on some of the Armitage fortune."

"Good. Then it's a date. Speaking of which, should we invite Bernie to ride along with us?" teased LeeAnne. "Maggie and I could be chaperones so there's no more hand-kissing hanky-panky."

"Ha ha. Very funny. You're right, though. It wouldn't hurt to have an extra driver along. Savannah is about an hour away, and who knows how long this pet rescue shindig will last."

LeeAnne and Maggie raised their eyebrows and grinned. I put my hands on my hips and said, "Let me assure both of you, there definitely will not be any hanky-panky going on!"

"We know," said LeeAnne, "because we'll be watching!" They laughed at my discomfort.

We made plans for our upcoming road trip. LeeAnne, always the good hostess, steeped cups of tea and set them in front of us before seating herself.

Maggie glanced at me. "Where is it, Helen?"

"Where is what?"

"That yellow legal pad of yours. I know you don't go anywhere without it."

"Right," added LeeAnne. "It's the first thing you drag out – even at the dinner table. It's like an extra fork or a napkin."

"No," said Maggie. "It's more like oxygen. Helen doesn't take a breath without consulting her notes."

"You two talk as though I have a serious problem – like my keeping notes is a lifeline to my sanity or something." I pulled the notepad out of my bag and slapped it onto the table. "There! Are you two happy now?"

Maggie nodded. "Our meeting has officially come to order."

She winked at LeeAnne. "Helen, could your read the minutes from our last meeting for approval, please!"

I dug my gel pen from my bag. "You two are having a great time at my expense, and you can stop at any time!"

They both burst out laughing. Maggie finally managed to control herself enough to answer. "Fine. But you've got to admit that yellow pad and your gel pen are almost extensions of your arm, maybe out of sight, but never out of reach."

"Yes," agreed LeeAnne. "It's like a pace-maker. You function better when you are plugged into it."

"I'm not that bad, am I?"

"Yes!" said my two friends in unison.

I shook my head, clicked my pen, and doodled 'conspiracy' on the edge of my note pad. My friends, it seemed, were out to get me.

"According to my 'lifeline', as you two so succinctly put it, our suspect list is pretty small."

"Right. We've ruled out Vincent," said LeeAnne.

I underlined his name. "I don't know. He may not have hired Mr. Reddy, but it doesn't mean he didn't kill the guy – especially if he thought the P.I. was endangering Cindy and Reesie."

"But even Cindy said he wasn't the kind of man who would do such a thing," argued LeeAnne.

"Who really knows what a man in love is capable of?" I said. "Guys have been known to do really stupid things to protect the women they love."

"That's true," said Maggie. "Artie Stoltz, who held a gun on you a while back on our vacation to Stone Mountain, only did it to protect the love of his life, Bunny Ambrozzi. (See '<u>No Stone Unturned</u>')

"You may be right," argued LeeAnne, "but Vincent isn't Artie Stoltz. Vincent has class."

"Oh, you think because he was born rich it excludes him from stooping to murder?"

Maggie held up her hands. "Girls, we've gone over this before. Arguing the pros and cons of Vincent's involvement will get us nowhere. We need proof!"

"Right. He stays on my list until we have proof he didn't do it."

Leeanne crossed her arms. "Okay. But put him on the bottom of that list as a least-likely-suspect."

"Are we good now?" Maggie asked.

LeeAnne and I both nodded.

"Great. Let's concentrate on our fact-finding mission. What do we hope to accomplish?"

"Well," drawled LeeAnne, "maybe we can find out if Vincent's family is aware of Cindy and Reesie."

"Right," I added. "And perhaps we can discover how they feel about the possibility of ReeAnn dipping into the Armitage fortune."

"I agree, but how do we do that?" asked LeeAnne. "We can't very well go up to them and ask what they think about Vincent having an illegitimate daughter."

"Of course not," agreed Maggie. "But perhaps we can get the information in a more tactful way."

"That lets me out," I said. "I'm all for the direct approach."

LeeAnne smiled. "Guess that leaves it up to you, Maggie.

121

You're always the voice of tact and reason in our group."

"Gee, thanks. Okay, I'll try to think of a tactful way to breach the subject. And what will your roles be, my co-conspirators?"

"We can take my car," said LeeAnne. "And Helen can convince Bernie to ride along to help drive home."

"One question, Mags," I said. 'What about Elsworth? Are you going to fill him in on our trip? And, if so, what excuse are you going to give for excluding him?"

Maggie chewed on her lower lip. "I hadn't considered that. I don't like doing things behind his back."

"Why not let him ride along, too?" said LeeAnne. "My car will easily seat five passengers. And that will make one more driver for the trip."

"What about George? Will your car fit six people? This sounds like it's turning into a fiasco before it ever gets on the road," I grumbled.

"George is tied up all next week with board meetings. He said he would be pretty much out of touch the whole week. And if he knows El and Bernie will be with us he won't worry."

"It's settled, then. I'll talk to El, and, Helen, you talk to Bernie. We can tell them we are going to support the unwanted pet rescue fund-raiser."

"Yeah, like Elsworth will believe that," I said. "You and I both know neither he nor Bernie will fall for that. We might as well be honest with them."

"Wow!" said Maggie. "Look at you being all up front and open. I think I like the new Helen."

"Yeah, well don't get used to it. I'm only thinking we might need some backup for this operation. Who better than an ex-spy, or whatever he is, to help us out if we get into trouble."

LeeAnne grinned. "And I think Bernie would walk through fire or take a bullet to protect you, Helen."

I smiled, rubbed the back of my hand again, and whispered, "You may be right. But let's hope it doesn't come to that."

Chapter 15

All the Homeless Puppies

I wandered back to my place upset that I had told my meddling friends about Bernie's hand-kissing incident. Not that it was a bad thing, really, but I knew my friends would be more insistent than ever about pushing me in his direction. I really didn't have the time or energy to pursue the subject of my involvement with Bernie Cox. I'd never been good with the touchy-feely stuff. One had only to ask my daughter, Emily, who claimed my aloofness had led her into years of therapy.

I unlocked my door and dropped my bag on the nearest piece of furniture. Perhaps she was right. Maybe I did need to learn to express my feelings. I grabbed my phone from my bag, plopped down into my recliner and hit Emily's number before I could argue myself out of it.

She picked up on the third ring. "Hello, Mother. What's going on? You don't usually call this time of day."

I cleared my throat, which suddenly seemed as dry and scratchy as a day in the Gobi Desert. "I just called to say hello."

"Oh, okay. Wait. What's wrong, Mother? You never call just to say hello. What's the real reason? Are you ill? OMG, you're sick, aren't you? You're calling with bad news. Wait. Don't tell me. Let me sit down first."

"Yes, you should sit down."

She sighed. "Alright, Mother, I'm sitting. Tell me what's wrong."

I echoed her long-suffering sigh. "Nothing's wrong. I just called to say I love you."

I quickly hung up before she could begin to analyze my response and question my sanity.

The phone rang before I had a chance to put it down. Probably Emily, full of questions about my confession. But, no, it wasn't her. Caller ID said 'Blocked Call'. Curiosity beat out good judgment and I answered.

"Mrs. Patterson?" the female voice asked.

"Yes, this is she."

"I represent the Armitage family. As a courtesy, I'm calling to suggest you refrain from further unwarranted contact with any member of the family."

I held the phone away from my ear as if looking at it would put me face-to-face with this 'representative'.

"Just who are you? And where do you get off threatening me?" I shouted.

"This is not a threat, Mrs. Patterson, merely a strong suggestion."

"Who are..." I started to ask again before I realized the woman had abruptly disconnected.

At breakfast the next day I filled my friends in on the suspicious call. "The woman said she represented the Armitage's. Maybe she's their attorney."

"It's possible," said Elsworth. "But, in my experience, an

attorney usually gives their credentials. I've never known a lawyer to be shy about being a name dropper. It's all part of the status."

"I agree," added George. "But if the woman isn't a lawyer, who is she? And how did she get Helen's number?"

Maggie spoke up. "I don't know who she is, but she probably got the number from the business card Helen gave Vincent."

"Right," said LeeAnne. "Maybe the woman is Vincent's step-mother."

"But why would he give her the business card?" asked Bernie. "You all implied that Vincent didn't seem to like her. Why would he share information with her?"

"Like I've been saying, Vincent may not be the nice guy LeeAnne and Maggie think he is," I said.

"Hopefully we can answer some of these questions when we go to Savannah on Saturday," Elsworth added. "Helen, would you recognize the woman's voice if you heard it again?"

I thought about it. "Yes, I think so. The woman on the phone had a soft, breathy tone, refined, yet with a deep-south timbre. Like the aristocratic tone didn't come naturally. If I had to guess, I'd say she was closer kin to one of us than to the nose-in-the-air Armitage's."

"Wow!" said LeeAnne. "You got all that from one phone call?"

I shrugged.

"That's really good, Helen," Elsworth said. "Perhaps you will be able to distinguish if the voice was that of the step-mother, Constance Armitage."

A compliment from Maggie's beau? I might learn to like this guy! And such a finding would definitely move the wicked step-mother up a notch on my suspect list.

126

Saturday morning found us on the road to Savannah. Since Elsworth volunteered to drive, that put Maggie in my usual place in the front seat. Bernie offered to ride center backseat since it was the least comfortable spot, with LeeAnne and me flanking him. If I couldn't ride shotgun, I was thankful to at least have a window seat.

The ride was uneventful, and, at my insistence, we only had to make one rest stop along the way. I wanted to stop at the 200-pump gas station/convenience store that featured billboards every ten miles along our route. While Elsworth topped off the gas tank, the rest of us went inside to use the facilities.

"Wow!" said Maggie. "This isn't a convenience store, it's a small city!"

She was right. The place bustled with customers. Some, like us, looked lost. Others had their arms loaded with snacks, stuffed animals, and T-shirts emblazoned with the place's logo, a smiling, big-toothed, big-eared animal of unknown origin. Small children ran amok through the place whining, 'Mom, why can't I have the stuffed bear?' And 'I want candy!'

Mothers wailed, 'That giant bear costs more than my weekly salary', and, 'You've already eaten enough sugar to keep the Hershey company in business for a year.'

Bernie patted my arm. "Why don't you ladies go powder your noses. I'll grab us some bottled water and meet you back here."

As we edged away, he hollered, "Don't get lost."

That was a distinct possibility. If it hadn't been for the giant neon sign with an arrow announcing 'Restrooms' we might have wandered aimlessly for hours in search of the correct door.

When we exited the restroom Maggie and LeeAnne got distracted by the myriad shelves, tables and glass cases of

127

merchandise. The store offered not only pegboards stacked with snacks, but counters with hot food, sandwiches and drinks.

"That bar-b-que smells delicious," said Maggie.

"I am not going to eat lunch in a gas station," I huffed. "Let's see if we can find our way out of this place."

Maggie and LeeAnne oohed and aahed at all the displays geared to make shoppers part with their money. I latched onto Maggie's arm and pulled her in the direction I thought we had left Bernie. "Come on, you two, we're on a fact-finding mission, not a shopping spree."

"I know, I know," she said. "But look at all these beautiful wall decorations."

"And the jewelry is exquisite," cooed LeeAnne.

"And overpriced," I groused. "I'd better not see any gifts for me under the Christmas tree that came from this place!"

"What makes you think you're going to get any presents?" Maggie teased. "Have you been a good girl?"

She picked up a box from the shelf beside her. "LeAnne, what do you think about this big-eared bobble-head for Helen?"

LeeAnne took the box, shook it, tilted her head, and smiled. "It's perfect! See how his little head bobs back and forth – he'll agree with everything Helen says. The ideal Yes-man."

I grabbed the box from her and slammed it back on the shelf. Its head bobbled back and forth in a mesmerizing way. I shook my mind free of the action and scanned the room. "Come on, you two comedians, let's get out of here. Which way is the door?"

Bernie stood right where we had left him. He handed us each a bottled water as we got back to the car. "The smell of bar-b-que in that place made me hungry. I hope there's food at this place we're going. I could eat my weight in cheese and crackers right now."

"Huh! For twenty-five dollars, there had better be something better than cheese and crackers," I said.

"Helen," said LeeAnne, "the money is for the animal shelter, not to feed the contributors."

"Yeah, but rich people expect to be treated royally when they give up their ill-gotten gains. They never give anything unless they get something in return."

"Don't be so cynical," said LeeAnne. "Let's relax and enjoy the day."

I stared out the window. "Bernie just reminded me I'm hungry. As much as I like a good bar-b-que sandwich, I hope Mrs. Armitage didn't cater this affair from that gas station!"

Elsworth pulled in and parked next to a sleek black car, beside which stood a uniformed man, obviously someone's chauffer. I gasped and all the old doubts and memories came rushing back. Ambrose Pennington III's face clouded my vision, my insecurities resurfaced. My hand froze on the door handle and I couldn't breathe. I looked at my clothes, way too pedestrian for this crowd. Neither Cynthia Walberg nor I would ever fit in with these people!

Bernie took my free hand in his. "You've got this, Helen. Take a deep breath and open the door. You are a strong, independent woman, and you are every bit as important as anyone here. Remember," he smirked, "we're doing this for all the homeless puppies in Savannah."

I finally managed to open the door. "You may be doing it for the puppies, but I'm here to catch a killer!"

He grinned. "Whatever gets you out the door and into that buffet line works for me."

Elsworth, with Maggie on one arm and LeeAnne on the other, followed us as we went through the door to mingle with the upper crust of Savannah.

Chapter 16

Always the Well-Dressed Dog

Tables lined the wall to the right inside the entrance. Six people sat at the tables behind laptop computers, took pertinent information, accepted donations, and issued name tags.

One of them looked up at me. "Hello. Welcome to STAF. Could I get your name, address and donation amount for our records, please?"

I frowned at her perfectly made-up face. "What is this *staff* thing? It sounds like an infection! Why do you need my name? And I thought this shindig cost twenty-five dollars."

The flustered girl looked from me to a gentleman sitting behind the last computer, and called, "Mr. Lamond, I need some help, please."

He stood and nodded to her. "I'll handle this, Stephanie." He motioned to Bernie and me. "If you can step down here, I'll try to answer your questions."

We stepped down the line and received stares from many in the crowd.

The young man held out his hand. "My name is Brian Lamond. Do you have an enquiry? We at STAF are here to answer any questions. How may I help?"

"Okay, Brian. First, what, or WHO is this staff you keep talking about?"

He addressed me as though I was a six-year-old he had to talk down to. "STAF is an acronym for Save The Animals Foundation. It's Mrs. Armitage's foundation for humane, no-kill animal shelters."

"Oh, that makes sense. Why do I have to give you my name and address? I don't even live in Savannah."

He flashed me a condescending smile. "We want to be able to thank our donors, and also send updates on the progress of STAF."

Bernie whispered, "Helen, we're holding up the line. Let's pay the nice man and move on."

He pulled out his wallet, handed Brian twenty-five dollars, and gave his information. The man entered the data into his computer, wrote Bernie's name on a white nametag and handed it to him. I noticed there were other colored tags on the table, and asked about them.

Brian rolled his eyes. "The pink is for a one hundred dollar donation, the blue for five hundred dollars, and the gold for one thousand dollars or more." He sighed. "How much can I put you down for?"

I handed him my twenty-five dollars.

He took the money from me as if it wasn't worth his time. "Under what name should I put the donation?"

"Anonymous," I said, as I stormed off, leaving him with a white nametag pinched between his fingers.

I took Bernie's arm and pulled him down the hallway to catch up with our group. Casually dressed attendants lined the entry to the large reception room; all held leashed animals or stood beside caged furry little beasts. The banners overhead announced: *Adopt a Pet. Spayed/Neutered. All vaccinations current.* Each attendant held a clipboard. Some spoke with prospective adoptive pet owners.

We caught up with Maggie, LeeAnne, and Elsworth. Maggie turned to me, smiled, and said, "Look, Helen. Isn't he the cutest thing?"

The "cutest thing" she held in her arms was a wriggling ball of fur, blonde on both ends with a black and tan middle. I couldn't tell the yapping end from the wagging end. "What is it?" I asked.

The attendant, whose nametag read, *Tom*, scratched the ball of fur and said, "He's a Yorkshire Terrier, and his name is Blinky."

"Blinky? That's a dumb name. Does it have eye problems?" I took another look at the ball of fur, focusing on the spot I thought its head should be.

Maggie gently lifted the animal up to me. "He only has one eye. The owners didn't want him because he would never be a show dog. They dumped him at the shelter. Isn't that sad?" She pulled the thing close and it snuggled into her shoulder. "See," she said, "he needs me."

"It's so small. Aren't you afraid you'll step on it, or trip over it? Jeez, I've got shoes bigger than that thing!"

Maggie covered what I assumed were the furball's ears. "Hush, Helen! Don't call him a Thing! He's precious. You'll give him a complex."

She handed the animal to Elsworth and began to fill out the paperwork. I looked at El and he shrugged.

"Looks like you've got some competition for Maggie's

attention, Big Guy." I punched him on the arm and the furball growled.

"Hmmm. Looks to me like you're the one with the competition, Helen. He growled at you."

I reached out to touch it and it jumped forward and barked. I pulled my hand back. "You may be right. But at least when it barks I can tell which end is which."

Maggie handed the clipboard back to Tom, the attendant, and he gave her a copy. "Take this to the front table and Mr. Lamond will get everything settled. If you check out okay, you can come pick Blinky up when you're ready to leave."

"What? You mean she's got to have a background check and be approved before she's allowed to take home a one-eyed dog?"

Maggie grabbed my arm. "Please don't make a scene, Helen. It's procedure."

"Make a scene? Me?" I turned to the offending Tom. "I'll have you know my friend is the kindest-hearted person I know. She will be a wonderful adoptive parent to – to…"

"Blinky," Tom said, as he reached out to take the furball from Elsworth.

"Yeah, to Blinky." I looked at Maggie. "You really need to rename it. In today's politically correct world, that name could be offensive."

"I'll consider that," she said as she dragged me away toward the front table and her background check. She turned and called over her shoulder, "We'll meet you three at the entrance as soon as we're finished."

"Do you have to give them your fingerprints, too?" I whispered. "After all, you could be an International Disabled Dog Dealer, or something sinister like that."

When we reached the head of the interrogation line, the man who would determine Maggie's fitness for pet ownership looked up and rolled his eyes.

"Oh, it's you," he said. He picked up a white nametag by his thumb and forefinger like it had cooties. "You came back for this?"

I took it, glanced at the name, and shoved it back at him. "You spelled the name wrong. It's AnonYmous – with a Y, not an O!"

He grabbed a magic marker, scribbled a Y over the O and thrust the nametag back toward me. "Will there be anything else, Ms. Anonymous?"

"That's *Mrs.* Anonymous," I shot back. "And, yes, my friend, Maggie Taylor, wants to adopt one of your fur…" Maggie scowled at me and I corrected, "one of your animals."

"I see." He reached out and took the paperwork from her.

"Yes," she gushed, "Blinky is such a sweet little thing. It's so sad that his owners simply disposed of him because he wasn't perfect. Why, if all imperfections were treated like that, most of us wouldn't be around. It's a crime!"

I patted her arm. "Easy, Mags. You can get off your soapbox. This isn't a debate, and I don't think you have to convince this guy of doggie indignities. Right, Mr.…" I checked his badge, "…Mr. Lamond?"

He looked up from the paperwork. "What? Oh, right. Now, Ms. Taylor, pet ownership is a big responsibility. Have you ever owned a dog before?"

"Oh, yes. My husband and I always had pets. You see, we had no children; our pets were our family. After Bill died, and I moved into my apartment, I didn't consider getting another. But when

Blinky looked at me, I couldn't resist. I really want to give him a forever home. Please?"

"Okay, Mags. You don't need to oversell yourself. No need to beg," I whispered.

Mr. Lamond signed the paperwork and handed it to a young woman beside him. "The adoption fee is thirty-five dollars today. Blinky has been neutered, and his shots are current. Kimberly will take care of payment and give you his medical records." He held out his hand and smiled at my friend. "I can tell Blinky is going into a loving home."

He turned to me, nose in the air. "Mrs. Anonymous, have a good day."

Maggie handed the girl her credit card and signed for her visually-impaired dog. "Isn't it exciting, Helen? I agree with you that Blinky needs a new name - something regal to build his confidence."

"Yeah, yeah. You can call him King Kong. We've been here nearly an hour and we haven't gotten through the doors to the reception yet. C'mon, I'm starved. I hope they've got something decent to eat at this shindig."

I pulled her toward the rest of our group. "And, in case you've forgotten, we came here to try to solve a murder, not rescue wayward puppies!"

We met our friends at the entrance to the reception hall and were handed maps and program information as we walked in. We entered the world of the over-dressed, self-indulgent elite.

"And here we have a fine display of 'Savannah Snobs'," I whispered to Bernie.

A lot of people milled around. Some visited with acquaintances, others checked out booths that displayed every animal product known to man. We saw leashes and collars that were possibly bedazzled with real jewels, if the prices posted were any indication. One booth displayed fresh, frozen food and Alaskan salmon treats.

"Those salmon must have taken a private jet here," I said. "I could fly to Alaska and pick them up at the source cheaper than that."

"Hush, Helen," Maggie said.

"LeeAnne grabbed Maggie's arm and dragged her to a booth that featured clothing – DOG clothing! She held up an item in blue. "Oh, look, Maggie. It's a little sweater."

She latched onto another thing, this one in bright yellow. "And here's a little rain slicker," she gushed. "Isn't it adorable?"

The girl tending the booth lifted up a small package, and smiled. "That coat comes with matching boots." They oohed and aahed over the 'darling clothes'.

"Boots? For a dog? What self-respecting dog would wear such a thing?" I asked as I looked around for something – anything! – that was the least bit interesting or appetizing.

Bernie took my arm and guided me to the next booth, and we checked out a table of homemade dog treats.

I looked at Bernie and shook my head. "Really? People actually go to all this trouble for their dogs?"

He shrugged. "To a lot of people, pets are part of the family."

"Humph. I never baked treats for my family. Store-bought cookies are a lot faster and easier. It seems to me 'some people' spoil their pets rotten."

I glanced around the room. "Where's the people food? I'm hungry enough to munch on one of those dog biscuits."

Bernie checked the map and pointed to the opposite end of

the building. "It's down there. But, according to the program, Mrs. Armitage is going to say a few words in about," he checked his watch, "about five minutes. We don't want to miss that."

"You're right," I agreed. "We need to acquaint ourselves with another of our suspects."

I told Maggie we were headed to the podium if she and LeeAnne wanted to drag themselves away from their clothes-shopping and join us.

Elsworth said, "I'm in," and they followed us to where the "Grand Lady of Savannah' (as the program described her) was about to speak.

Chapter 17

The Grand Lady of Savannah

We joined the group of Savannah elite to get our first glimpse of Constance Armitage. First, though, we had to listen to the mayor gush her praises. He droned on about all the boards and city projects in which the Armitage family had played a part. He turned and acknowledged Mrs. Armitage.

A smattering of polite applause arose from the crowd.

"Doesn't sound like the rousing applause one would expect for one of Savannah's finest, does it?" I whispered to Bernie.

He shook his head. "No, it doesn't. More like an expected response than a natural one."

At long last the mayor wound down and announced, "And now, our guest of honor, Mrs. Constance Armitage!"

More polite applause. I glanced to my right. The two ladies beside me glared at the stage as a petite blonde walked to the microphone dressed in red from her stilettos to her blood red fingernails and lips.

Hussy!" sneered the one beside me.

"Man-chaser," said the other. "She drove poor Nathaniel to his grave."

"I heard she was seen at bars and nightclubs – always in the company of younger men," said the first.

The second nodded. "You know she ran around with Nicholas before he got himself killed."

This was the kind of information I needed! Forget Constance Armitage! I pulled one of our Tricycle Girls business cards from my bag, tapped the nearest woman on the shoulder, and handed it to her.

"I couldn't help overhearing. I take it you aren't fans of Mrs. Armitage."

She looked at the card, then at me, and frowned. "You could say that. Why?"

"My company has been consulted on another matter, and the Armitage family name came up in our investigation. Could you spare a few minutes to answer a couple of questions?"

I poked Bernie and he looked my way.

"My name is Helen Patterson, and this is my associate, Bernie Cox."

He leaned forward and held out his hand. "How do you do?"

I smiled at him. "These ladies might have some information about the Armitage's. If they would be willing to answer some questions, we might be able to close our case."

He picked up the conversation. "Yes, anything you could tell us about dynamics in the family would be a big help."

The people in the row ahead of us turned and scowled. Bernie suggested we meet with the ladies after Mrs. Armitage finished her presentation.

They nodded. I let my eyes wander around the room while the voice of our Lady in Red droned on. The voice was similar to the one I heard on my phone, but there was something different about the put-on elite accent. The way her eyes skirted those gathered, told me she was aware she was not one of them – she was an outsider. She knew it, and she knew *they* knew it. Her whole demeanor was faked. She was definitely not 'to the manor born' – as they say. However, I didn't think she had been my threatening caller. Her voice was too high-pitched and whiny. I whispered as much to Bernie, and he nodded.

On one side of the room stood Vincent Armitage, arms folded across his chest, and looking either bored or angry – it was difficult to say. But his stance suggested he was not happy to be here. Behind him another woman, also in red, took turns first glaring at Constance then eyeing Vincent. What was that all about, I wondered? Relative? Vincent's girlfriend?

I caught a glimpse on the other side of the room of a very self-satisfied David Armitage who was smiling at our Lady in Red. I pointed him out to Bernie.

"Hmmm," he whispered. "That's the way a man looks at a possession. If I'm not mistaken, David Armitage either possesses – or hopes to possess – the Grand Lady of Savannah."

"Really? That might explain some things."

The voice of the grand lady broke any further thoughts or comments.

"…and I'm very proud to announce that I've commissioned a statue in the Armitage name by one of Savannah's foremost sculptors. It will stand outside the new Armitage Animal Shelter. Would you like to see it?"

She gave a nervous laugh. "Of course I don't have it here, but I do have life-sized photos. Gentlemen, dim the lights and project the images."

She continued her commentary while photos of a bronze sculpture of a child playing with a kitten and a puppy flashed before us.

More polite applause, this time a bit more enthusiastic. For some reason, people get all misty-eyed about small people and small animals.

Finally she finished the presentation and asked that the lights be brought back up. She smiled to the audience. "Thank you all for coming to support this worthy cause. Our shelter should be up and running by spring. Tell all your friends."

Everyone stood to leave as she clip-clopped her stilettos across the stage. I turned to the two ladies I had overheard, just in time to watch them move swiftly away.

"Guess they decided they didn't want to talk to us underlings," I said to Bernie.

"You did point out earlier that the rich protect their own. It's alright for them to discuss each other among themselves, but it's something else to talk to outsiders about their foibles," replied Bernie.

"I suppose you're right. But I'm sure it's not Constance they're protecting. It's the Armitage name. Old money demands respect."

We exited the staging area and went in search of the buffet line, where we munched our way through enough food to at least take the edge off my hunger.

Maggie then said she had to retrieve her dog. She had purchased several items, all of which she held up for me to examine. The items included clothes, boots, food and water dishes, and homemade treats.

I shook my head.

She waved a note card in my face. "Look, Helen, I even got the recipe for the dog treats. I can make Blinky more of these if he likes them."

"Oh, goodie. You'll probably start serving them for our get-togethers."

She laughed. "Why not? The girl said they are people-friendly."

She handed everything to Elsworth but the small purse/carrier she had bought to stuff the poor, disabled dog into.

"While you go finish your dog business, I'm going to find a ladies room. It's a long ride back home."

"Good idea," said LeeAnne. She called over her shoulder as she followed me, "We'll meet you at the door where we came in." We moved deeper into the mass of people who stepped aside as if they didn't want to be tainted by rubbing elbows with the commoners.

As we rounded a corner, I saw two figures who looked familiar. Locked in an embrace, the man had his back to me. Though they stood in the shadows, I thought it was David Armitage. I held up my hand to stop LeeAnne.

The woman in his arms stepped back and hissed, "Not here, you fool. People will see us."

We backed into an alcove where we couldn't be seen.

"That's David Armitage and his so-called aunt, Constance Armitage," I whispered to LeeAnne.

Their conversation continued. "Quite a show you put on in there," he growled. "And I'm not the fool here. You are, if you think you can worm your way into the upper class this way. The Armitage family is not so easily infiltrated."

"Oh, David," Constance whined, "I'm sorry. This has been such a stressful time. I'm so confused right now."

There was a lull in the conversation; LeeAnne mouthed the words, 'Hanky panky'. I nodded.

After a time we heard more talking. "I like that dress. I told you red is your color," David said.

"Yes, you did," she cooed. "Now I really must go mingle. We'll talk later."

The door behind us opened and a man stepped out. "Sorry, ladies, this is the men's. Ladies is down the hall."

Flustered, we moved into the hall and nearly collided with the Grand Lady of Savannah, who sauntered by, stilettos clicking, while a very smug, cat-that-ate-the-canary smile played on those blood-red lips.

Dog Treats

4 ½ cups oatmeal
1 egg
1 medium apple
1 cup canned pumpkin

Grind oatmeal in food processor to consistency of course flour. Place in large mixing bowl.

Core and grate apple, add egg and pumpkin. Mix well. Mixture will be thick and sticky.

Roll dough to ½ inch thickness, cut into doggy bone shapes and place on lined baking sheet.

Bake at 400 degrees for 12-15 minutes, or until golden and crispy.

Cool and store in airtight container for up to a week.

Quantity depends on size of treats.

Chapter 18

Not Again?!

LeeAnne and I found the ladies room right next door to the men's.

"We'd better hurry, Helen. We've been gone a long time. Blinky may be getting restless in that carrier Maggie bought."

I hurriedly dried my hands and followed her into the hall. "If he's not already antsy, he sure will be after an hour's ride in the car. I just hope he doesn't get car sick like one of the dogs my kids brought home years ago."

We finally caught sight of our traveling companions and headed to the car. The little dog seemed to accept his confinement without complaint. He peeked out of the little doggie window to check his surroundings, curious but quiet.

We passed a dog run that had been set up for today's gala. It sported small trees in pots, fire hydrants, and even a stand that held rolls of plastic bags for waste disposal.

Elsworth suggested Blinky might need to take a run before the long ride back to Loblolly.

"I'll wait in the car," I said. "I've already taken my run."

I sat down and tried to get comfortable, but something didn't feel right. I squirmed and turned in the seat while Bernie went around to the opposite door to claim his spot in the middle.

"Well," he said, "except for Maggie's dog, we didn't get much out of our trip."

"I guess not. I did overhear those ladies talking about Constance. And LeeAnne and I caught her and David Armitage in a serious lip-lock when we went to find the ladies room. She's obviously up to something, but I'm not sure what, if anything, it has to do with ReeAnn or the dead P.I." I reached for my bag. "I'm going to write down our findings while they're still fresh in my mind. Oh no! It's gone!"

I jumped out of the car. "LeeAnne!" I hollered. "Do you remember if I had my bag when we left the ladies room?"

She stepped over to where I stood. "What did you say, Helen?"

"My bag! Did I leave my tote bag in the ladies room? My legal pad and all my notes are in that bag. My *whole life* is in that bag!"

I gasped for breath and grabbed my chest. This might be a real heart attack. Not a reaction brought on by a kiss, but by panic. Maggie might be right. Maybe I did have an unhealthy attachment to my legal pad.

Bernie took my arm and guided me back toward the car. "Sit for a minute and catch your breath. Then I'll go back inside with you to find your bag."

Soon my breathing slowed and I was able to stand up. Maggie and Bernie judged me fit to travel, so he and I headed back inside against all the outgoing traffic. The general noise of tables being disassembled, and work crews shouting orders, filled the halls.

"I guess the party's over," I said.

146

"Yes, it's amazing how fast these people can get in and out. It's like a chaotic dance."

"Well, I don't have time to dance. Let's get my bag and get out of here."

Bernie stopped at one of the tables to ask if anyone had turned in a purse or tote bag. The young man eyed us as if we had spoken to him in a foreign language, and finally managed to say, "Uh, you might ask someone else. I'm just here to break down tables."

I grabbed Bernie's arm. "Come on. We can go check the ladies room. I'm sure I put it on the counter when I washed my hands."

We walked down the hall. The crowd had thinned, so there wasn't as much traffic as earlier. When we got to the sign that said MEN, Bernie touched my arm. "I'm going to stop here while you go check the ladies room."

"Okay. I'll only be a minute. I'll meet you back here."

I reached the ladies room, pushed the door open, and noticed a metallic odor that hadn't been there earlier. I stepped around the partition and heard someone scream. I grabbed for the wall.

Lying on the floor, her head wreathed in blood, was Constance Armitage, her eyes open, her red lips the only color to her pale face. Her hands clutched my tote bag, its contents haphazardly strewn around the room. My yellow legal pad lay open beside her, soaked in her blood.

Only when I heard someone bang on the door did the screams stop. I swallowed. My throat ached, and I realized those screams had been mine.

Bernie burst into the room. "Helen, what's wrong. I heard screaming."

He grabbed my arm and, as he did, his eyes caught sight of Constance. I stood there, transfixed, unable to take my eyes off the horrible sight.

"Helen," he shouted. "Let's get you out of here and call the police."

"Yes," I croaked, "you can't be in here, it's the ladies room."

Bernie took over, found a chair, sat me down and called 9-1-1. Then he dialed Maggie to fill her and the others in on the situation.

All the while I sat in a daze. Every time I tried to rest my eyes or swallow, that halo of blood around Constance Armitage's head brought bile up to my sore throat.

Maggie rushed to me, grabbed my hand, and asked if I was alright.

Bernie took my other hand. "I think she's in shock, Maggie. The EMT's will be here soon, we can have them take a look at her."

"Is she hurt?" Maggie cried.

"No, just shaken, I think. No one else was around. Whoever attacked Mrs. Armitage had already left."

Behind Maggie I heard Elsworth mutter, "Not again?!"

She scowled at him and patted my hand. "That's good. She will be alright then, as soon as we get her home."

"You're talking about me again like I've checked out," I whispered. "I'm fine, or I will be, as soon as I get my voice back. There might be a small problem, though. The contents of my tote bag are all over the floor in that room." I shuddered at the memory of Constance Armitage's body, my bag in her hand, and my bloody legal pad beside her.

Medics and other emergency personnel soon swarmed the

area. They checked on Constance Armitage and whispered among themselves.

Against my protestations, Maggie told Bernie to corral one of the EMT's to come look me over. He got the attention of a young woman, about the age of my granddaughter, Ellyn – much too young to be giving me medical advice -who checked my vitals, peered at my throat, and declared I would eventually heal. She did caution me to not speak unless absolutely necessary, and said I should go see my personal physician to make sure everything was healing properly. Then she brought me a bottled water and disappeared into the influx of people milling around.

Finally a suave-looking young man in a sports jacket sauntered up to our group. His blonde hair curled above his shirt collar. His dark eyes bored into me as though I had interrupted his personal life for something as negligible as a body in a bathroom. My friends all huddled around me like some kind of protective shield. He pulled out his badge and introduced himself. "I'm Captain Andrew Justice, head of the homicide division with Savannah P.D. I understand one of you discovered Mrs. Armitage."

I tried to speak, but Bernie put his hand on my shoulder. "Yes, Captain. My friend, Mrs. Helen Patterson, entered the ladies room and found Mrs. Armitage on the floor."

The man scowled at Bernie. "I'd like to hear the account from Mrs. Patterson, if you don't mind." He arched his eyebrows at Bernie, "Unless you escorted her into the ladies room."

"No, Sir, I didn't."

He turned and smiled down at me. "Now, then, Mrs. Patterson, could I get your statement?" He pulled a small pad and pen out of his pocket.

I massaged my throat and began to squeak out a response.

Maggie spoke up. "Captain Justice, I understand your urgency to get to the bottom of Mrs. Armitage's accident, but Helen has sustained a terrible shock. She screamed so much she's lost her voice. The EMT person told her not to talk."

He eyed Maggie. "And you are...?"

"Oh," she stammered, "I'm Maggie Taylor, Helen's friend. We've known each other all our lives. She's like a sister to me."

"Maggie," I whispered, "you're overselling yourself, again."

I flashed the captain what I considered my best smile and held my throat as I spoke, my voice no more than a hoarse whisper. "You have the perfect name for an officer of the law, Captain Justice. And I'll gladly answer your questions if you can get me a pen and paper. Mine seem to be in there," I pointed to the ladies room, "with Mrs. Armitage."

"What? Those are the contents of your purse? We assumed they belonged to the deceased. Why did she have your bag, Mrs. Patterson?"

I shrugged and mimed writing on a note pad.

"Deceased?" Elsworth asked. "She's dead?"

Justice looked into Elsworth's steel-gray eyes. Evidently that look was enough to convince him to take Elsworth into his confidence. "Yes, sir. Very dead."

He turned his gaze on Maggie. "And it was no accident. Mrs. Armitage was murdered."

Maggie gasped. A tear ran down LeeAnne's cheek. Bernie held tightly to my hand.

And Elsworth muttered under his breath, "And the body count rises."

The captain rolled his eyes and ran his large hands through his sandy blonde hair. "Ladies and gentlemen," he nodded toward us, "is there anything you can tell me about Mrs. Armitage?"

"She was Vincent Armitage's step-mother," offered LeeAnne.

Maggie added, "She set this gala up today to raise money for a no-kill animal shelter."

Justice ground his bicuspids against each other and looked to Elsworth for help. "Anything pertinent to this case?"

We all shook our heads and admitted we really didn't know the woman.

"Why, then, did you five travel all the way from – where did you say?"

"Loblolly," Bernie said. "It's about an hour's drive from here."

"Yes, Loblolly. Why drive an hour to save Savannah's homeless dog population?"

"We came on Vincent Armitage's behalf," Maggie said.

"Vincent Armitage invited you here?"

"Not exactly," Maggie replied.

"What exactly, then? Help me out here. What is your connection to the Armitage family?"

"Do you suspect us of killing Constance Armitage?" I croaked.

He paced back and forth in front of us. "I don't know what or who I suspect. Everyone here is a suspect. That's the way investigations work. People tell me what they know, and I put the pieces together." His agitation grew, as did the volume of his voice, as he paced.

He finally stopped, took a breath and smiled at us. "You seem like nice folks. I've got elderly grandparents, and I sympathize. I hate to ask you all these questions, but," he pointed to the gurney with the covered body rolling past us, "I have a murder to solve. And I feel like you're giving me the run-around."

Elsworth stepped up. "Excuse me, Captain, but there's really no subterfuge here.   Let my colleagues straighten out this situation."

Elsworth definitely had clout! Justice shut up and nodded to him. I was impressed!

He turned to Maggie. "Will you and LeeAnne please fill the detective in on our reason for coming to Savannah?"

I glared at him.

He caught my look and apologized, "I didn't mean to exclude you, Helen. I merely felt you shouldn't strain you vocal cords. Feel free to add anything Maggie and LeeAnne might forget."

My friends filled Justice in on our investigation into the Bunny Caper. They included their plan to try to hook Vincent Armitage up with Reesie's mom, Cindy.

"Let me get this straight," he said, when they had wound down, "You came all this way to make a love connection for Mr. Armitage?"

"Uh, not entirely," Bernie said. "Helen and I want to try to solve the murder of the P.I., Ivan Reddy. We figure it's got to be tied to the Armitage's somehow."

"Because this dead guy had the little girl's bunny in his hands?" Justice asked.

I nodded.

He loomed over me. "If that's the case, then maybe Constance Armitage having your tote bag in her hand has something to do with you! Did you kill her, Mrs. Patterson?"

"Of course not! I didn't even know the woman," I squeaked.

LeeAnne stepped up beside me. "Helen and I saw her and David Armitage in a very intimate embrace after her presentation. And, as she walked away, Mr. Armitage made a comment about her being a fool if she thought she could worm her way into the

Armitage fortune. It sounded very threatening to Helen and me."

"You believe that people in one of Savannah's finest families are mixed up in a murder? Or maybe two murders?"

He turned to Elsworth. "You seem like a very reasonable man, Mr. Lumley. What is your take on the ladies assumptions."

Elsworth took a long time before answering. Finally he said, "I must admit I've not always agreed with Helen's tactics. But I have been around her long enough to learn her skill at solving mysteries is quite exceptional."

"Oh? This isn't the first time she's been mixed up in a crime?"

"Mixed up in a crime?" I croaked. "You make it sound as if I'm a felon – or a murderer!"

Bernie took my hand. "Now, Helen, don't get yourself all worked up. You've got to take care of your voice."

"I can take care of my voice just fine!" I Scribbled on the note pad the detective had given me.

"Actually," LeeAnne said proudly, "Helen, Maggie, and I have solved a couple of crimes in the last year. Check her legal pad, she keeps all our notes on it."

He slapped his notepad on his hand and crammed it in his pocket. "I definitely intend to do just that! Colbert," he shouted, "get these people's information and send them home to Loblolly – and out of my sight!"

I scribbled a note on the pad and held it up to him. "When can I get my belongings back?"

"They are part of a murder investigation. You will get them when I'm convinced you aren't mixed up in this crime!"

"I sure hope you show your grandparents more respect than you've shown us." I instantly regretted my outburst because it aggravated my aching throat.

He stomped off. Officer Colbert got our names, addresses, and phone numbers. As I rose to leave, he reminded me to not strain my voice, and to be sure to see a doctor when we got back to Loblolly.

"Thank you," I whispered.

"Oh," he added, "the department will probably release your stuff in a few days." He handed me a card. "Call this number. And don't be offended by Captain Justice's abrupt behavior. High profile cases like this get the big brass's attention. Captain Justice has a lot on the line."

Bernie shook Colbert's hand. "Thank you, Captain." He took my arm. "Come on, Helen. Let's go home. We've had quite enough excitement for one day."

Blinky had remained quiet through this whole ordeal. Maggie let him out for one last run.

Bernie sat down beside me while we waited. I leaned my head back on the head rest and started a mental list of all the information I was going to have to transfer to a new legal pad. Even if I got my other one back, there was no way I'd ever touch it again.

Chapter 19

Silent Partner

I had hoped to enjoy a quiet ride back to Loblolly. The ordeal we had been through had exhausted me. Without paper to jot notes on, I wanted to mull over the events of the day. I leaned my head back against the seat and closed my eyes.

Unfortunately, rest was out of the question, as my friends kept a running conversation going about a new name for Blinky, the one-eyed furball.

Forced, as I was, into silence, and with no legal pad handy, I couldn't join in or give my personal opinions on some of their possible choices.

King? That name was too big for such a small dog.

Alphie – Really? That wasn't even a decent movie!

Greystokes – Wasn't that Tarzan's family name? What kind of name is that?

And on and on.

Maggie turned from her position riding shotgun and smiled at me. "Helen, the conversation isn't nearly as lively without your input."

I touched my head with my forefinger.

"Oh," she laughed, "you're committing everything to memory?"

I nodded.

My friends joined in the revelry about my inability to argue or give voice to my opinions – all of them except Bernie, who came to my defense. "It's okay, Helen. When we get home, I'll get you a new legal pad and you can write down all your pithy answers."

"It won't have quite the same acerbic effect as when she verbalizes, though," Elsworth said.

"No," added LeeAnne, "but I'm sure we'll all be properly chastised."

I crossed my arms and stared out the window, upset about being the butt of their jokes.

"Come on, Helen," coaxed Maggie. "Don't be angry. We don't know quite how to deal with you as a silent partner. We're used to you as the leading voice in our group."

"Yes," agreed Elsworth, "a conversation without your input is like dinner without dessert. It's not complete."

I nodded my approval to Maggie. That was the nicest thing her beau had ever said to me. I must be growing on him. "Tell him thank you," I mouthed.

Maggie and LeeAnne hijacked me Monday morning and spirited me off to see a doctor. Those two would not be satisfied until I paid someone to tell me what I already knew – my throat would heal in about a week.

I'd checked in my handy medical reference encyclopedia when we got back from Savannah on Saturday. I ruled out mono, meningitis, and gonorrhea as too ludicrous to even consider.

All I had to do was drink warm liquids, gargle with salt water, and refrain from talking for a few days. The first two things would be easy enough, but my friends had a wager on how many days I could go without inserting my opinion into conversations.

Elsworth's and George's money was on two days, max. LeeAnne and Maggie thought I could hold out for three days.

Only Bernie had faith that I could go the distance. "You know how determined Helen can be," he began.

"The word is stubborn, Bernie," laughed George. "Helen is the most stubborn woman I've ever met!"

"Ha ha!" I wrote on the brand-new legal pad Bernie had given me.

"You may be right, George," Maggie added. "Helen will refuse to talk if for no other reason than to aggravate us and prove us wrong."

"You all are getting a kick out of this, aren't you?" I scribbled.

Everyone laughed, but all was forgiven when they encircled me in a group hug and let me know they all cared about my well-being.

This writing stuff down wasn't going to be easy. Maybe I'd have to stay away from my friends for a while to keep my silence. I'm not a fan of awkward displays of emotion in public – or in private either, for that matter. The hugs were uncalled for.

So now I sat, flanked by my two best friends, waiting for a summons from the doctor. My legal pad rested on my lap and I doodled on it to pass the time.

"Should LeeAnne or I go in with you to answer the doctor's questions?" Maggie asked.

I nodded and pointed my gel pen at her.

"That's a good idea, Maggie," said LeeAnne. "You can fill the doctor in on what happened, and find out for sure how long before Helen can speak."

"Right," agreed Maggie. "I can be a witness to make sure she follows the doctor's orders."

I scribbled something on my pad and nudged her. She read the words aloud. "I'm still here. Quit talking about me in the third person, as though I'm dead or in a vegetative state!"

I added to my words. "I've already passed George and Elsworth's guesses on how long I'd remain a mute. You two want to make sure you win the bet."

Maggie gave me a smug look. "Technically, the guys have until the end of the day for you to crack. I'm supposed to keep a close eye on you today."

"How much is this wager?" I wrote. "I might just fold if there's something good in it."

"Trust us," LeeAnne said. "You'll enjoy winning the bet."

"Helen Patterson."

Our labor-intensive conversation halted with the announcement of my name.

Maggie jumped up. "That's us. Come on, Helen."

The issuer of the summons led us into the exam room after humiliating me by making me stand on the scales in the hallway. "I'm Angela, Dr. Powell's nurse. What seems to be the problem, Mrs. Patterson?"

I held up my legal pad on which I'd written, "Ask my friend."

She cast a questioning gaze in Maggie's direction.

Maggie filled her in on the reason for my silence, and ended by stating, "We wanted to make sure there are no serious problems."

Angela nodded. "I see."

She took my vitals, entered the information on the computer, and said, "Dr. Powell will be in to see you shortly."

I fidgeted and doodled on my legal pad, until Maggie touched my arm and asked, "What's wrong, Helen?"

"I hate doctor's offices" I wrote. "I think there's some kind of doctor code that says they have to wait until the patient's blood pressure has risen twenty points before they make their entrance."

"You're exaggerating. It hasn't been that long. Your impatience will definitely cause a spike in your blood pressure. Try to relax."

At that moment, Dr. Powell breezed into the room. Her blonde hair, petite build, and easy smile did nothing to ingratiate her to me.

"Hello, Mrs. Patterson. What seems to be the problem? It's been a while since I've seen you."

I pointed to my designated spokesperson, Maggie, who repeated what she had already told the nurse.

"Okay. Let's get a look at that throat. Do you think you can step up and sit here?" she patted the exam table.

I scowled and scribbled, "I'm hoarse, not decrepit."

"I see you haven't lost your wit along with your voice."

She peered into my throat with her little light, uttered a couple of aha's and finally announced, "Your vocal cords are definitely strained."

Well, DUH!

"Unfortunately," she continued, "there's no quick fix. Healing will take time."

"How much time?" I wrote.

"That's hard to say. A few days – maybe up to a week. In the meantime speak as little as possible." She tapped my legal pad. "That notepad is a good idea. Keep it with you – and use it!"

"There aren't any medications that will speed up the healing process. I'll give you a list of things you can do at home that will ease the symptoms. Drink lots of water to hydrate your vocal cords. Oh, and don't eat dry or crunchy things such as chips. They will irritate your throat."

She rose to leave. "Any questions?"

"Should Helen schedule another appointment?" Maggie asked.

The doctor smiled. "I don't think it's necessary unless after a week she still can't talk. If that's the case I would refer her to a specialist to check for underlying problems. Personally, I think she'll be fine."

"Still here," I wrote.

"It's always a pleasure to see you, Mrs. Patterson. You make my day. I wish I had more patients like you." She patted my shoulder. "Okay, let me go print out this information. I'll be right back."

She was as good as her word. She handed me an overview of my visit plus several pages of suggestions for healing strained vocal cords.

She winked and whispered conspiratorially, "I pulled this stuff off the internet. There's a lot of information, and it won't all apply to your situation. I've checked the ones that might possibly help."

She looked at Maggie. "Please call if you have any questions or problems." She smiled and moved toward the door. "Oh, one more thing. Try to not find any more dead bodies."

"Good plan," I mouthed.

With that she exited. I stuffed the papers into my bag, and we met LeeAnne in the waiting room.

"What's the verdict?" she asked.

"She'll live in silence for up to a week," Maggie answered as we made our way back to the car.

I scanned the papers on our way home and finally handed Maggie a note. "Most of these remedies call for honey, lemon or ginger. I need to go pick up some things."

We made a side trip to the grocery store and headed home so I could heal myself.

Maggie was as determined as a first-time mother with a sick child. She hovered. She flitted. She tried to force gallons of lemony water down my throat.

I finally rebelled. "For crying out loud, Maggie," I wrote on my new legal pad, which was fast filling up with my protestations of her mothering. "Go home – PLEASE! Let me rest. If I drink any more water you're going to have to build an ark to accommodate the overflow!"

"But, Helen," she pouted, "I'm worried about you. You're never sick. I want to help, but I don't know how." She plopped down at the table and wrung her hands.

"I know," I squeaked.

"She shook a finger at me. "Ah, ah. No talking."

I rolled my eyes, much like my granddaughter, Ellyn, did when I tried to impart some of my wisdom to her.

"The doctor said I need to test my voice a little each day," I wrote, "so I'll know if it's healing."

"Just a few words, though," she admonished.

From my bag my phone jingled. I reached for it and checked

the number. No name came up on the caller ID, just a number.

Maggie grabbed it from me and answered.

"Hello."

"No, this isn't Mrs. Patterson. This is her friend, Maggie Taylor."

I jumped. Had our anonymous caller struck again?

"Oh, hello, Sweetie." A pause while she listened to the voice on the other end.

Definitely not the alleged Armitage representative. Maggie wouldn't call her 'sweetie'. The call continued.

"No, she's not able to talk right now, she's not feeling well."

Another pause. I tried to decipher the one-sided conversation.

"That was nice of her."

"Yes, I'll tell her."

"Goodbye."

When the call finally ended, she pocketed the phone. I drew a big question mark on my pad.

"That was Reesie," she said. "She wanted to let us know she has a phone now, and she thought you should have the number."

I held up the big question mark again.

"Well, evidently, Vincent Armitage gave Reesie's mom a *fancy new phone* - Reesie's words – and Cindy gave Reesie her old one. She's only supposed to use it for emergencies."

Again I flashed the sign.

Maggie laughed. "To her, getting Ariadne back constitutes an emergency."

"Kids!" I scribbled.

"Oh, she said she hopes you'll be better soon."

"Yeah, me too," I wrote. "Now will you please go home? I need some rest. Your helpfulness is killing me."

She stood and kissed my cheek; she figured I wouldn't bother to write down my disdain of such an expression. "Fine, I'll go. See you at dinner."

"Supper," I wrote.

"Whatever," she mumbled.

She patted her pocket when she got to the door. "I'll keep your phone. That way you won't be tempted to answer it."

I shrugged. It was easier than writing 'Whatever.' Besides, unless the Armitage representative tried to contact me again, who would call? Most everyone who bothered to talk to me lived here at Golden Harvest. Maggie had notified my kids about my encounter and subsequent hoarseness. All had expressed mild concern. My daughter, Emily, in her over-dramatic way, claimed it was another way I had embarrassed her. Good thing she had her therapist on speed-dial.

My friends had put out the word that no one was to try to engage me in conversation until further notice. The residents feared me enough to heed to the warnings, to the point I felt like a pariah. I'd never felt the need to interact with most of these people, but the exclusion bothered me in a way that puzzled me. Heaven forbid I somehow sought these people's approval all of a sudden.

The thought unnerved me.

After I shooed my hovering friend, Maggie, away, my friends left me alone. We still took meals together, but even there, conversation was subdued. We put our investigation on hold for a few days to allow my voice box to heal. That left me with nowhere to place my energy. I paced, tried to read my latest nursery rhyme mystery, 'Bang, Bang Black Sheep'. I drank and gargled so much honey and lemon water I was in danger of floating away.

Only Bernie continued to come around. I suspected the girls had made him the designated Helen-sitter. He coaxed me into leisurely walks around the courtyard, despite my aversion to exercise.

"Don't think of it as exercise," he laughed. "Pretend we're strolling somewhere."

He handed me my constant companion, my legal pad. "If you could take a walk anywhere, where would you go?"

"To my recliner," I wrote.

"No, not happening. Think of a place."

I blushed and scribbled, "Paris."

He nodded. "Oui, oui, mam'selle." He held out his hand. "Come. We will stroll the Streets of Paris; perhaps climb the Eiffel Tower, or gaze at Notre Dame."

He held out his arm and we walked out into the evening arm in arm. Bernie kept a running commentary on the beauty of Paris, only asking questions I could answer with a shake or nod of my head.

One evening our imaginary stroll took us to London, where we listened to the chimes of Big Ben.

"I hear it's always raining in London," I wrote on my new petite yellow legal pad Bernie had found somewhere. It was small enough to carry in my pocket. Very handy! "Should we take an umbrella?"

"Pish posh, woman! Only tourists use umbrellas. Come, let us sally forth unencumbered."

By week's end, our walks had taken us to the pyramids of Egypt, the Irish countryside, even a ghostly castle in Scotland. Bernie was good – no, he was the best medicine for my injured voice and haunted memory of a week ago. Each evening he allowed me to utter a few words, and by Saturday my voice sounded almost normal.

I announced to my friends at supper that Bernie and I were back from our forced vacation and ready to get on with our investigation.

Maggie and LeeAnne grinned at me.

"What's with you two?" I asked.

"Did you enjoy your gift?" Maggie crooned. "It was Bernie's idea to take you on a whirlwind stay-at-home vacation to keep you from worrying too much about your 'case'. "

"Yes," agreed LeeAnne. "And the trip seems to have done you a 'world' of good, too."

I looked from them to Bernie and had to smile. "Yeah, it was great. But I'm more than ready to start conversing without the use of a pen and paper."

Bernie took my hand. "Take it slow, Helen. Don't over-exert your voice."

"That's right," added Maggie. "Just because you haven't spoken for a week doesn't mean you have to do seven days of catch-up all at once."

I assured her I was fine, but by the time we finished our meal and discussed our next steps, the strain had crept back into my voice.

"Okay, that's enough for tonight," Elsworth announced. "Let's meet at my place tomorrow afternoon. Our notes await."

"Yes," said Maggie. "He won't let me move those infernal boards with the notes. He stares at them constantly." She grinned at him, then at me. "Kind of reminds me of you, Helen, when you're involved in a project. Are you sure you two aren't related?"

I frowned and everyone else laughed.

Sunday morning, George, LeeAnne, Maggie, and Elsworth headed out to the church service at the big non-denominational church in town. Bernie joined me for the smaller service presented at Golden Harvest. The speaker talked of sharing our abundance. I had to agree, we were all abundantly blessed.

After services, we sat down to a delicious Sunday meal of roast beef, mashed potatoes and creamed peas. All that was topped off with hearty slices of Dutch apple pie.

Satiated, Bernie leaned back and patted his stomach. "What time are we supposed to meet for our discussion? I think I need to go take a nap after that meal. Otherwise my only input will be a snore or two."

We all agreed and decided to meet at Elsworth's apartment around three-thirty. At which time I intended to bring up my anonymous caller.

Chapter 20

Pandora's Box

We assembled at Elsworth's apartment in a Sunday-afternoon frame of mind. Even Maggie's little furball lolled lazily on his doggie bed in the corner. I wondered how long it would be before Maggie and the furball took up permanent residence with Elsworth Lumley.

My after-dinner nap and done nothing to freshen my mind. The lack of enthusiasm on the faces of the rest of the group assured me their mental faculties were no clearer than my own. But we had let our investigation slide long enough. It was time to regroup.

We sat around the table, Elsworth stood at the head beside our clues. I noted they had overflowed from our original corkboard to another surface. This one a dry erase board with various names, dates, and lines that stretched and ran every which way connecting some of the names. The P.I., Ivan Reddy, took the top spot on the left, with Constance Armitage's name beside his.

Elsworth pointed to the names. "I thought it wise to place our two victims at the top and try to determine how, or if, their lives intersected with our suspects."

"Yes," said Maggie. "He's been arranging and rearranging lines and names all week. Like I said, Helen, he's as bad as you." She smiled at me and blew Elsworth a kiss.

He smiled back, cleared his throat, and continued. "As you all know, Helen received a call warning her to back off from harassing the Armitage's. The female caller didn't leave a name, but we suspected it might have been Constance Armitage who made that call."

He turned to me. "Helen, after listening to Mrs. Armitage on Saturday, do you believe hers was the voice you heard?"

I shook my head. "On the contrary, I'm sure my caller was *not* Constance Armitage. I do believe the two women came from similar backgrounds, but Mrs. Armitage spoke with a more practiced, refined voice. My caller spoke with a hesitancy, almost apologetically, as if she was aware she didn't belong."

"Wow! You got all that from one phone call?" asked Bernie.

I turned to him. "No, it only hit me after we heard Constance Armitage speak. Her voice held none of the hesitancy of my caller. Even though she obviously stepped up a notch or two from her beginnings, Constance Armitage had convinced herself she was the queen and all in Savannah were her subjects."

"What name do we give our mystery caller?" asked LeeAnne. "Madame X?"

"NO," said Maggie. "That sounds like a spy."

"Well, she might be a spy for the Armitage's," LeeAnne argued.

"How about using your term, Mystery Caller? That about says it all."

"Good idea, George," Elsworth said as he wrote the name on the board.

I scribbled 'Mystery Caller' on a file card and pinned it to the corkboard. I preferred the cards. I could move them around without having to go to the trouble to erase and rewrite. However, I had to admit the dry erase board was eye-catching. The two victims' names were in red at the top, the Armitage's in black, and Reesie's and Cindy's in blue.

Elsworth had added 'Mystery Caller' in purple. He stepped back to survey his work and read the suspect names. Only four were on the list, David Armitage, Gus from the bar, Mystery Caller, and Vincent Armitage.

"That's not much of a suspect list," said George.

"It only takes one," replied Elsworth.

"That's assuming the same person committed both murders," I said.

LeeAnne crossed her arms defiantly. "I don't think Vincent's name should even be on that list."

Maggie raised her hand in agreement. "LeeAnne's right. This started as a mission to help get Vincent and Cindy together, and it's spiraled into an attempt to solve not one, but two, murders. It's gotten out of control! I'm all for letting the authorities solve the crimes and us returning to our original plan to help Reesie."

"We already helped her find her rabbit," I argued. "We did our job. Any matchmaking on yours and LeeAnne's parts is over and above our job description. Getting Vincent Armitage and Cindy Walberg together is just some romantic pipedream cooked up by you two."

Maggie folded her arms across her chest; she and LeeAnne both glared at me like twin volcanoes ready to erupt. By the set of her jaw I could tell she had clamped her mouth shut to keep from tearing into me. She closed her eyes, jutted out her chin, and took a deep breath in preparation for her next remarks.

Elsworth quietly strode over behind her, put his hands on her shoulders, and began to slowly massage her neck.

Bernie patted my arm and made eye contact across the table at George who had draped his arm over LeeAnne's chair. We all sat in silence, no one willing to speak.

Finally I broke the staring contest. "Okay, okay, I recognize a Mexican standoff when I see one. I also see I'm in the minority here. I'm sorry, Mags. I know you and LeeAnne mean well, and I hope the matchmaking thing works out. Reesie deserves to have her father in her life."

Maggie visibly relaxed, but didn't smile. She wasn't ready to concede. I hadn't won back my friend yet. And my next words didn't help the situation much.

"I still think it's a lost cause, but I'll go along with you. I just hope your attempts don't do more damage than good." I pointed my gel pen in her direction. "I caution you to not get the little redhead's hopes up that she might get a dad out of this deal."

Maggie lowered her eyes and no one else said another word.

Bernie finally stood up and said, "I think we need to cap off the meeting for today. How about a trip to the Ice Cream Palace? We can all relax and cool off. My treat."

"Good idea," George agreed. "Who wants to ride with LeeAnne and me?"

"Helen and I will hitch a ride," Bernie said as he helped me to my feet.

Elsworth pulled Maggie's chair back. "Maggie and I will meet you there."

Bernie sighed. "Okay, come on folks, it's ice cream time."

"Thanks for the diversion, Bernie," I said as we walked to George's car. "I guess I'm more caught up in trying to solve the murders than in finding a love connection between Cindy and Vincent. Besides," I laughed as I hooked my arm in his, "murder is easier to handle. It's usually more straightforward than love."

He squeezed my arm. "Ain't it the truth."

Monday morning I thought I'd skip breakfast with the gang. I scanned my cupboards. Like Mother Hubbard's, mine were almost bare. Nothing of interest – not even a spoonful of instant coffee to jumpstart my day. I had lived on soft foods for a week and was ready to sink my teeth into something that required dedicated chewing. Toast drenched in butter and honey sounded good. I made my way to the dining room, plopped into a chair, and noticed tiny bowls of yogurt mixed with fruit in front of Maggie and LeeAnne.

"How do you two expect to make it until lunchtime on that little bit of stuff? Don't you know breakfast is the most important meal of the day?"

I put my order in for two eggs over easy, sausage, and a double order of wheat toast. "And lots of coffee," I added. "Oh, and could you bring me some honey for that toast, please? Some fruit would be good, too, but leave the sour milk product out of it."

"My, you have a hearty appetite today," LeeAnne said.

"Yeah, I've hardly eaten anything for a week that couldn't be sucked through a straw. I'm ready to chow down on some real food."

"It wasn't that bad, Helen," Maggie laughed. "You only had to stay away from coarse foods. I didn't see you drinking your baked chicken or chopped steak through a straw."

"No, but gargling and drinking all that lemon water was

definitely a hardship. All that liquid took the edge off my appetite, and I couldn't savor food the way I like."

Maggie choked and I smiled sweetly back at her. "You know that eating is one of my few indulgences, and I really missed it."

One of the waitstaff set my breakfast in front of me. I took a sip of my coffee then picked up my fork. "Now, if you'll excuse me, I'm going to *savor* my breakfast."

When we'd finished eating, I asked about everyone's plans for the day. George had a budget meeting, Elsworth and Bernie said they were going to hit the golf course for a round or two. Maggie and LeeAnne had planned a shoe-shopping excursion for some sandals that were on sale.

"Come with us, Helen," LeeAnne said. "It will be a fun outing."

I shook my head. "No thanks. Women, shoes, and sales. Three words that spell disaster. I'll pass."

"Okay, but if you change your mind, let us know. We won't leave before ten."

"Don't hold your breath waiting for a call," I called over my shoulder as I made my way back to my apartment. I wasn't sure how I'd spend my morning, but whatever it ended up being, it had to be better than fighting over sale sandals.

Back in my apartment I retrieved my legal pad from my new bag. I still hadn't gotten my stuff back from the Savannah cops. I needed to check with them to find out when I could expect my belongings. I located the card I'd been given by that cop – what was his name? Oh, right Justice. Captain Justice – and dialed the number. The person I reached checked the records and assured me my purse and belongings had been overnighted on Saturday and should be in my hands by day's end. "My name is Tracy. If you don't receive your belongings today, give me a call and I'll put a trace on them for you."

I thanked her and turned to the pad with my new notes. I had bought a pack of multi-colored file cards and proceeded to duplicate the names from our murder boards, using different colors for victims, suspects, and random people. Elsworth wasn't the only one who could create colorful lists!

I shuffled the cards, dealt them out, stacked them in piles by color. Finally I pulled them all together and set them aside. The exercise did nothing but frustrate me. I'd read enough mysteries to know I must be missing something – or someone. The rules for solving a murder were basically: Means, Motive, and Opportunity. Oh, and don't leave out Love and Money.

I had gotten the distinct impression of dislike of Constance Armitage. Our Grand Lady of Savannah hadn't been particularly enveloped by the elite rich of the community, but it was a long stretch from disdain to murder.

All our talks, hashing and rehashing, hadn't brought our group any closer to a motive for Constance's murder. And, as for our other victim, we knew next to nothing about the private investigator. Maybe he should be the next one to check out.

I sorted my cards again, but couldn't tie I. M. Reddy with anyone but Cindy Walberg. There had to be a connection, we just hadn't made it yet.

I restacked the cards, pulled out the one with his name and wrote: Who hired this man? What was he looking for? Why was he murdered? And why did he have the little redhead's bunny?

I slapped it back on the card pile just as my phone rang. I figured it was Maggie or LeeAnne begging me to go shoe shopping, and was prepared to voice my protest once again. But it was the reception desk letting me know a package for me had come in and was waiting for me at the front desk.

I made my way to the front for my package. Sure enough, it was from the Savannah P.D. I carried it to my place, glad to have my things back. My ID, insurance cards, banking information – my life pretty much fit into one small box. It was enough to depress a lesser person. Fortunately I am, in no way, a lesser person. I set it on my table, hesitant to open it. What if they had sent back that bloody legal pad? I had specifically asked that it be destroyed. In fact, I signed an affidavit giving Savannah police permission to discard that particular piece of my belongings. But there was no way of knowing, short of tearing into the box, if my request had been honored.

I checked the clock. Ten-thirty. Maggie and LeeAnne wouldn't be back for hours. George was in a meeting, and there was no telling how long Bernie would be out hitting golf balls around.

I sat down and stared at it like it was Pandora's Box and opening it might set the whole world a-kilter. If that infernal yellow pad was inside, it would definitely set *my* world a-kilter.

I took a deep breath. *Okay, Helen, you're a big girl. You can do this!* I rubbed my hands together, rose and went to fetch a knife to cut the tape that secured the box. While up, I grabbed a trash bag, just in case. If my notes were in there, I'd quickly shove them into the bag. Armed with my tools, I approached the package, tentatively cut the tape, held my breath as I opened the flaps, and peeked inside.

Chapter 21

Helen's Got a Brand-New Bag

The pouch with all my cards and change, two gel pens, a small bottle of pain relievers, and the rest of the loose items I always carried, had been placed in a ziplock bag and lay atop my cloth carryall. I placed the plastic bag on the table, peeked under the edge of my carryall and breathed a sigh of relief. I hadn't realized I'd been holding my breath. No legal pad in sight.

The cloth bag went straight to the laundry basket. I didn't look to see if there were any telltale spatters of blood on it. Ignorance is bliss, they say. What I didn't know wouldn't haunt my dreams.

Next, I dumped the contents of the plastic bag on the table and opened my card pouch to insure all my life's information was still inside. I pulled out I. M. Reddy's business card that I had taken from Charlie at the bar. Detective Metcalf had confiscated mine. What good would it do to try the phone number? Elsworth had said the PI ran a one-man operation out of his home. If that was the case, no one would answer if I called. But what if he had an answering service? Perhaps I could get some information from whoever took his calls. It couldn't hurt to try.

I dialed the number, and after four rings a questioning voice picked up.

"Hello?"

"Yes, is this the number for the private investigator, Ivan Reddy?"

"Yes, it is. At least it was," the voice stammered. "Mr. Reddy is no longer – uh – taking cases."

There was something strange, almost familiar, about that voice. Also, the girl sounded as if she was about to burst into tears.

"Well, I was recommended by," I ventured a guess, "someone in the Armitage family. There's a sticky little matter I'd like to get to the bottom of. When might Mr. Reddy be able to take cases again?"

"Never!" she sobbed, before bursting into full-fledged bawling in my ear.

What should I do now? Maggie would console the poor child, LeeAnne would give her a hug if she was within hugging distance.

I couldn't very well hand her a tissue, so I was lost.

"What seems to be the problem, Dear? What did you say your name was?"

"Evelyn," she sniffed. "Evelyn James."

"Alright, Evelyn. May I call you Evelyn?"

"Uh huh."

"Why are you crying, Evelyn?"

"Ivan's dead," she sobbed again.

"Oh, my. That's too bad. I assume it was recent, as my friends said they had used his services only a few weeks ago." I hoped my surprise and my condolences sounded sincere. I'm sure Janine the Snow Queen would have panned my acting abilities, but she wasn't here, and I was ad-libbing. It sounded like Evelyn had more than a passing interest in our P.I. This was worth investigating!

"You and Mr. Reddy must have been pretty close, since you worked for him," I said.

"Kind of." She spoke so quietly I could barely hear her.

"Are you an investigator, too?" I asked. "I was under the impression Mr. Reddy worked alone."

"Who of us is completely alone," she sighed. "Ivan, uh, Mr. Reddy, used to say that. No, I'm not a P.I., just, uh, an answering service. But he did have a part-time investigator when his caseload got heavy."

"Who might that be? Could I possibly contact him?"

"Uh, I don't know. His name's Jerry. Jerry James. But I'm not sure where he is at the moment. I, uh, think he's on another case."

"Jerry James. Any relation to you, Dear? A brother, perhaps?"

"No," she sighed, "my ex-husband."

"Well, that is interesting. It must be difficult working with an ex." I cleared my throat and laughed. "At least I know it would be difficult for me."

I finally broke the silence on the other end. "I'm calling from Loblolly. I've had problems with some people here in town and hoped to find a way to make them pay restitution. I won't bother you with details, since you aren't involved with investigating. But if Mr. James shows up and would care to discuss my situation, have him give me a call."

"Uh, sure."

The girl didn't seem very articulate for an answering service. She stammered a lot. She seemed to be measuring her words for fear of saying something incriminating. What was she hiding?

"Are you aware of the work Mr. Reddy was involved in for the

177

Armitage's here in Loblolly?" I ventured.

"Uh, not really. Something to do with a woman, no doubt. It was always another woman," she said with disgust.

"You didn't approve?"

"It wasn't my place to approve or disapprove of where he went or what he did," she huffed. "He made that very clear!"

"I see. Can you tell me anything more about Mr. Reddy?"

"Why? What difference would it make? And why would knowing about him possibly help with whatever problem you have? He's dead! Now, if you'll excuse me, I have to clear this line. I *am* an answering service, not Ivan's biographer."

Since I wasn't going to get any more out of her, I gave her my name and phone number and hung up. What that call had accomplished, I had no idea. It sounded like she had more than a passing interest in Mr. Reddy. But enough to commit a double homicide? Maybe.

Perhaps her ex, Jerry, would get back with me and fill in some blanks - if Miss Evelyn gave him the message.

I added both their names to my slowly growing stack of cards. If nothing else, they were another connection to Mr. Reddy.

I put the rainbow of cards aside and began to transfer the loose items I'd dumped onto the table into my new bag. It had several pockets and, until I got used to it, I was sure I'd be continually hunting for things. I placed my pens in one of the pockets; I was glad to have them back. One can't have too many writing tools.

After everything else had been properly pocketed, I was left with one item. I picked it up. One gold hoop earring. Not mine – My ears aren't pierced. I placed the earring back in the plastic bag. Perhaps it belonged to Constance Armitage. I probably should let

Captain Justice know, but first I'd talk to my friends about it. This might be a clue.

The phone rang and interrupted my thoughts. I.M. Reddy's name popped up on my caller ID. Maybe Evelyn had remembered something she wanted to tell me.

I picked up. "Hello?"

"Mrs. Patterson? This is Jerry James returning your call. Exactly what can I do for you? Evelyn said you're in need of some investigating services."

His voice had a forced semi-professionalism, and coming so soon after my talk with his ex, puzzled me. Evelyn must have had him on speed dial. I had to think fast and ad lib again.

"Yes, Mr. James. I was really hoping to speak with your employer, Mr. Reddy."

"Well, like Evelyn told you, that's not possible, since he's dead. He ain't speaking to anyone – except maybe St. Peter as the angel turns the old con man away from the Pearly Gates." He laughed, and I felt the hairs on my neck rise.

"Con man, you say? Was Mr. Reddy not a legitimate private investigator?"

"Ha!" he said. "That depends on your definition of the word. He had a license tacked on his wall like he was some bigtime operator, but that doesn't mean he was legit."

"It was my understanding from Evelyn that you worked for Mr. Reddy. Are you also a private investigator, Mr. James?"

"Nah. Ivan called me his flunky. I did most of his legwork for him. He sort of trained me. Always meant to get my license, but never did. Ivan said it didn't matter – it was just a piece of paper."

"Hmm," I said, in an attempt to keep him dishing dirt on his former employer, "it sounds as though Mr. Reddy had double standards."

"Huh?" he replied.

"What I mean is, him having a license and denying you one kept you in his servitude. Perhaps he wanted to keep you from going off on your own."

"Yeah, you're right," he said, as if suddenly aware he'd been taken advantage of. "If I had my P.I. license me and Evelyn coulda walked out on the cheapskate."

"You and Evelyn? I thought you two were divorced."

"We are. But I'm trying to win her back. She was too good for him. But she kept telling me she couldn't leave Reddy. She said he needed her."

"Needed her for what? Didn't she just answer the phone?"

"No," Jerry said. "She did practically everything for him – not that he appreciated any of it. She kept his books, made deposits when and if he got paid, even went to clients to get his money sometimes. Why, the dame even cooked for him!"

"Wow! She did a lot."

"Yeah. Between her and me, we ran the guy's whole business."

"Sounds like Evelyn took pretty good care of his personal life too," I said to test his reaction.

"Yeah," he growled, "the dirty old womanizer took advantage of her. Made her think he couldn't do without her. And she ate it up. It was disgusting!"

"I see," I said.

"Say, lady, just what was the job you needed done? I can handle it, whatever it is."

"I'm sure you can, Mr. James. But it's not something I want to discuss on the phone. Would you and Evelyn be available to come to Loblolly to discuss the matter later this week?"

"Uh, sure. Just call Evelyn and she'll get ahold of me."

"Alright, then. Thank you for returning the call so promptly. That speaks well of your professionalism." I laid the compliment on thick so he wouldn't question my motive too closely. Although I figured that if Reddy had been able to dupe him he probably was easily manipulated.

"I'll be in touch, Mr. James."

My phone call had raised more questions to a case already long on questions and short on answers. Jerry James was not a big fan of our Mr. Reddy. And, if I was correct, he was more than a little jealous of his former employer's attentions to his ex, Evelyn.

I absent-mindedly fondled the earring in its plastic bag and wished my friends would get back home from shoe-shopping. I was anxious to fill them in on the latest news.

Chapter 22

Lord of the Earring

I paced. Time moved like a slug across pavement while I waited for my friends to return. I paced some more. I needed to share this new information with my crime-solving confederates. That thought stopped me in my tracks. I had always prided myself on my go-it-alone way of life. It was disconcerting to realize I'd become somewhat dependent on someone else's – several someone else's – points of view.

Maybe dependent was too strong a word, but I had to admit I valued their judgments. And, of course, Elsworth's covert connections didn't hurt, either. His contacts could ferret out information a lot faster and more accurately than the rest of us could do on our own. Yes, he was a good asset to our crime-solving operation.

And the smile he put on Maggie's face was an added plus. He was definitely good for her. I no longer feared his intentions weren't on the up-and-up. His face lit up as bright as hers when they were together. He even liked her new little furball.

The ring of my cell phone brought me back to the present. I scratched my head with my gel pen as I twisted around where I stood in the middle of the room. I looked for the blasted thing, and finally located it under my pile of notes just as the message went to voicemail. Caller ID said it was Maggie, so I called her back.

"Sorry," I said when she picked up. "I was busy and couldn't find my phone. Back so soon? Didn't you and LeeAnne find any good buys on your outing?"

"It's three o'clock, Helen. We've been gone for hours. And, to answer your question, we found some really cute sandals. You should have come along."

"Three o'clock, huh? I've been busy and lost track of time."

"Right," she said. "Busy doing what? Reading or napping?"

"I'll have you know, I have plenty to keep me busy when you're not around. In fact, I've got some information on our case to share with y'all. When do you think the guys will be back from the golf course?"

"El said he'd call when they were on their way home."

"Good. This information is really important – I think."

"Helen, you have a one-track mind. You need to get out and enjoy life more. I'll bet you've been sitting in your apartment working out murder scenarios all day."

"Not all day," I said in my defense.

"Right. What else have you done? Did you even eat lunch?"

"Lunch? Of course I ate lunch! I always eat lunch."

"LeeAnne and I went to Mabel's and had spinach wraps. What did you eat?"

"Uh, fig bars." To discourage her from harassment of my lunch choice I asked, "Did you have some of Mabel's yummy peach cobbler, too?"

"As a matter of fact, we shared a bowl. Don't you wish you'd been with us?" she teased.

"Hmph. Not if I'd have to share my peach cobbler. I don't share!"

"I know that's right," she laughed. "Oops. Got to go. I'm getting another call. It's probably El. I'll tell him you've got information to share. Bye."

"Okay, bye," I said to dead air.

Thirty minutes later Maggie called and said El and Bernie had returned and would meet us at his apartment.

"What about George?" I asked.

"LeeAnne left him a message. Hopefully his budget meeting is over, and he'll be there. I'm taking Blinky for a walk and I'll meet you at El's."

"You still haven't given that poor animal a decent name? He's probably scarred for life!"

Maggie laughed. "If that's the case, he was scarred before I got him. I'm waiting for the perfect name. He and I will both know when it's right."

"Okay," I said. "But at the rate you're going, he'll go his grave as Blinky the One-Eyed Furball. Go walk the sad little thing. I'm going to gather up my stuff and head to Elsworth's place."

"Thanks," Maggie said.

"Thanks for what? For pointing out that you're giving your rescue animal a complex?"

"No," she said. "Thanks for finally calling El by his first name instead of constantly referring to him as Lumley."

"Oh. Okay. Sure," I stammered. "I've got to admit, he's kind of growing on me."

She sighed. "Yeah. Me too."

"I know."

I'd still have to put a stake through his heart if he ever hurt my friend, but no sense telling her that. Some things are better left unsaid.

I put a rubber band around my file cards, dropped them, my notes, and the earring into my new bag, and headed to Elsworth's apartment.

Bernie and I reached the door at the same time. He flashed me a sunny smile. "Good afternoon, Beautiful," he said.

"Beautiful, huh? You must have done well on the golf course. Either that or you got too much sun and it addled your brain. Unless you're hallucinating, there is no one beautiful here."

A frown took the place of the smile, so I quickly added, "However, hallucinating or not, I appreciate the compliment. No one but you has ever called me beautiful."

"Their loss," he said as he knocked on the door, the smile back in place.

LeeAnne appeared beside us just at the door opened. "Hi, y'all."

I cocked my head. "Listen to you. Keep talking like that and we might make a Southern Lady of you yet!" I shook my head. "Now, if you'd learn to enjoy the elixir of the southern gods, sweet tea, I'd feel I'd done a proper job of initiating you to perfect southern manners."

Her joyful, lilting laugh echoed down the hallway. "Sorry, but I'm afraid I'm a lost cause to that initiation."

She gave me a hug and looked past me to Bernie. "You must have gotten a little sun today, Bernie. Your cheeks are red."

He rubbed his face. "Yeah, that's probably it."

"Ha!" said Elsworth, who stood in the open doorway. "That's the red of humiliation for the trouncing I gave him on the golf course."

Bernie nodded. "That's true. But I'm getting closer. I'm waiting for you to get complacent, then I'll make my move."

"Uh, oh. Sounds like a challenge. I'll be waiting," he said as he led us to his conference table.

"And I challenge the winner of that match," said George.

Bernie and El nodded to each other and said in unison, "We'd better practice!"

LeeAnne pulled up a chair beside George. "Hello, George. I see you got through your budget meeting intact."

"Yes, it's not my favorite thing to do, but is one of those necessary things. I'm ready to hear something stimulating. That budget meeting nearly put me to sleep."

Maggie chose that moment to join us. Hmm. I noticed she didn't even bother to knock when she arrived – just waltzed right in. Before long she and Elsworth would be cohabitating. I wasn't sure I was ready for that step in my friend's life.

Elsworth pulled out a chair and she sat beside him, Blinky, the One-Eyed Furball, in her lap. I sat to her left. Blinky looked at me and growled under his breath. I leaned down and growled back. I'd show him who was the alpha dog here.

Everyone laughed. The furball settled back down on Maggie's lap, content to let me believe I was in charge.

Elsworth glanced at me. "Alright, Helen. Maggie said you have some important news on our case. What is it?"

I pulled out my set of file cards. I'd made extras of the two new names and handed them to him.

He read them aloud. "Who are Evelyn James and Jerry James? And how did you come up with the names?"

I laid my legal pad on the table. "I called I.M. Reddy's number from his business card and Evelyn James answered." I filled them in on my conversation with her, and my subsequent talk with Evelyn's ex, Jerry.

"According to Jerry, he and Evelyn practically ran Reddy's business, and didn't feel they were treated as equals. At least that's the impression I got from him. I also think he resented the time and attention Evelyn gave Mr. Reddy."

"Hmm," said Bernie, "jealousy is a very good motive for murder."

"Yes," said LeeAnne, "but what about Constance Armitage? If we believe the two deaths are related, what's the motive for her murder?"

I shrugged. "I haven't figured that one out yet."

"Maybe they're not tied together," said Maggie. "Maybe hers was a random murder."

"Perhaps," said Elsworth, "but I'm not a believer in coincidences. My gut tells me there's a connection."

He nodded to me. "Good work, Helen. I only told my sources to check out the P.I. I should have asked them to dig deeper. I'll make a call."

"Is that all the news you had, Helen?" asked George.

I reached into my purse and laid the earring on the table beside me. "Not quite. I got my stuff back from the Savannah police today. This lone earring was mixed in with the other loose items from my bag. Since it's not mine, it might belong to Mrs. Armitage. It's also possible it belongs to whoever attacked her."

LeeAnne picked it up, pulled a jeweler's loupe from her purse, studied the earring, and handed it and the loupe to Elsworth. "El, does that look like blood?"

He studied the earring, set it back on the table. "Helen, you need to call Captain Justice. There's more than blood on this earring. This could be evidence."

"Yeah, I was going to do that as soon as we all had a look at it."

Blinky put his paws on the table, sniffed the earring, and grabbed the bag. He jumped off Maggie's lap, ran to his doggie bed, and tucked his prize under his blanket. I got up to retrieve it and he growled as I reached out my hand.

George laughed. "Guess he doesn't want you to steal his new toy."

Maggie walked over and he allowed her to pick up both him and the earring. She scratched his head and he snugged into her shoulder. She turned to all of us, a huge smile playing on her lips. "I know what Blinky's new name is," she announced. "It's Frodo, Lord of the Earring!"

"Good one," said George.

"Are we about done here?" LeeAnne asked. "It's nearly time for dinner, and my spinach wrap from lunch wore off long ago."

Elsworth looked at me. "Is there anything else you needed to share, Helen?"

I shook my head. I didn't mention I'd tentatively asked to meet with Evelyn and Jerry James. That could wait until Elsworth had his 'friends' do a deeper dive into the duo's backgrounds. It wouldn't be smart to walk blind into a meeting with a possible killer or killers.

We tabled our discussion for the time being and headed to the dining room. As we left, everyone but me scratched Maggie's furball behind his ears. He only growled a little as I passed by. I stared at him and he tucked his head under Maggie's arm.

One thing we all agreed on, though: Frodo was the perfect name for the new addition to our group.

Chapter 23

Sanity is Overrated

Bernie trailed down the hall after me until I finally slowed so he could catch up.

He reached my side breathing deep and holding his chest.

"You seem pretty excited to go to dinner tonight," he said. "Did you get word there's a special treat this evening?"

"It's *supper*. And one can only hope there's a decent desert in store," I sighed. "Sorry I ran off and left you in the dust back there. This case has got me all flubber-dubbed, I guess. I keep running things through my mind, trying to make connections, and all I get are more questions."

He laughed. "I know. You and El are a pair. That's about all we talked about during our golf game. It's probably why I came close to beating him, something that doesn't happen often. His mind was off in Savannah trying to solve a murder."

I took his arm. "Next time you two go play golf I'll give him another puzzle to work on and maybe you'll beat him."

He patted my hand. "Good idea. Maybe I should challenge him to a game right now, while he's distracted. His mental wheels started turning when you pulled out that earring. I could tell he thinks it's significant."

I stopped and turned to him. "Do you think it's important?"

He shrugged as we continued walking. "Could be. El thought so. And so did Maggie's dog. Maybe he's a spy, like El and his former companions. And," he continued, "speaking of the dog, I think Frodo is a perfect name for the little guy. Small but feisty and determined."

"Yeah, well," I laughed, "at least she didn't name him after the Gollum in that book."

Bernie smiled and nodded. "Right. Smeagol is a much more humiliating name than Blinky."

We all met in the dining room and took our usual seats together. The meal consisted of typical summertime fare – way too many salad greens topped with indistinguishable chunks of meat. After my lunch of fig bars, the skimpy portion hardly made a dent in my appetite. The dessert, though, helped fill up the empty space in my stomach.

I eyed Bernie's slice of the rich apple spice cake drizzled with a brown-sugar, caramel glaze. "The server must have a crush on you. Your piece of cake is bigger than the rest of ours."

He grinned and exchanged his dessert for mine. "There you go, Beautiful. Enjoy. I know your appreciation of the sweet things in life is greater than mine."

I thanked him and glared at Maggie who had opened her mouth to speak. My look shut her up – at least temporarily. She raised an eyebrow and mouthed, *Beautiful?* I was sure I'd get an earful from her later about the 'cake exchange'.

I attempted to discuss our case while we ate but no one took the bait. In fact, every time I said a word, one of my friends changed the topic to something mundane like the weather – hot and muggy – or Bernie's and Elsworth's golf game – Bernie lost again – or Maggie's new furball, now named Frodo.

"Fine!" I huffed. "I get the point. You don't want to discuss the case."

"It's not that, Helen," Maggie said. "But there are other things we can talk about besides murder, especially at the dinner table."

"Yeah, yeah. Hot weather, Bernie's lack of golfing skills, your dog."

Maggie's smile faded; I'd hurt her feelings again. "All wonderful, interesting topics, to be sure," I sighed. "But I can't get these murders out of my head, and they're driving me crazy!"

Maggie smiled. "You know, there are some who think you've already driven to the end of that crazy road – present company excepted, of course."

I looked around at the smiling faces of my friends. "Of course. Thanks, I think."

George spoke up. "Your dogged persistence is one of the things we love about you. I've always admired your never-give-up attitude."

"Right," added Bernie. "We like your craziness. Besides," he smiled at me, "I think sanity is overrated."

I stood up and Bernie followed suit. "Okay. I can't take any more of these back-handed compliments. If no one cares to share the remainder of their dessert with me, I'm going to adjourn to my apartment and work on my insanity."

Maggie stood up too. "El and I promised Frodo we'd take him for a walk."

George helped LeeAnne to her feet and asked her, "Would you be up for a game of Gin Rummy?"

She smiled and blushed. "That sounds like fun."

As they all went in different directions, Bernie grinned at me.

"That leaves us. Do you play Gin Rummy, Helen?"

"Yes, I do, and no I won't. But I will challenge you to a game of Scrabble. How's your spelling?"

"About on par with my golfing skills, I imagine."

I took his arm as we walked down the hall. "Good. I won't need to distract you too much to throw off your game."

"I accept that challenge," he said. "It's no embarrassment to get beaten by the best."

Back in my apartment I pulled out the Scrabble board and placed the velvet pouch with all the tiles on the table beside it. Then I retrieved my Scrabble Dictionary from the bookshelf.

He pointed to the book. "This looks serious. But I doubt you'll have to check that thing for any words I'll use."

I grinned and handed him the book. "Oh, this is for you to verify *my* words."

"Uh oh, I think I'm in over my head!"

"Think of it as a learning experience, like golfing with Elsworth."

I picked a 'J' out of the pouch and handed him the bag. "Your turn. Beat a 'J'."

He pulled out a 'D'. "What does this mean?"

"Oh boy, this is going to be easier than I thought. You got the tile closest to 'A', so you start." I dropped my tile back in the pouch. "Draw seven letters and make a word."

Bernie wasn't the novice he claimed to be, and the game was well-matched. I managed to squeak by with a win by placing 'zoospore' across his word 'bias'. He had to look up the word but admitted defeat after he read: "A spore of some algae and fungi."

"Why would you even know that, Helen? He laughed. "Are you a closet botanist?"

"Actually, the word came up in one of my mysteries. A chemist tried to mix elements to create a poison of global proportions. I wrote the word down as a possible Scrabble word. 'X' and 'Z' words can often defeat even the best of opponents. I've got to admit, you gave me a run for my money."

He shrugged off the compliment as he looked at his watch and stood to leave. "Do you realize you haven't mentioned the murders for nearly two hours?"

"Wow! You're right. Maybe this mess hasn't completely driven me insane after all."

I walked him to the door. "Thanks for an enjoyable evening."

He kissed my cheek and said, "Anything to be of service. But to be honest, I kind of like your form of insanity; it keeps the rest of us on our toes. Sweet dreams, Beautiful."

I patted his cheek. "You really need to stop with the beautiful comments. Maggie is going to grill me about that. Did you see the look she gave me at the table tonight?"

He smiled. "As a matter of fact, I did. Is that such a bad thing?"

He had me there. What was the harm of him calling me beautiful – aside from the fact I wasn't!

I shook my head and watched Bernie saunter down the hall whistling "Everything is Beautiful". I closed the door and leaned back against it. What was I going to do with that man? Maggie and LeeAnne were right – he was definitely persistent. He needed new bifocals, though, if he thought I was beautiful. But, in a way, it was flattering. I'd never before felt – or been told that – I was beautiful.

I pushed myself away from the door. I didn't have time for this sentimental, mushy stuff! Leave that to my partners in crime-fighting, Maggie and LeeAnne, whose romances seemed to be blossoming nicely.

My phone jangled in my pocket. I plopped into my recliner and answered it. "Hello, Maggie. I was just thinking about you."

"Hello to you, too. Did you and your beautiful admirer have a good time?"

"Give it a rest, Mags. Quit trying to be a match-maker. Did you, Elsworth, and Frodo have a nice walk?"

"As a matter of fact, we did. It's a beautiful evening, beautiful night sky full of stars. In fact, Everything is Beautiful," she chuckled.

"Okay," I sighed. "You must have heard Bernie whistling his way down the hall. I told him to stop that."

"Why?" she asked. "I think it's sweet. What's wrong with him saying you're beautiful?"

I shrugged, even though she couldn't see me through the phone. "Nothing's wrong with it, I guess. Except we all know I'm not beautiful!"

"It seems Bernie thinks otherwise, and that's all that matters. What did you two beautiful people do for fun? Did you go back to your place and try to solve the case?"

"No. If you must know, we played Scrabble. Bernie even commented that I went for nearly two hours without even mentioning the murders."

"Wow!" she said. "That's got to be a record! Either you were having fun, or your competitive side took over and forced you to try to beat him."

I laughed. "A little of both, I think. Bernie is really easy to be around. And he's a good listener. I did manage to beat him, but not by much."

"The ability to be a good listener is imperative around you," she teased. "But seriously, I'm happy for you. Bernie is a really nice guy."

"Yes, he is," I agreed. "Did you call to grill me about my evening, or did you have something important to say?"

"As a matter of fact, I do have some information. El kept talking about that earring you showed us. I swear, Helen, he's as bad as you about this case."

"Maybe that's what attracted you to him, I said. "He's the male equivalent of your best friend."

"Eww," she said. "That's too weird to even think about."

"What about Elsworth and the earring?"

"He said there's something besides blood on it."

"Yuk. Like what, exactly?"

"Now don't freak out, Helen."

"What's freaking me out is you not telling me what's going on."

She took a deep breath. "He thinks it might be flesh. He said it might have been torn from someone's ear during the struggle that killed Constance Armitage."

"Double yuk! Why didn't he say that at the meeting?" I shouted. "That thing might belong to her killer!"

I began to hyperventilate and grabbed my chest. "Maggie, this is *Huge!*"

I got up and dumped my bag to retrieve the evidence. My hands shook as I picked it up. "This could be the key the police need to solve this case!" I shouted again.

"Calm down, Helen. You may be right. Or, as El said, the earring might belong to Mrs. Armitage, not the killer. He didn't want to upset you – or worse – cause you to do something stupid."

"Something stupid!" I screamed. "Something stupid like what?"

"Like trying to confront the killer on your own," she said.

"Uh," I stammered.

"Uh, what, Helen? What have you done?"

"I, uh, made a tentative appointment with Jerry and Evelyn James."

It was Maggie's turn to raise her voice. "You what?"

"Well, not an exact appointment. I asked to meet with them sometime this week to talk about a case."

"What case would that be?" she questioned.

I knew, from experience, she was running her hand through her hair and pacing in her place much as I was in mine.

"What case would that be, Helen?" she repeated.

"I made up a bogus case. I was very vague and told them I wanted to talk to them in person here in Loblolly."

"Oh no! I've got to call El and let him know. Don't you dare set up a meeting with them on your own!"

"I have no intention of calling them tonight. It's too late. I promise to contact Captain Justice in the morning, and we'll play it by ear-ring from there," I joked.

"Very funny. Now, let me call El. I'll see you at breakfast. Sweet dreams."

"You too."

I dropped the earring into my bag and headed to bed. I feared my dreams would be anything but sweet.

Easy Apple Spice Cake

One boxed Apple-spice cake mix
1 cup Applesauce
½ cup Buttermilk
1/3 cup butter, room temp
1 tsp Lemon zest
1/3 Cup solid shortening
1 tsp. Vanilla
2 Eggs
1 cup chopped, peeled apples
1 cup chopped pecans

Preheat oven to 350 degrees. Mix all ingredients except chopped apples and pecans. Mix well. Fold in pecans and apples. Place in greased Bundt pan. Bake 50-55 minutes or until cake is golden and springs back when lightly pressed. Cool, Remove from pan. Spread warm brown sugar, caramel glaze over cake.

Glaze:

3 Tbsp. butter
3 Tbsp. light brown sugar
3 Tbsp. granulated sugar
3 Tbsp. heavy whipping cream
½ tsp. vanilla

Place all ingredients in saucepan. Bring to a boil. Let boil for one minute, stirring often. Remove from heat and spoon over cooled cake.

Chapter 24

From Match-making to Murder?

I spent a restless night filled with dreams of dogs and earrings and dogs wearing earrings. As soon as I dragged myself out of bed in the morning, I put in a call to Captain Justice. He wasn't in his office yet. I told the officer I spoke with it was imperative he call me. I gave my name and phone number. "Tell him it's about the Constance Armitage case," I said.

Maggie eyed me when I pulled up my chair at the breakfast table. "You look like you didn't sleep well, Helen."

I merely nodded in silence as Bernie handed me a cup of coffee. I took a sip. It was flavored exactly the way I like it. I raised it to him and mouthed, "Thanks," as he sat down beside me.

He beamed. He'd obviously been more observant of me than I had of him. I had no idea how he took his coffee.

I yawned, filled the group in on my dreams, and told them I had put a call in to Captain Justice. From the looks on their faces, Maggie and Elsworth had already filled them in on the possible significance of the earring.

"He's supposed to call…" My phone jangled and I dug it out of my bag. "That's probably him now."

I checked, but caller ID said 'blocked call' again. I answered and got only dead air. I dropped the phone back in my purse. "Blocked call," I said. "Guess it was a wrong number."

"Or maybe it was that woman who called and threatened you," LeeAnne said. "Wasn't hers a blocked number?"

I shrugged. "If it was her, I guess she didn't want to talk to me."

I toyed with my food. "These last few days have really messed with my appetite. At this rate, I'm liable to waste away to nothing."

They all laughed. Bernie patted my hand. "I could ask if there's any of that spice cake left from supper. You managed to get that down last night."

I shook my head. "Thanks anyway."

"How about another cup of coffee, then?" He grabbed my near-empty cup.

My phone rang again. "Yes, that would be good." I checked caller ID. This time it registered Captain Justice's number.

I tapped Bernie's arm as I got up to take the call. "Could you fix me another cup just like the last one while I talk to the captain? I'll be right back."

I explained to the captain about the earring I found in my returned belongings and suggested its possible connection to Mrs. Armitage and his case.

He was not happy that his officers had missed a possible clue and said he would personally come to Loblolly to pick it up.

"Please secure it so no more evidence is lost," he demanded.

"I put it in a plastic bag as soon as I opened the box. That's as secure as I can make it. Any lost evidence came from your end," I huffed.

"You're correct. I apologize. It's not your fault we missed the clue. I can be there by eleven o'clock. Will that be convenient?"

"The sooner, the better, Captain. I'll let the front desk know to expect you. Ring the buzzer and someone will let you in the gate."

I hung up and returned to the table. My friends all waited patiently as I sipped my fresh cup of coffee and nodded my approval to Bernie for his coffee-making skills.

Finally Maggie folded her hands on the table and said, "Okay, Helen, out with it. What did the captain say?"

I set my cup down. "Aren't we impatient today?"

She stared across at me, waiting for me to say something. I stared right back at her. Two could play this game!

Finally I responded. "First he demanded that I secure the earring so no more evidence would be lost."

"I'll bet that went well," Bernie laughed.

I nodded. "I informed him that any lost evidence came from his end, and he apologized."

Bernie patted my back. "That's my girl. Keep the guy straight on the facts."

"Did he ask you to mail it back to him?" LeeAnne asked.

"No, he's coming here to pick it up. He said he'll be here before noon."

Maggie leaned forward. "Did you mention your talk with Mr. Reddy's helpers?"

I copied her movement, leaned across and looked her in the eyes. "No, I didn't. He wouldn't be interested in those two. I.M. Reddy is not his case."

"Helen's right," added George. "We believe the two murders are connected, but we have no proof. He'd only think Helen was meddling."

"I agree with George," said Elsworth. He turned to me. "Maggie told us you set up an appointment with Mr. and Mrs. James."

I glared at her and she shrugged. "You didn't say to keep it a secret. Besides, you agreed to let El check on them before you meet with them."

I raised my cup. "To be clear, I didn't exactly agree to anything. But…"

She began to protest. "Helen, you're going to raise my blood pressure to dangerous levels if you keep jumping headlong into scary situations."

She pointed at Bernie. "Please convince her she's not Nancy Drew or some other crime-fighting hero before she gets herself hurt." She sat back, deflated, teary-eyed.

I reached across the table and took her hand. "Calm down Mags and let me finish. First of all," I said with a smile, "I would be a crime-fighting *heroine*, not hero."

She tried to pull her hand away. "This isn't a joke, Helen."

"Let me finish what I was saying before you get all worked up. I think it's a good idea to let Elsworth have his friends run a check on the James's. I'll not set up a meet with them until we know more. And I promise I won't meet them alone."

I sat back and folded my arms. "Satisfied?"

She pulled a tissue from her purse and wiped her eyes. "Yes," she nodded. "Thank you."

We all got up to leave the table. I surprised her with a hug, and whispered in her ear, "Don't worry about me. I plan to hang around for years to annoy you."

She laughed and hugged me back. "I can hardly wait."

Bernie knocked on my door at 10:30 and insisted on going with me to meet Captain Justice.

"Did Maggie put you up to this?" I asked.

He shrugged. "She did mention it, but I had already decided to accompany you. It's always best to have two sets of eyes and ears on a conversation. You don't mind, do you?"

"No. I guess you're right. But it's not like I'll be walking into trouble. Justice is a policeman, not one of our suspects. What's Maggie afraid of? Does she think I'll irritate him to the point he'll arrest me?"

He laughed. "She did say something to that effect, but I'm sure she was joking."

"Sure she was. She thinks I'm going to do something stupid if she's not around to run interference."

I took his arm. "Let's go sit in the lobby and wait for the captain."

"Your wish is my command."

I grabbed my bag and we headed for the front.

The lobby was more aptly a sitting room. Small couches and chairs dotted the area. To one side sat a bookcase with a few novels from the library. Another shelf held knickknacks, and a potted plant soaked up sunlight in the large front window.

We sat on a couch and Bernie picked up one of the magazines scattered across an end table. He looked around. "This is a nice little room, but I seldom see people sitting out here."

"No privacy," I huffed. "Sitting out here implies to anyone who walks by that you either don't know the way back to your apartment, or you've got absolutely nothing to do. Neither scenario appeals to me. If you look bored, Carolyn is liable to swoop in and drag you off to some scary game or craft project."

"And what happens if you're simply lost?" he asked.

"That's even worse. I don't know this for a fact," I whispered conspiratorially, "but I think there's a padded room under the building where lost keys, lost socks, and lost souls end up." I cocked my head and smiled into his blue eyes. "It's just a theory. Like with our investigation, I have no proof, but I'm taking lots of notes."

His laugh echoed through the room, and the receptionist at the front desk eyed us as if we'd disturbed her nail filing.

"Helen," he said, "you really should write a novel. You have a wonderful, crazy, quirky imagination."

"Ha! I'm too old to write a book."

"You're the perfect age. You have a mature, positive perspective on life."

"Right. Like I said, I'm too old."

I had informed Tammee (with two m's and two e's, as she told everyone – even if they couldn't care less) that we were expecting the captain, and promptly at eleven she buzzed him in. Bernie suggested we go to the library and sit at one of the tables. Captain Justice waited for us to sit, and hesitated before taking a chair across from us where he could look directly into our eyes.

"Thank you for calling my office about the earring, Mrs. Patterson. May I see it, please?"

I dug in my bag, pulled out my legal pad, my pen, and the bag containing the earring. I handed him the evidence. "My friends and I think it belongs either to Mrs. Armitage or the person who attacked her."

He took the plastic bag, looked it over, but remained silent.

Finally he removed an evidence bag from his pocket, dropped the earring inside and scribbled some notes on the bag.

"Well," I asked, "do you think it might be important?"

He glanced at the legal pad on the table as if trying to read my notes upside down. "I can tell you this much, Mrs. Patterson, the earring does not belong to Mrs. Armitage. She was wearing diamond studs."

Bernie sat forward. "Is it possible it could belong to the killer?"

"It's possible, yes. Or it could have been a random piece of jewelry left lying on the floor," Justice said.

"Oh, come on, Captain. You don't really believe that nonsense, do you?" I asked. "It's got to belong to her killer!"

His dark eyes glared at me. "Unlike you, Mrs. Patterson, I can't jump to that conclusion. I must have facts."

"Here's a fact for you..." I began.

Bernie touched my arm and gave a slight shake of his head. I clamped my mouth shut.

Bernie spoke. "Do you know how Mrs. Armitage died, Captain?"

"It appears to have been blunt force trauma," he said. "It looks like she fell during a struggle and hit her head on the edge of the sink."

"She must have fallen quite hard." I jotted the information down.

Justice tapped my note pad. "I would appreciate it if you did not play amateur sleuth. I read the notes from your other pad. Why were you really in Savannah checking on the Armitage's? Who is I. M. Reddy, and what does he have to do with Constance Armitage?"

I couldn't look at the man. Instead I doodled bunnies and guns and earrings in the margins of my new pad. "It's a different case, entirely," I mumbled.

He pushed back his chair, stood up, and loomed over me. "Different case entirely? Then why are there so many of the Armitage's listed in your notes? I took time to check out Mr. Reddy. It seems he's also dead."

"We already explained that to you, the day of Mrs. Armitage's death. Weren't you listening? Or did you merely dismiss us because we reminded you of," I turned to Bernie, "How did he say it? Oh Yes, his grandparents. His *elderly* grandparents."

By this time the captain's face had turned red; he paced back and forth and ran his hands through his curly blonde hair.

Bernie stood and touched the captain's arm. "If you will have a seat, Helen and I will try to explain again."

He sat. Bernie and I went through the whole story one more time about Reesie's lost bunny and finding Reddy's dead body.

Captain Justice shook his head. "Let me get this straight. You were hired by an eight-year-old girl to find a stuffed animal, and you ended up tripping over a dead body? Then you came to *my* town and just happened upon another body?"

He stood up again. "Do people often turn up dead around you, Mrs. Patterson?"

"Not too often," I muttered.

"But we did solve a murder in Atlanta a few months ago," Bernie bragged.

I elbowed him in the ribs. I feared much more stress and the captain might have a coronary.

Bernie cringed with pain. "All we intended to do was to find out if we could get Vincent Armitage and Reesie's mom together."

"Match-making to murder," the captain sighed. "Just when

you think you've heard it all!" He rubbed his hands across his face. "Do you have anything else to add?"

"As a matter of fact, yes. We think the murders of Mr. Reddy and Mrs. Armitage are tied together somehow," I said.

"Detective Metcalf is in charge of Reddy's case here. You might check with him and compare notes," Bernie suggested.

His eyes brightened. "Dale Metcalf?"

I nodded.

"I know him from the academy. Have you managed to make him want to tear his hair out, too? I might go talk to him while I'm in town, just to sympathize. Now, if there's nothing more, I really must get going."

We walked him to the front. He stopped and turned as he reached the door. "Try to not fall over any more bodies." He pointed to Bernie. "And one last caution to you both. This is not a mystery game where Mr. Green did it with a rope in the library. Nor is it some murder mystery and dinner theater. This is the real thing. *Real* people are *really* dead! I don't want to go to the scene of a crime and find a senior citizen is the victim because they thought this was a parlor game! Be careful. If you're right and the same person or persons are responsible for both murders, one more body added to the count won't matter to them."

Chapter 25

You're Not Too Annoying

I growled as we turned to go back to my place. "The nerve of that man!"

Bernie grabbed my arm as I stomped down the hall. "The captain is right. We don't know who's responsible for the murders. We need to be careful."

"We aren't doing anything dangerous," I grumbled. "All we've done is ask a few questions."

He stepped ahead of me, put his hands on my shoulders and looked up into my eyes. "Someone must believe differently," he said. "Otherwise why would that mystery woman have called to threaten you?"

I pulled away and continued walking. "Maybe she's protecting the Armitage's interests. People with money don't like their names linked with anything tawdry like illegitimacy and murder."

"Looks like that's likely to change since Mrs. Armitage's demise."

I pulled my key card out to unlock my door. "Perhaps. But you've got to remember, Constance was only an Armitage by marriage. She can easily be swept away like an unwanted dust bunny. If what I overheard from those ladies at the gala is any indication, she wasn't well liked or accepted by the 'old money', even if she was funding an animal shelter."

He followed me inside and closed the door. "That's awfully cynical," he said.

"Maybe. But I've had a little experience with *those people...*"

"Yes, I know. A bad experience," he sighed. "I'm sorry about that. But you shouldn't let it color your view of all *those people*, as you call them."

"*Those people*," I continued, "only care about their wealth and standing. A home for wayward dogs doesn't enhance their wealth. Nor would it endear Constance Armitage to them. She would never be able to buy her way into their good graces, no matter how many wayward puppies she saved."

Bernie glanced at his watch. "Let's put the whole mess aside for a while. It's nearly lunchtime. Shall we head to the dining room and see what's on the menu for the day? I'm sure the others will be anxious to hear about our visit with Captain Justice."

"With my luck it's probably another salad! I'm ready for cool weather and some good, hearty, stick-to-your-ribs food. I'm liable to turn into a rabbit myself. I could end up being the little redhead's new fluffy bunny."

Bernie laughed. "The little redhead's name is Reesie. And if you ended up as her new bunny, I know you would be well loved." He cocked his head and looked me up and down.

"What?" I asked. "Why are you staring at me?"

He grinned. "You don't look like an Ariadne. Reesie would have to give you a different name."

I slapped his arm. "Very funny. Come on, let's go check out the salad bar."

Our friends were already seated when Bernie and I entered

the dining room. Happily, instead of rabbit food, club sandwiches were on the menu. At least there was meat involved in our lunch. The group all waited without asking questions until I finished my sandwich and dove into my bowl of fresh fruit.

Maggie latched onto my arm halfway to my mouth with a forkful of melon. "Alright, Helen. We've been patient long enough. What did Captain Justice have to say about the earring?"

I pulled my arm away and popped the melon into my mouth. After I had sufficiently chewed and leisurely swallowed the bite, I cleared my throat and wiped my mouth with my napkin. I could see Elsworth grinding his teeth, and Maggie nearly had smoke coming out of her ears as they waited.

Bernie leaned over and whispered in my ear, "Maybe you should fill them in before Maggie erupts like Mt. Etna, and El grinds his teeth down to the gums."

I grabbed my legal pad from my bag. "Okay, here it is. Number one, the earring was not Constance's. That means it probably belongs to her killer."

LeeAnne gasped. "Did the captain say that?"

"No, not exactly. He said Constance was wearing diamond studs. He tried to say it could have been a stray earring lying on the floor."

"Of course, Helen called him on that point," Bernie added. "But he couldn't confirm anything without proof."

Elsworth glared at me. "Wise man."

I continued. "He had also read the notes from my other pad and questioned me about why I had a list of the Armitage family. Bernie and I explained about the little redhead…"

"Reesie," Maggie muttered.

"Yeah, Reesie. We told him Vincent Armitage is her biological father and you and LeeAnne are trying to play match-maker."

Bernie spoke up. "He also asked about the private detective, and his involvement with the case. Helen explained to him about finding Reddy's body and that he had Reesie's stuffed bunny in his hand. When he questioned us about that case, Helen told him to check with Detective Metcalf here in Loblolly about it."

"He knows Metcalf and said he'd go talk to him while he's in town," I added.

"Our assumption from all of this is that Constance Armitage's attacker is a woman, am I right?" George asked.

Elsworth nodded. "That's the natural conclusion. But, like Captain Justice, we have no proof. And," he added, "no viable suspects."

"Last, but not least," I added, "Justice believes we're a bunch of old people playing a parlor game. He warned Bernie and me to stay out of the investigation."

I pounded my fist on the table. "Old people indeed! I say, let's go find some viable suspects and show the captain we're still capable of solving crimes."

LeeAnne shrugged, Maggie shook her head. Elsworth sighed, and Bernie grinned like a kid who's just been handed the keys to the candy store.

Maggie raised her hand. "Can we have just one meal without bringing up the subjects of dead bodies and murder, please?"

"You started it!" I pouted like a petulant child.

She glared at me and smiled shyly at Elsworth. "El, I know you and Helen get wrapped up in this macabre stuff, but not everyone shares your fascination with mayhem. I'd like to sit down to a meal where the worst subject discussed is the weather. All this talk of death is depressing!"

Elsworth slipped his arm over Maggie's shoulders. "You're absolutely right, my dear." He looked around the table. "Let's make a rule there will be no more murder discussions at the dinner table."

Everyone nodded.

"That's reasonable." I grinned at Maggie. "What about the breakfast and lunch tables?"

"Helen," she growled.

"Okay, okay. I get it. No more murder talk while we eat. Will that make you happy?"

She nodded and we finished lunch in silence, no one able to find a topic that didn't center around the case.

Elsworth stood and helped Maggie to her feet. He glanced at his watch. "How about we meet at my place to continue our discussion? Maggie and I promised Frodo a run at the dog park after lunch. We will be back by three o'clock. Does that fit with everyone's schedules?"

LeeAnne, George, and Bernie all agreed.

Maggie eyed me. "What about you, Helen?"

I jumped at the sound of my name as I returned my legal pad to my bag. "Loblolly has a dog park? What's next, dog college?"

Everyone laughed.

"Probably elementary and high school first," Maggie deadpanned. "And the dog park is all you got out of the conversation? The question asked was if three o'clock works with your schedule."

"Oh, yeah. Sure. The only thing on my agenda is the newsletter. Several people have submitted articles, and Carolyn asked me to print a calendar of events for the month. Other than that the only things that await me are my recliner and my latest nursery rhyme mystery."

"That's so sad and lonely," said LeeAnne. "Maybe you should get a dog like Maggie did. You need something to take care of and give you unconditional love."

"Hah! That's the last thing I need. Ask my daughter, Emily. To hear her tell it, my kids had to practically raise themselves. What I considered giving them independence, she calls abandonment!" I shook my head. "No dogs. No way!"

George spoke up as they all meandered down the hall behind me. "How about a cat, then. Cats are aloof and independent."

I stopped, turned and said, "No cats. No dogs. No guinea pigs, snakes, or any other living thing! I can't even keep a houseplant alive! I don't want the responsibility. Got it?"

I turned and marched toward my apartment.

"Got it," they all laughed as they wandered off to their various activities.

I fumbled for my key card, not sure why my hands were shaking. Bernie touched my arm and I jumped. "Sorry," I apologized. "I didn't know you were still here. I thought you'd left with the others."

He reached out his hand for my key card. "It looked as though you needed a bit of help. Want me to get that door for you?"

I handed him the card. He opened the door and motioned for me to enter. "Would you like some company, or do you want to be alone?"

I sighed. "Come on in. Having you around is kind of like being alone." My hand flew to my mouth. That hadn't come out quite the way I meant it.

He chuckled. "Thanks, I think."

I threw my bag on the table and plopped down. He sat beside me. "What I meant was that you're not too annoying."

He cocked an eyebrow. "That's good, I guess."

"Of course it's good. You don't push me to do things. You go along with my hair-brained ideas. You listen to me without offering advice – most of the time. And when you do offer, it's in the nicest way."

His blue eyes sparkled.

"And," I continued, "you've never once told me I need a dog!" I finished with a grin. "All in all, you and your cute bow tie are nice to have around."

"I can live with that. Now, would you like some help putting your newsletter together? Ben Franklin told me I was a pretty good typesetter back in the day."

I laughed. "Sounds like a plan. Ben and I could use a good typesetter."

We sorted and pasted poems and articles into the computer for the next two hours. Finally Bernie stood and stretched. He checked his watch. "Almost time to meet the gang. Are we at a stopping place?"

I saved the material, shut down the computer, and we headed to Elsworth's and our murder investigation.

Chapter 26

I Should Be CEO

Everyone settled around the table like high-ranking members of the board. I looked at all the well-worn faces. Which one of us was the DMSO? Chief Murder-solving Officer? I figured Elsworth, with his background, as secretive as it was, earned that title.

I supposed I would be the head of information collecting – that sounded better than secretary.

Maggie would be Human Resources, LeeAnne Entertainment Coordinator. That left George and Bernie. George could be COO - Chief of Operations, but what about Bernie? We didn't need a financial officer, we didn't have any finances.

"Helen!"

At the sharp voice, I shook my head and came out of my reverie. "What?"

"Where were you?" Maggie asked. "El asked you a question and you stared off into space with a silly grin on your face. Is something wrong? Are you ill?"

Yup. Maggie would be perfect in HR.

I laughed. "I looked around this conference table at all of you and tried to decide where you all fit in this investigating organization."

Everyone looked at me puzzled.

I held out my hands. "Think about it." I placed my hands on my chest. "I could be the CEO ... "

"Wait a minute," Maggie interrupted. "Why should you make yourself CEO? LeeAnne and I have been right there with you since the beginning of this crazy escapade!"

"Yeah, but I was the one who made the business cards that got us started."

"Whatever." Maggie sat back and crossed her arms over her chest. "Who else is on this board of yours?"

"Well, I think Elsworth should be the designated CMSO."

"What's a CMSO?" El laughed.

Chief Murder Solving Officer," I answered.

"Humph," Maggie groused. "I'm surprised you didn't give yourself that title, too."

"No," I smiled at her, "Elsworth gets that title because he has access to information we couldn't find on our own."

Maggie nodded. "That makes sense. What positions do you have planned for the rest of us?"

"You're definitely HR because you're good with people. You steer me back on course when I get off on tangents."

I could see she was beginning to come around. "I tell you what, let's make this a limited partnership with you, LeeAnne, and me as equal partners."

I glanced at everyone. "George could be CEO; he's the executive in our bunch."

Bernie spoke up. "LeeAnne did such a good job coordinating

that talent show a while back, she would be entertainment coordinator."

I nodded. "And I guess if I can't be CEO, I'll be CIC – Chief Information Collector." I held up my legal pad and fanned it at in front of them. Everyone agreed that was very appropriate.

"What about Bernie?" LeeAnne asked. "He's the only one who doesn't have a title."

Bernie held up his hands. "I'm content to be an Indian in this powwow. It seems as though we have plenty of chiefs already."

George stood and cleared his throat." As the designated CEO, I suggest we table this discussion for now and let our CMSO have the floor. All in favor please raise your hands."

We all chuckled at his formal request, raised our hands, and turned to Elsworth.

He nodded. "I spoke with my friends about the James's. It may take a day or two to get any information from that source." He pointed his finger in my direction. "Helen, do not set up a meeting with them yet. I want to know exactly who we're dealing with before you approach them."

I saluted. "Got it. I've already been cautioned by our new head of HR." I grinned at Maggie and she smiled.

My phone jangled in my purse. I pulled it out. Caller ID indicated it was Vincent Armitage. I answered and laid the phone on the table. "Yes, Mr. Armitage. How may I help you? First, let me tell you my phone is on speaker so my friends can hear you. It will save me having to repeat what you tell me."

"That is fine, Mrs. Patterson. I understand."

"Why the sudden call?"

He continued. "I just received a very disturbing call from

ReeAnn. Did one of you ladies tell her about Constance Armitage's death?"

We all gasped. "Definitely not, Mr. Armitage!" Maggie said.

"Someone did. Whoever it was told her that a person very close to her – her grandmother - had died and they thought she should know."

"It wasn't any of us, I assure you."

Elsworth spoke up. "Elsworth Lumley, here, Mr. Armitage. I'm sure it wasn't the police either. That's not the way they handle things. Did ReeAnn say whether the voice was male or female?"

"Female. She said a lady called. She did not recognize the voice."

"Can you think of anyone who may have made that call, Mr. Armitage?" Elsworth asked.

"No. I have no idea who would do such a thing."

"Well, if you think of anyone, let us know."

"I will. Also, Mrs. Patterson, ReeAnn wants me to come see her, but she made a request. She would like for you, Mrs. Warner, and Mrs. Taylor to accompany me. Could you possibly manage that? I told her if it is alright with you ladies, we could come tomorrow morning before her mother goes to work. I'm sure Cynthia needs to be a part of the conversation."

Maggie spoke first. "Yes, we'd be glad to."

"What time?" LeeAnne asked.

"I can pick you up at ten. I told her I would be there by 10:30. Cynthia leaves for work before noon."

We agreed and he thanked us and hung up.

My phone rang again before I could return it to my bag. This time Reesie's name popped up. I answered and put the phone on speaker again.

"Hello, Reesie. How are you?"

I heard a sniffle.

"What's wrong, Sweetie?" Maggie asked.

"Someone called me and told me my grandma was dead and I should be sad," she wailed.

"I'm so sorry. What can we do?"

"I need Ariadne! When am I going to get my friend back? I'm sad. I know she's sad too, without me."

I pushed the phone closer to Maggie and LeeAnne. They were better at the TLC stuff than I.

LeeAnne spoke. "How about I give Detective Metcalf a call right now. Miss Helen, Miss Maggie, and I are coming to see you tomorrow. I'll see if the detective will let us bring Ariadne back to you. How does that sound?"

Another sniffle, then a quiet, "Okay. You promise?"

"I promise to try really hard. See you tomorrow. Goodbye, Sweetie."

Before they could hand the phone back to me, it rang again. "What's with all these calls? Usually my phone only rings when one of you calls to bug me."

Maggie picked it up. "Blocked number," she said and handed the phone to Elsworth. He laid it in front of me. "Put it on speaker again. Helen, you speak. Everyone else stay quiet."

"Hello," I said. "Who is this?"

"An Armitage representative," the overbearing voice said. "You have been asked repeatedly to stay out of the Armitage's business. I am making that request once more, and strongly suggest you take heed."

"Or what?" I hollered. "Exactly what do you intend to do if I don't 'take heed'?"

"In that case," the threatening voice continued, "things could get very unpleasant for you."

"What kind of threat is that?"

A click and silence indicated the caller had disconnected.

"The nerve of that woman," I seethed.

Bernie left my side and returned with a glass of ice water. "Here, drink this and take a deep breath – or several deep breaths."

Until I reached for the glass, I hadn't realized how upset that call had made me. I grabbed the glass with shaking hands, took a big gulp, and set it on the table.

Bernie took my hand. "Now, how about those nice, deep breaths."

I placed my free hand on my chest and did as he asked.

Finally LeeAnne spoke up. "Good, your face is regaining a more natural color. Wow! That was intense! What do you think it was all about?"

My eyes surveyed the faces around the table. Elsworth had his arm around Maggie. Obviously, she was nearly as upset as I about that call.

"Helen, do you feel up to answering a few questions?" he asked.

I nodded. Bernie still held onto my hand, and I didn't attempt to remove it.

"Was that the same voice you heard the last time?"

I nodded.

"For obvious reasons, we can rule out Mrs. Armitage."

Everyone laughed half-heartedly.

He continued. "Could the voice have been Evelyn James, Mr. Reddy's secretary?"

"No," I said. "Evelyn didn't sound that hateful. Besides, her voice is in a higher range. I'm sure this was not Evelyn James. I think this is someone close to the Armitage's."

"In that case, we have an unknown in our mix of suspects." He slammed his fist down on the table and we all jumped. "I don't like unknowns. They put too many variables in an investigation!"

Wow! The mystery caller had even managed to fluster our cool Mr. Elsworth Lumley.

Bernie pushed his chair back and stood up. "Sounds like we ought to close the meeting for today. Everyone is out of sorts." He helped me to my feet. "Would you do me the honor of dining with me, Madame?"

I took his arm. "Well, it is supper time and we're going in the same direction. We may as well go together."

LeeAnne snapped her fingers. "I have the perfect board assignment for Bernie!"

We all turned to her.

She held out her hands. "CHC!"

"Exactly what is a CHC?" I asked.

"Chief Helen Calmer," she laughed.

Bernie grinned. "Yeah, I can do that!" His myopic blue eyes looked into mine. "That is, if she'll let me."

I could feel my face flush and my ears burn red. I practically dragged him to the door as my friends all cheered behind me.

Chapter 27

Ariadne Comes Home

I was in a foul mood the next morning. My sleep had been haunted by ringing phones and disembodied voices shouting, "This is going to get very unpleasant." Obscure threats tend to unnerve me.

I finally got up and sat at the table checking my notes and rearranging my rainbow of suspect cards. Elsworth was right, our mystery caller had definitely brought questions to our investigation. We needed to be very cautious and keep our eyes and ears open. The trouble was, we had no idea who to watch out for.

I dressed and staggered down to breakfast. I needed coffee, and lots of it! I was the first one to the table. Coffee in hand, I sat down and fanned my rainbow of cards out around me. Bernie showed up next, then LeeAnne, and finally Maggie and Elsworth joined the group.

Maggie raised her eyebrows at the sight of the suspect cards. "I thought mealtimes were off-limits for talk of murder."

I gathered up the cards, rubber banded them, and dropped them into my bag. "Sorry. No one else was around. Those phone calls yesterday kept me up half the night. I thought maybe I'd see something we'd missed if I stared at these cards long enough."

She nodded and patted Elsworth's arm. "You and El. He did the same thing last night. I threatened to hide them…"

El spoke up, a sheepish grin played on his lips. "Actually, she threatened to *burn* them if I didn't get away from that murder board."

We laughed and she shrugged. He draped his arm over her shoulders and gave her a kiss on the cheek. "She was right. That mystery call unnerved me, too."

I guess I wasn't the only one obsessed with this case.

"Should we tell the police about the mysterious caller?" LeeAnne asked. "Her message sounded like a threat, no matter how veiled it was. Oh, by the way," She added, "I talked to Detective Metcalf about getting Ariadne back for Reesie. He said he would come by her place this morning while we're there. He wants to speak with Vincent Armitage again, anyway."

"Yes," Elsworth agreed. "We need to inform Detective Metcalf and Captain Justice, even though with so little information, there's not much to tell them."

George sat down beside LeeAnne. "Good morning everyone. I agree with Elsworth. The phone call needs to be entered into police records.

"Helen, Maggie, and I will be seeing Detective Metcalf this morning. We can fill him in on the phone call."

"Good," said Elsworth. "I'll give Captain Justice a call. I only wish we had some idea who the woman is, and what her relationship is to the Armitage's."

We tabled our discussion and dug into our breakfast of eggs, turkey bacon, and wheat toast. Even LeeAnne and Maggie, who generally disgusted me with their morning meal of fruit and yogurt, shared in the repast. Afterwards, we three gals made plans to meet at the front of the building a little before ten.

Punctual as the last time, Vincent showed up promptly at 10. He opened the passenger and back doors of his roomy Lexus and I jumped into the front seat.

Maggie shook her head as she and LeeAnne climbed in the back. Leeanne leaned forward and explained to Vincent that the Captain would be meeting us at the shelter to bring Reesie's bunny home.

"That is wonderful. ReeAnn has been very distressed. Perhaps having Ariadne back will help calm her." A sad smile crossed his lips.

"By the way," I asked, "have you thought anymore about that mysterious caller?"

He didn't take his eyes off the road. I noticed, though, that his hands suddenly had a death-grip on the steering wheel. "No," he said, "I have no idea who the caller might have been. If I find out it is someone in my employ, I assure you they will be terminated immediately! I wasn't even aware that others knew about my relationship, or that I had a daughter."

"It's difficult to keep those kinds of secrets," LeeAnne said. "People always have a way of locating skeletons in your closets – especially if you have money or fame."

He sighed. "I suppose that is true." He glanced at her through the rearview mirror. "You speak as though you have experienced some of those closet-poking people."

"Many times," she sighed.

She didn't offer any more information, and far be it from me to bring up her fan-dancing past. I hadn't thought about that aspect of LeeAnne's life since she became a part of our lives, and I would challenge anyone who dared to speak badly about her.

"How do you suppose the woman got both my phone number and Reesie's?" I asked. "That is, assuming it's the same person."

He jerked his head toward me and said, "Someone has called you, also? What did she say?"

"Only that she represented the Armitage's and things could get very unpleasant if we didn't back off from harassing the family."

He pulled up to the shelter, parked, and looked me in the eye. "I assure you, Mrs. Patterson, that woman, whoever she is, does not legally represent my family!"

His hands shook as he disengaged his choke hold on the steering wheel. "I will find out who is behind this!" He slammed his hands against the wheel, and we all jumped.

"Be careful," Maggie said, and patted his shoulder. "These people have killed twice already."

"These *people*?" He shouted. "You think there is more than one?"

"We believe so, yes. We're going to discuss the calls to Helen with Detective Metcalf this morning," Maggie added.

I looked out the car window. "Speaking of the good captain, there he is now."

The policeman crossed the lot with the determined stride of a man in charge. It might have been intimidating, except for the bright blue gift bag in his hand. We exited Vincent's car and he tipped his hat. "Ladies, Mr. Armitage. Good to see all of you."

Vincent shook his hand. "The ladies said you have some questions, Captain. I also have some questions for you."

Metcalf nodded. "My questions will only take a few minutes. You go first."

Vincent filled him in on the call to ReeAnn, and asked what measures were being taken to assure her safety.

Metcalf, in turn, assured him the call certainly did not come from his office. As for ReeAnn's safety, he had men patrolling the area frequently.

LeeAnne told him our concerns about the anonymous calls to my phone. "We felt they should be added to the police report, even though we have no idea who made the calls, or why. Mr. Armitage – Vincent – assured us the woman did not represent his family."

Metcalf took a note pad from his pocket and scribbled the information on it. "I will certainly add it to the report." He turned to Vincent. "Now, Mr. Armitage, could I speak privately with you for a moment?"

Vincent checked his watch. "Will this take long? I promised ReeAnn I would be here to see her by 10:30."

"No, no. Just a couple of questions." Metcalf took Vincent's arm and led him away. I shrugged. "Guess it's a private conversation. Let's go wait on the porch."

Reesie ran out the door as we approached and threw her arms around LeeAnne and Maggie. She looked up anxiously into LeeAnne's eyes. "Did you get her? Did you bring Ariadne home?"

She checked both LeeAnne's and Maggie's hands for any sign of her bunny.

LeeAnne pointed to Metcalf and Vincent engaged in conversation. "See that gift bag the captain is holding? I'm not sure, but I think Ariadne might be in there."

The little redhead started to run but Maggie caught her by the shoulder. "Give them a minute to talk, okay? They're having a grownup conversation."

Her smile faded, but she continued to bounce up and down on her toes. "Okay, but I hope they hurry!"

At that moment the captain turned, smiled, waved to her, and held up the gift bag. As the two men walked our way, he said, "I have someone here who says she missed you very much."

ReeAnn bolted down the steps and ran to them. "Is it really Ariadne?"

"Why don't you check and see?" He smiled as he handed her the bag. She tore into it, pulled the stuffed rabbit out, and hugged it tightly to her chest.

Vincent put his hand on her shoulder. "What do you say to the captain, ReeAnn?"

"Oh, yeah, I forgot. Thank you, thank you, for bringing Ariadne home!" She turned and ran back to introduce us to her friend.

As the men ambled toward the building, the door flew open. Cindy Walberg stood in the doorway, hands on hips.

"Okay, Vincent. What's this all about? Who called and upset my kid?"

"Our kid," he sighed.

"Right," she scoffed. Her voice spoke words of anger, but the look that passed between the two of them spoke volumes of hurt and regret.

Chapter 28

You Could Always Abdicate

There was an awkward pause, Cindy glared at Vincent, he held her gaze, and the rest of us adults fidgeted. Finally ReeAnn broke the silence. "Look, Mom, the policeman brought Ariadne home!" She held the bunny above her head and twirled around so we could all see.

"That's nice, honey. Take it inside and put it away," Cindy ordered.

Reesie hugged the stuffed animal close. "But she wants to stay with me," she whined.

"Okay, okay." She scowled at her daughter. "But what did I say about whining?"

"Don't whine. It's not ladylike," The child said.

"Right. Now you folks all come into the house so we can have a chat."

She turned and led us into the sitting room. ReeAnn held tight to her bunny in one hand and LeeAnne's hand in the other. Cindy told her daughter to bring some chairs from the dining area and we all settled onto the uncomfortable furniture.

ReeAnn sat on the arm of the couch, her father on a wooden chair to her right, LeeAnne and Maggie on the couch to her left.

Cindy addressed the captain. "What's this all about? Does it have something to do with the dead guy who had ReeAnn's toy?"

Reesie opened her mouth to argue, but a look from Cindy made her clamp her lips shut. She hugged the bunny closer and whispered in its ear. It appeared she and her mother had definite differences where Ariadne was concerned.

Captain Metcalf spoke. "We aren't sure, at this time, what the connection might be, or if there is any. But we will be looking into the possibility. I've been in contact with Captain Justice in Savannah."

Cindy posed her next question to Vincent. "Alright, who died? ReeAnn said the person on the phone told her it was her grandmother, but you told me your mother was dead. And my mother drank herself to death years ago. Just who is this mystery grandmother?"

Vincent shifted in his chair and put his arm over his daughter's shoulders. He cleared his throat and began his explanation. "My father remarried a few years ago. Her name was Constance. She died last week, under, uh, questionable circumstances."

Cindy's face fell. "Oh, I'm sorry, Vincent."

He held up his hands. "Don't be sorry. She was not well liked. In fact, it's the family's belief she only married my father for the prestige and the money." The weight of his words hit him, and he looked into Cindy's eyes.

"Now do you understand why I wouldn't marry you? I'd never be accepted by your family."

She burst into tears and Reesie looked from her mother to Vincent. "Did you make Mom cry?" she asked.

He shrugged and draped his arm over Reesie's shoulders. "I suppose I did. But that was definitely not my intent."

His eyes searched the room for some help to quell Cindy's tears. Finally he spoke again. "Cynthia, you are not anything like that woman! I have never known you to take advantage of anyone. Why, you will barely allow me to do anything to help you and ReeAnn. And, Lord knows, I would move mountains to make life easier for the two of you."

Her crying eased and she looked across the room at him. "I can make it on my own!" she said defiantly.

"Yes, you can. I have watched you make it on your own for the last eight years," he sighed. "But you don't have to!" A tentative smile played on his lips. "You are a very stubborn lady."

She opened her mouth to speak and he held up his hands again to stop her. "Please don't take that the wrong way. I admire that stubbornness. You are the strongest woman I have ever met. It is that strength that caused me to first fall in love with you."

LeeAnne put her hand in Reesie's, and Maggie's face showed pure satisfaction as she smiled at me.

Cindy glanced at Vincent then cast her eyes down. "This isn't some fairytale," she mumbled. Her lower lip trembled. "In real life, love doesn't conquer all."

Vincent turned and smiled at his daughter. "Your mother is a wonderfully stubborn woman, ReeAnn."

"Is that a good thing?" she asked.

He laughed. "It is a really good thing. And I am sure you will grow up every bit as strong as she."

Cindy looked embarrassed. "Can we get on with this? I have to leave for work soon. Just to be clear, this dead woman, whoever she was, has no connection to my kid."

Vincent looked her in the eyes and said, "Our kid, Cynthia.

ReeAnn is my child, also. But you are correct that Constance had no connection to the two of you."

"Then how did that person get ReeAnn's phone number?" She pointed a finger at him. "Was it you?"

"Absolutely not! You gave your permission and I have phoned ReeAnn on occasion. But I did not at any time give anyone else the number."

"Excuse me, Mr. Armitage – Vincent," I said. "Has anyone else had access to your phone? Is it possible someone might have scrolled through your contacts to get ReeAnn's number?"

After a long pause he answered. "Uh, no. Not that I can recall."

He abruptly changed the subject and reached into his jacket pocket. "I brought a new phone for ReeAnn, if you will allow her to have it. He handed it to Cindy. "As a precaution, I had her old phone disconnected. She will receive no more threatening calls, you have my word. I took the liberty of programming three numbers into the phone; yours, mine, and Mrs. Patterson's."

Cindy dropped the phone into her smock pocket.

Reesie jumped up and ran to her mother. "Can I have my new phone, Mom. Please?"

All eyes were on Cindy. She reluctantly took the phone out of her pocket and handed it over. "Alright. But remember, this is for emergencies only. Don't call and bother people. And don't answer calls from any unknown numbers. Understand?"

Reesie nodded her head and grabbed the phone. "Yes, Ma'am." She ran back and plopped down beside Vincent. "Thank you, uh, Mr. Armitage, Sir. Thank you for the new phone. And it's blue, my favorite color!"

"You are very welcome. And, if it is okay with your mother,

you may call me Vincent." He gazed expectantly at Cindy and she nodded.

He smiled down at Reesie. "Oh, and I also loaded a math and spelling game on your phone. The man at the store said it is both fun and educational."

Cindy frowned, and he added, "Be sure to follow your mom's rules, and do not play on the phone all the time. Can you do that?"

"Yes, Sir," She nodded, as she turned on the phone and began to scroll through the apps.

Cindy stood. "If there's nothing else, I need to get ready for work."

Seemed as though we had been dismissed. We all stood to leave. Reesie hugged LeeAnne and Maggie, then walked over to me. I patted her on the head and said, "Call and send me your new number... in case you lose your bunny again."

She smiled. "Okay." She threw her arms around my waist. "You're a really good detective – just like Encyclopedia Brown!"

"Uh, thanks."

The detective smiled at me. "High praise, indeed," he said as he patted the little redhead's shoulder. He looked at her. "Take good care of Ariadne, okay?"

"Yes, Sir."

Lastly, she timidly approached her father and reached out her arms. He squatted down and enveloped her in a hug. "You can call me anytime," he said. He glanced at Cindy. "As long as your mother says it is okay."

Cindy silently nodded again.

He stood, pulled a monogrammed handkerchief from his pocket, and wiped it across his face. "There must be some pollen in the air stirring up my allergies."

"Yes, I'm sure that's it," smiled LeeAnne.

He cleared his throat. "Shall we go, ladies? I will drop you at your apartments, then I must head back to Savannah."

Detective Metcalf followed us to the car. "I'm depending on you ladies to not interfere with this investigation. Whoever is behind this is very dangerous, and I don't want to have to worry about your safety."

"Yes, Sir," said Maggie.

"You don't have to worry about us," agreed LeeAnne.

As we walked to the car, my friends seemed wrapped up in their match-making mode. Personally, I thought the encounter between Vincent and Cindy had been a sickening sweet display of emotions. As much as my friends wanted to push them together, I wanted to solve these murders.

And, for starters, I had a couple more questions for Mr. Vincent Armitage!

Vincent opened the back doors for Maggie and LeeAnne while I took my place in the front passenger's seat. He drove in silence, the only sound in the car the tapping of my gel pen against my legal pad. Maggie and LeeAnne began to engage themselves in discussion of the little redhead's excitement on the return of her 'friend'.

"Seeing ReeAnn's face light up was priceless," LeeAnne said.

"Yes," agreed Maggie. "I've never been as happy about our investigating group as I was today. I feel as though we did something really special."

LeeAnne leaned forward and addressed Vincent. "ReeAnn loves that little rabbit. It's her physical connection to you. She was devastated when she lost that connection."

He cleared his throat. "I had no idea until today how much the gift meant to her. Perhaps Cynthia will allow me to be a bigger part of her life once this mess is cleared up."

"It may have taken this mess, as you call it, to help Cindy see how much you really care for her and Reesie," Maggie added.

He sighed. "Perhaps you're right. I only hope it didn't drive a further wedge into an already precarious relationship."

He turned to me. "You have been quiet, Mrs. Patterson. What is going on in that problem-solving brain of yours?"

"Who? Me?" I pointed my pen ahead. "Please keep your eyes on the road."

He smiled and faced forward. "Yes, Ma'am. What is on your mind?"

"See, Helen," Maggie said, "you're an open book. Even people who hardly know you can see right through you."

"Hmph! You're mixing your metaphors, again. You don't see through an open book - you read it!"

"Right," she laughed. "And you're trying to change the subject. Tell Vincent what's on your mind."

"Alright, I do have a couple of questions. First, who was the woman lurking in the background at your step-mother's gala?"

Vincent's hands gripped tighter to the steering wheel. "I want to be perfectly clear about one thing, Mrs. Patterson, Constance Armitage was not my step-mother. She was merely my father's wife. She never had any intention of being anything other than that, nor did I want or expect her to be.

"But that does not answer your question. You will have to be more specific. To what woman are your referring? I don't recall seeing anyone lurking at that self-serving production of Constance's."

"The woman stood behind you at the back of the stage. She

was blonde, about your step... Mrs. Armitage's height and build, and she wore a red dress similar to Constance's. She had her arms folded across her chest and, I might add, she didn't look any happier to be there than you did."

A grim smile passed his lips. "Ah. That must have been Catherine. She's Constance's younger sister. Constance hired her as her secretary – or assistant – I'm not sure what her job description was. She mostly followed Constance around and did whatever the Queen Bee told her to do – bring coffee, lunch, take her clothes to the cleaners, answer the phone, make appointments. From my observation, Constance treated her much the same as she did everyone – her sister was someone else to be stepped on to get where she thought she belonged – at the top, looking down on the rest of the world," he spat out.

"Ouch," I said. "Was the sister resentful? Do you think she may have killed Constance?"

Vincent thought for a moment before answering. "No, I cannot see Catherine as a killer. She idolized her sister. But, she may have been the person who called ReeAnn. She was very distraught and may have wanted someone to share in her pain."

I nodded. "That was my second question. I could tell you were holding something back when I asked if anyone else had access to your phone. Were you thinking of Constance's sister?"

He glanced at me then turned his eyes back to the road. "You *are* very observant, Mrs. Patterson." He smiled. "As ReeAnn said, you are a good investigator – almost as good as Encyclopedia Brown."

"Yeah, I'm flattered. But you didn't answer my question."

He sighed. "No, I was not thinking of Catherine; it was my

cousin David. He asked to borrow my phone recently. He said he had to make a call and his phone needed to be charged. It's probably nothing, but your question did bring the incident to mind."

LeeAnne spoke up from the back seat. "Since the person who called both Reesie and Helen was a woman, that lets your cousin out."

"Unless," said my logical friend, Maggie, "he gave ReeAnn's phone number to someone else."

Nothing else was said until Vincent pulled into the parking area of Golden Harvest.

"Thank you for taking the time to go with me," he said. "It meant a great deal to ReeAnn. I can see she has grown quite fond of you ladies. If you don't mind my saying, I think she has adopted you as surrogate grandmothers." He sighed. "It's unfortunate she never got to know her real grandparents."

LeeAnne patted his shoulder. "That's not your fault."

"Oh, but you're wrong. It's entirely my fault. I was unable to see the situation from Cynthia's point of view." He let out a bitter laugh. "It's the curse of being born into money. Cynthia was right. You begin to believe because you have it, money can fix everything."

"I wouldn't know," I said. "I've never had money."

"Exactly!" Vincent shouted. He sighed again. "That's what I couldn't understand. Until today, I couldn't see how difficult that transition would be for Cynthia. She is correct – there are those who would not easily accept her. And not only my family – the whole elitist, snobbish hierarchy would look down their collective noses at her. She would hate that – and by association, come to hate me for putting her in that position." He rested his head on the steering wheel, his whole body appeared to deflate at the realization.

LeeAnne and Maggie leaned forward with reassuring pats and comments. I sat and reconsidered my previous assessment of the rich and famous. Vincent Armitage didn't fit my preconceived notions. He really seemed to care for Cindy and the little redhead.

"You could always abdicate," I said when Maggie's and LeeAnne's reassuring comments had reached an end.

He lifted his head and turned toward me. "Pardon?"

"You know – abdicate. Like Prince Edward did when he wanted to marry Wallis Simpson. He decided love was more important than being King of England."

I opened my door and exited the car. Maggie and LeeAnne, stunned into silence for once, looked from me to Vincent and followed suit.

He nodded and cleared his throat. "Thank you again, ladies." He checked his watch. "I have an important meeting in Savannah. I really must be going."

"Humph!" I said as he drove off and we entered the building. "I guess he's not ready to abdicate."

"I'm not so sure," said LeeAnne. "At the very least, you gave him something to think about."

"Yes," agreed Maggie. "That was brilliant. LeeAnne is right. You gave Vincent a lot to think about." She playfully punched my arm. "You're getting the hang of this matchmaking."

"Yeah, maybe. That doesn't mean he'll act on the suggestion. Nor does it ensure Cindy will accept it if he does."

Chapter 29

The Champ Got KO'd

We met the guys in the dining room for lunch, Maggie and LeeAnne both still swooning about having helped their love connection along.

"…and Helen actually suggested Vincent could abdicate his position for Cindy," LeeAnne gushed.

"Abdicate?" George laughed. "Vincent Armitage isn't a king."

"No," said Maggie, "but he is Savannah royalty. And, in Cindy's eyes, that's pretty close."

Elsworth took a sip of his tea and asked, "How did Mr. Armitage take that suggestion?"

"Ha! He didn't say anything!" I scoffed. "I don't think he's ready to give up his throne any time soon."

Maggie placed her hand over mine. "You don't know that, Helen. Why do you always have to be so negative?"

I removed my hand from under hers and picked up one of the chocolate macadamia cookies that posed as dessert. "Somebody has to play devil's advocate. You and LeeAnne are so caught up in trying to make those two fall in love, you've lost sight of reality."

She folded her hands on the table and whispered, "That's not true." She raised her head, jutted out her chin, looked at me and spoke louder. "Vincent and Cindy *do* love each other, whether you can see it or not. They are both miserable playing their roles – Cindy the hard, I-can-do-it- alone person, and Vincent wanting to help but not knowing how to go about it."

I opened my mouth to argue but she stopped me. "After meeting with Cindy and ReeAnn today – and your little abdication speech – I believe he recognized the underlying problem. He can't fix his relationship with money. LeeAnne is right, you gave him a lot to think about."

"Yeah. But, like I said, it remains to be seen how that will play out." I grabbed another cookie and pushed my chair back. "I'm going back to my apartment to transcribe my notes from this morning. We still have a couple murders to solve."

Maggie spoke up. "Helen, did you not hear Detective Metcalf tell us again to not interfere in his investigation?"

I latched onto one more cookie. "Yes, but that never stopped us before. We're not interfering in his investigation – we have our own investigation going. Besides," I said as I rescued the last of the cookies from the plate and dropped them all into an empty pocket in my new bag, "I have a vested interest in this case. People have called and threatened me – or us – if you haven't forgotten. And I don't like being threatened!"

Bernie, always my defender, stood and linked his arm in mine. "Mind if I come along? I'd like to know how our case is coming."

Elsworth stood and helped Maggie to her feet. "As a matter of fact, I have some news to report also. How about we all meet at my place at three o'clock?"

"Why not now while we're all out?" I whined.

"Because," he said, "Frodo needs an outing. And," he added, "Maggie and I have some things to discuss."

Maggie looked into his eyes and frowned.

Uh oh. What if this was going to be the big let-down – the 'I'm sorry, but I think we should just be friends' speech. If so, and he hurt my friend, there might be one more body for Captain Metcalf to deal with!

I hoisted my bag onto my shoulder and stomped down the hall with Bernie double-timing it to keep up.

"What's your hurry, Helen? Did something get you spooked?" he asked as he caught my arm. "Slow down. You're breathing hard and your face is as red as if you've been out staring into the sun."

We stopped at my door, I grabbed my chest and gasped to catch my breath.

Bernie took my key card and opened the door. "C'mon. Sit down and tell Uncle Bernie what's bothering you."

I plopped down at the table and dropped my bag on the floor. "It's Lumley," I said through clenched teeth.

"Elsworth? What on earth did he do to get you all riled up? You seemed fine and then suddenly turned into an Olympic sprinter." He sat down beside me and took my hand.

"He said he needed to have a talk with Maggie," I shouted.

Bernie tilted his head and furrowed his brow. With his cute little bow tie, horn-rimmed glasses, and that pensive stare, he resembled a diminutive college professor. His puzzled frown indicated he was attempting to determine what his student's answer had to do with the question he had asked.

"Okay," he finally said. "But I believe Elsworth's exact quote was, "Maggie and I have some things to discuss.""

"Same thing," I groused in my defense.

"Why does it upset you so much?" he asked. "They discuss lots of things."

"Well, Maggie had no idea what he was talking about. I saw the look on her face."

"And again I ask: Why does it upset you."

"Because he's probably going to give her the, 'Let's just be friends' speech, and that will break her heart!"

Bernie nodded and patted my hand. "I see. You want to protect your friend. What would you say if I told you I believe your worry is unfounded?"

"I'd say prove it!"

"I guess I can't actually prove it. What I can tell you is that Elsworth speaks very fondly of Maggie. In fact, outside of talk about this murder mess, Maggie is his main topic of conversation when we're together. He mentioned the other day while we were golfing, that he can't believe his good luck that someone as beautiful and intelligent as Maggie actually cares for him. Does that sound like he's getting ready to dump her?"

I relaxed a bit. "I guess not. I'm only looking out for Maggie. She and I have been friends since we were five years old, and I don't want to see her get hurt."

He chuckled. "Might I offer an alternate suggestion without being tossed out of here on my ear?"

I raised an eyebrow. "What?"

"Perhaps your concern is more that Elsworth will replace you in Maggie's eyes."

I pulled my hand out of his. "Absolutely not!"

I thought for a moment and said more quietly, "Maybe."

I wrung my hands together. "Do you think that might happen?" I whispered.

He smiled and pulled my hands to him. "To quote another beautiful lady, 'Absolutely not!' You can't be replaced. I know

Maggie's heart is big enough to encompass both you and Elsworth – not to mention the rest of our group."

I smiled and nodded. "You're right. She loves everybody. And everybody loves her. Why just today the little redhead…"

Bernie frowned and I sighed. "…Reesie ran out of her house and gave Maggie and LeeAnne big hugs. Vincent said she thinks of us as surrogate grandmothers. Maggie and LeeAnne were thrilled."

"How about you?"

I shrugged. "Not so much. But Maggie and LeeAnne never had kids, so the idea of a granddaughter has some appeal."

"I can understand that," he said.

"Yeah. They skipped the hassle of raising teen-agers and got right to the fun of spoiling a grandchild." I chuckled. "I saw a refrigerator magnet once that read: 'Grandchildren are our reward for not killing our children.' I can relate to that."

"Yes, that sounds like you. How many grandkids do you have, anyway?"

I closed my eyes and tried to visualize my off-springs' off-springs. "Twelve – no eleven, I think. I kind of lost count somewhere along the way. They're mostly all grown now. Steve's daughter, Ellyn is the only one who visits."

"Ah, yes, I met her. She helps you with your computer problems, right?"

I nodded, bent down to retrieve the cookies from my bag, and placed them on a paper towel in the center of the table. "Would you like something to drink with these refreshments? I have instant coffee, tea, and tap water."

He laughed. "My kind of lady. Only the best desserts for our high tea."

241

Bernie's presence had relieved me of some of my stress. I leaned over and gave him a peck on the cheek. "Thank you for being my friend."

Realizing my bold move, I cleared my throat and grabbed my legal pad. "Would you like to hear what we found out today?"

"Sure," he said as he grinned and rubbed his cheek.

Bernie propped his elbow on the table and rested his head on his hand. He smiled, his hand covering the tell-tale place I had planted that unexpected kiss.

Flustered, I transcribed what I recalled from our talk with Vincent, and filled Bernie in on what we had discovered.

"Do you think Mrs. Armitage's sister is behind the phone calls?"

"Probably. But Vincent wasn't sure how she got our phone numbers. He did seem pretty sure she wouldn't harm Constance. According to him, Catherine was really torn up about her sister's death."

"And what about his cousin, David?" Bernie asked.

I scribbled Catherine's name on two of the file cards before answering. I put one in my stack and one in my bag to place on the murder board at El's.

"I'm sure Vincent thinks David is up to something. He might confront him in an effort to keep any sordid details behind closed doors. That's what *they* do."

Bernie raised his eyebrows. "They?"

"Yeah, they," I said, waving my hands in the air. "The rich. The privileged. They make their own rules."

"Ah." He nodded. "And we're not talking about Vincent anymore, are we?"

I shrugged. "Maybe not." I dropped my pen and ran my hands

through my hair. "Ooh! Ambrose hadn't entered my mind for fifty years, and now he's there every time I turn around. No man should have that much power!"

Bernie took my hands and pulled them out of my hair. "You do know he only has that power because you allow it, right?"

"Huh?"

He caressed the backs of my hands with his thumbs, and I looked down at the unusually soothing action. He continued. "In every other aspect of your life, you are the strongest woman I have ever met. You face life head on."

He squeezed my hands and my stomach did flip-flops, like little butterflies tickling my insides. "Now, don't get angry when I say this, but it seems to me that when it comes to this Ambrose person, you allowed yourself to become a victim. You let him make you believe he's better than you."

He stopped, sighed, and continued. "That is *so* not true. You are equal to all the Ambrose-Whatever, the Third's in the world. You just have to believe it!"

He raised my hands to his lips and kissed each one. My breath, and any retaliatory words I might have considered, caught in my throat. I realized he was right. As of right now, I would never again be a victim of Ambrose Pennington the Third.

I jumped up and almost kissed him again. "Bernie, you're the best thing that's happened to me in a long time!"

He stood, a huge grin played on his lips. "Now, that is the best thing *I've heard* in a long time!"

He gestured toward the door. "Shall we head to El's place? Maybe he and Maggie will fill us in on their discussion."

"Right. I'll be able to tell immediately from the look on Maggie's face whether or not it was good news. If she looks unhappy, Mr. Elsworth Lumley and I will be going a few rounds."

I gathered up my things and tossed them in my bag. "Be ready to play referee in case things get out of hand."

"Okay," he said as he closed the door behind us. "Should we stop by my place and get my boxing gloves?"

I laced his arm in mine. "I don't think that will be necessary. Just whistle."

He bounced along beside me. "I can do that."

"I know you can. I've heard your stirring rendition of 'Everything is Beautiful'. Unfortunately for me, so did Maggie. And she won't let me live it down."

His grin was infectious, and I laughed in spite of myself as we stopped at Elsworth's door.

"Are you ready, Champ?" Bernie asked as we knocked.

"Yup." I took a deep breath as the door opened and framed my dearest friend, Maggie, with a thousand-watt smile on her face.

Bernie whispered as Maggie led us into the room, "Looks like El took this round, Champ."

We followed as she seemed to glide across the floor. I whispered as much to Bernie and asked if it was my imagination.

"Nope," he whispered back. "She's definitely gliding."

"Come, sit, you two," Maggie gushed. "Now that everyone's here, we can get started."

I glanced around the room. Sure enough, everyone else had already seated themselves around Elsworth's conference table. Even Frodo, the one-eyed earring-stealer, was present.

Maggie reached down, picked him up and snuggled him against her shoulder. As she scratched behind his ears, something caught eye.

"Maggie Taylor, you didn't!" I shouted.

She patted Frodo once more and sat him down. "Didn't what?" she chuckled. She held out her left hand that sported the largest diamond I'd ever laid eyes on, then placed her hand on Elsworth's shoulder. "El asked me to marry him."

LeeAnne jumped up and grabbed Maggie's hand to get a better look at the ring.

George congratulated Elsworth, and Bernie grinned and said, "It's about time!"

Elsworth beamed, but had the good sense to keep his mouth shut and allow Maggie to have the spotlight.

I sat there in stunned silence. Things around here were changing too fast, and I wasn't sure I liked the direction they were heading.

Chapter 30

What Have I Done?

Our meeting turned out to be pretty much a bust after Maggie's announcement. Aside from adding Constance's sister's name to our murder board, not much got accomplished. The conversation turned to wedding plans, showers, and bachelor parties.

I finally had my fill of the non-productive get-together. I stood and announced, "I'm going back to my apartment. When y'all are ready to discuss our case, give me a call!"

Maggie's face took on that look of disappointment I'd come to know well over the years. Everyone else stared at me as if I'd just stomped on baby chickens. I'd done it again, I'd hurt my oldest and dearest friend's feelings.

Finally Bernie stood and took my hand. "Helen, I know you're anxious to continue our investigation, but today is a special day for Maggie and El. Let's celebrate with them." He nudged me with his elbow. "What do you say? Let's drink a toast to life and love and new beginnings. Besides," he whispered, "those bodies aren't going anywhere."

He pulled out my chair and I plopped back down. "You're right," I sighed. "I'm sorry, Mags. I am happy for you. But as much as I have considered you might take this step, it was still a shock to me."

She relaxed and smiled. "I know, Helen. I should have been more thoughtful of your feelings and not hit you with this without warning." She placed one hand on mine and held Elsworth's with the other. "I was so excited I had to share the news with my nearest and dearest friends." She smiled. "Sorry if our announcement waylaid your murder investigation."

El cleared his throat. "How about we reconvene this evening about 7:30 to discuss our progress? Right now I'd like to propose a toast."

He poured flutes of bubbly champagne – the real deal, not our usual fake stuff – and we all took one. He raised his glass. "To Maggie Taylor who, happily for me, said yes to my proposal."

"To Maggie," we all chimed in as we lifted our glasses.

I raised mine again. "I'd like to add to that toast." I tipped my flute toward Elsworth. "May you always make Maggie happy. And, if you don't, you'll have to deal with me."

Everyone chuckled.

El smiled and touched his flute to mine. "Duly noted."

We all clinked glasses and drank to the happy couple.

Supper that evening consisted of lots of congratulations and hand shaking. It seemed the 'Over-the-Hilton' grapevine was in fine working order.

Janine Hopgood rushed over and gave Maggie a very big, very dramatic hug in full Snow Queen fashion. Since our trip to Stone Mountain awhile back, where Janine and I had been accused of murder, she had not been such a thorn in my side. That could be because she had been reacquainted with Jon Burkowitz, the guy who had been in love with her since grade school. Go figure. There's no accounting for some people's taste.

Some of the ladies, though, were not as happy. Maggie had removed the most eligible bachelor at Golden Harvest from the dating pool. Ora Price and her groupies had pursued Elsworth to the point of stalking the poor man. They even joined an exercise group so they could corner him in the workout room. To his credit, he hadn't acknowledged their attention. In fact, he didn't even recognize their intent until I pointed it out to him.

I caught Ora and some of her cronies eyeing Bernie, as if he might be the next-best candidate for their affections. I couldn't resist an unnatural urge, and laced my arm through his. He smiled up at me and patted my hand. I glanced down and my cheeks turned red.

What had I done? Had I just put my claim on Bernie Cox?

After all the well-wishing and cold stares, supper went quietly. The vow to abstain from our investigation, not to mention my faux pas with Bernie, caused me to be antsy, and so uncomfortable, I rushed through my meal. I only managed to slow down long enough to savor the dessert of tart-sweet rhubarb cake.

At last Elsworth helped Maggie to her feet and announced they would meet us at 7:30 as planned. They left to take Frodo for his evening stroll. My guess was they wanted some alone time after the revealing afternoon and all the attention it brought.

George and LeeAnne took off together in the opposite direction. That left me awkwardly still seated with Bernie to my right. I pushed the cake crumbs around on my plate until the kitchen staff gathered it up and left me with nothing to fiddle with.

I couldn't look Bernie in the eye; I peered down at the empty place on the table where my cake plate had recently been. "I guess

I should go back to my place and organize my notes." I pushed my chair back and, using the table for support, managed to hoist myself upright.

Bernie stood and pushed our chairs up to the table. "Would you like some company?"

I threw my bag over my shoulder. "Uh, no thanks. Like Maggie and Elsworth, I think I need a little alone time."

His look of dejection lasted only a moment – long enough for me to realize I'd been the cause of someone else's hurt feelings. Great! I was two-for-two. My eyes glanced over Bernie's head and around the room. There was no one left for me to upset and make it a trifecta. I stood there in silence until Bernie smiled, patted my arm and said, "Okay, Lovely Lady, I'll see you at 7:30."

At 7:25 there was a knock at my door. I peeked through the peephole at a smiling Bernie Cox and opened the door with a sigh.

"You're early," I grumbled. I stepped back and he meandered in.

"I know you like to be prompt," he said. "Did you manage to get your notes organized?"

"More or less. I spent a lot of time thinking about Maggie and Elsworth. Do you think they'll leave Golden Harvest when they get married? I moved into this place because of her."

"Ah," he said.

"And what does that mean?" I asked as I tossed my file cards in my bag, threw it over my shoulder, and headed for the door.

"Do you think this might be the tricycle syndrome all over again? Do you again think you're being replaced?"

I glared at him and then down at the floor. "You mean I'm making this about my happiness instead of Maggie's."

He took my arm. "Are you?"

"Of course not!" I stopped and thought for a moment. "Well, maybe." I sighed. "Okay, yes, I guess I am. Maggie is my oldest and dearest friend – my best friend."

He squeezed my arm. "I could be your second-best friend."

I smiled and kissed him on the cheek. "How about my third-best friend? LeeAnne has to come before you. After all, she and Maggie are on my business cards."

He grinned. "I'd be honored to take third place."

We continued down the hall to Elsworth's apartment. Bernie strolled confidently; I shuffled along beside him and wondered exactly what I had just committed myself to.

Everyone showed up promptly at 7:30 and sat around Elsworth's conference table. El set up our murder boards. I handed him the new cards I'd printed, and he rearranged them before he spoke. I retrieved my legal pad from my bag and prepared to take notes.

He nodded and pulled some papers from his pocket. "I received some information from my sources about Mr. and Mrs. James." He unfolded the papers and scanned them before relating the information. "They have been married for ten years, but apparently the relationship has been a rocky one. There have been allegations from both sides of infidelity. Jerry James has a past record of assault. Nothing too serious, mostly bar fights involving someone making passes at Evelyn."

"It sounds like he's the jealous type," George commented.

"Evidently they both are. Evelyn James also has a short temper." He checked his notes. "Accounts say she gave him a black eye one time for smiling at a waitress."

He laid the papers on the table. "There's more, but I think you get the picture. Both parties are volatile and seem relatively unstable."

We all nodded at that assessment.

"One more thing my sources noted," he said. "Evelyn appears to be the brains of the duo. Jerry pretty much does what she says."

"Would that include telling him to murder someone?" LeeAnne asked.

George put his arm over her shoulder. "Who knows what a person may be capable of – especially an unstable one."

Bernie spoke up. "But what's the motive? Why would either of the James' kill the P.I. or Mrs. Armitage?"

"Like Helen said, these things usually boil down to love or money," Elsworth answered.

We batted that idea around for a while. Mr. Reddy certainly didn't have any money, but there was the fact Jerry James wasn't happy with the attention his wife gave the man.

Constance Armitage had money through her deceased husband, but we couldn't make a connection between her and the James's.

I drew a graph on my legal pad with I.M. Reddy and Constance Armitage at the top. Under the P.I.'s name I placed the James', and wrote David and Vincent under Constance's name. I shook my head. Nothing connected or made sense.

"Did your 'sources'," I air-quoted the words, "find any further information about Constance or her sister?"

"As a matter of fact, yes." Elsworth picked up the papers, flipped to a new page and read: "Constance Armitage, nee Boder, and Carolyn Boder, are the oldest two of nine children born to Ellie and Carl Boder of Elmo, West Virginia."

Bernie whistled. "Nine kids. That must have been difficult. I've been through Elmo. It's a very poor, rural area. If Constance lived there, I can understand why she wanted out."

"Right," agreed Elsworth. "Her father was a coal miner before being disabled in a mining accident. Constance ran off to the big city to be 'discovered', according to neighbors, when she was sixteen. It's said she had beauty and ambition and eventually found a stage in the Miss West Virginia beauty pageant where she placed third. She found an agent and used the notoriety from the pageant to seek a career in modeling. That led her to a job modeling jewelry for Armitage Fine Jewelers."

Maggie placed her hand on her chest. "Rags to riches. A true Cinderella story."

"Perhaps at the outset," added Elsworth. "But it seems her name became linked with both of the older Armitage brothers, as well as innuendoes of other liaisons – both before and after tying the knot with Vincent's father. The common consensus was she settled on Nathaniel Armitage because he held controlling interest in the family business. His younger brother, Nicholas, was quite the ladies' man, with a need for speed, as they say. He died in an automobile accident. Constance and Nathaniel had been married a little over two years when he suddenly passed away."

"Wow! If she got control of the company, that puts Vincent back on the top of my list for her murder," I said.

"Ah, but that's not the case. Nathaniel Armitage's will stated the company and all holdings passed to his son, Vincent, and any and all heirs he might have."

"While we're tossing ideas around," said George, "what if someone found out about Vincent's illegitimate daughter and wanted to get rid of those 'any and all' heirs? Perhaps that's why the P.I. had staked out Reesie and her mom."

"You mean to discredit Vincent, void the will, and stage a take-over of the company?" LeeAnne asked.

George nodded. "Something like that. I've been in the money business for a lot of years. I've seen the terrible ways families behave over inheritance."

"Okay, that moves David up on my list," I said.

"I agree. We need to find out more about the James's and David Armitage," said Elsworth. "But nobody," he looked directly at me, "needs to go off alone to confront any of them!"

All eyes in the room stared at me.

I held my hands up in surrender. "Okay, okay. Point taken. I promise not to do anything dangerous."

Maggie crossed her arms in front of her and glared at me. "Or stupid!"

I glared back at her as I pushed my chair away from the table and crammed my legal pad into my bag.

Everyone else laughed to break the tension as they followed suit and stood to leave.

Elsworth shrugged. "I guess that concludes our meeting," he said. "Everyone have a nice evening."

Bernie dropped me off at my apartment. "I'd ask if you wanted company, but you're sending out serious Greta Garbo vibes!"

I looked at him, laughed, and dramatically threw my arm across my forehead. "Ah, 'I just want to be alone'. Thanks for noticing, Bernie. You know, you can read me nearly as well as Maggie."

He smiled and nodded. "I'll take that as a compliment."

I patted his shoulder. "It is. And you're right. This case has my mind in a muddle. I think I need to prop my feet up, read a book, and forget about it for a while."

"You mean one of your mysteries? Isn't that going to get you more wound up?"

I shook my head. "No, because there's always a solution. The bad guy – or gal – always gets found out in the end."

"That makes sense." He reached up and gave me a peck on the cheek. "Good night, Beautiful."

"No one beautiful here," I called to his back. "But thanks."

He didn't look back, merely waved nonchalantly over his shoulder as he strode on down the hallway.

Rhubarb Cake

1 cup shortening
2 cups flour
1 ½ Cups brown sugar
1 tsp. baking soda
1 Egg
1 tsp. salt
1 cup sour milk
1 ½ cups chopped rhubarb
1 tsp. Vanilla
1 cup nuts (optional)

Preheat oven to 350 degrees. Mix all ingredients well. Pour into 9 by 13-inch greased pan.

Mix together and sprinkle on top:
½ cup white sugar
1 tsp cinnamon.
Bake for 30 minutes.

Chapter 31

Going to the Dogs

I tossed and turned most of the night. Bernie's 'Beautiful' comment had thrown me for a loop. Seemed as though he'd been doing a lot of that lately. And, despite Elsworth's and Maggie's admonishments, I was determined to confront Vincent's cousin, David, and the James's. David might be a problem. I'd already set a plan in motion to get the James's to Loblolly where I could interrogate them. I'd call them tomorrow to come discuss the "case' I'd told them about, and offer them cash up front to sweeten the deal. I finally drifted off into an uneasy slumber for a couple of hours.

Morning and breakfast came much too early, but I forced myself up, dressed, and ran a brush through my hair. I had to talk to LeeAnne. She had a car, and I needed a ride and a driver to my appointment with the James gang.

Everyone headed in different directions after breakfast. I looked down at my empty bowl and realized I had no idea what I'd eaten.

Bernie still sat beside me. "You seem more distracted than usual this morning, Helen. Is something bothering you?"

"Uh, no, I'm fine", I stammered as I stood to leave.

He grinned. "I don't believe that for a minute."

I put my hands on my hips and glared at him. "Why would you think I lied?"

"Because you just ate yogurt and fruit for breakfast and didn't complain about it."

"What!?! I ate yogurt?"

He laughed. "You certainly did."

"Yuck. I must be more tired than I thought. I really didn't sleep well last night." I turned to go and, with a big yawn for emphasis, said, "Guess I'll head back to my place and take a nap."

I lumbered away feeling the effects of my lack of sleep. Possibly the yogurt I had ingested at breakfast also contributed to my general malaise. I saw LeeAnne ahead of me in the hallway and called to her.

She turned and smiled. "Good morning, Helen. How was your breakfast?"

"Don't even go there! I can't believe you and Maggie allowed me to eat yogurt. If I ever do that again grab the infernal stuff and slap me back to my senses. And if that doesn't work, call 9-1-1 because you'll know I must be having an episode!"

She patted my arm. "Calm down, Helen. I get it. Grab yogurt, slap, call 9-1-1. So," she added, "what has you distracted today?"

I let out what I hoped was a resigned sigh. "I think this investigation is getting to me. I thought maybe we could get out of this place for a while. What are you doing this afternoon?"

"Nothing, as far as I know."

At that moment Maggie walked up, Frodo cradled in her arms. "What's going on, girls? Where do you need to go?"

"Uh," I stammered, "I need to get out of this place and get

some fresh air. I think I'm losing my perspective on this investigation. I can't quit thinking about it. "

"Right," she replied. "You did seem far away at breakfast,"

LeeAnne leaned over and stage-whispered in her ear, "Don't mention the yogurt."

She nodded and scratched the dog behind the ears.

"Say," I cut in, "why don't we all go to that dog park you raved about? Furball could have a run and we could get out and not have to think about these murders for a while."

She huffed, "His name is Frodo. And why do I get the feeling you have an ulterior motive? The Bark Park doesn't seem like a place you would suggest we visit."

"Jeez. Do you think I have an ulterior motive every time I make a suggestion?"

"Yes!" they answered in unison.

I ignored the jab. "The three of us haven't done anything together lately. Wouldn't it be nice to escape from this place and do something different?"

They both eyed me. I added, "We could go to Mabel's later for peach cobbler. And maybe discuss your plans for getting Vincent and Cindy together."

That got their attention. We settled on the Bark Park at one o'clock, with a side trip to Mabel's afterward.

Maggie held the furball... Frodo... up and said, "How about it, little one? Want to go to the park?"

He barked and licked her nose. She laughed, "I guess that's a yes."

I called Reddy's number as soon as I got back to my apartment in hopes Evelyn could still be reached there.

She picked up on the fourth ring. I could tell from her

mumbled "Hello." I had wakened her. I reminded her who I was and asked if she and Jerry were available to discuss my 'case' at one thirty today. After another round of her arguing why it couldn't be handled over the phone, she finally acquiesced when I sweetened the deal with a promise of $5,000 up front.

I gave her the location of the dog park and she said they could find the place with GPS. "How will I know who you are?" she asked.

"I'll be the big, white-haired woman wearing a hibiscus outfit and walking a small dog. I'll be easy to spot."

"Fine! Bring cash," she said and ended the call.

Her abrupt dismissal was worrisome, but I decided she wasn't a morning person, and shook off my uneasiness. The dog park would be a safe enough place to meet, with lots of people out giving their mutts some fresh air. If these two were our murderers- and the more I thought about it, the more convinced I became – surely they wouldn't try anything sinister in a place full of witnesses. I crossed my fingers just in case.

Maggie, with Furb...Frodo, poking his head out of a small satchel she had tossed over her shoulder, LeeAnne, looking as lovely as ever, and me in my hibiscus outfit, met at one and headed for our little outing.

Maggie offered to ride in the backseat and spread out a small blanket for her Furbaby beside her. "I'm still curious why you volunteered to go to this dog park. You don't even like dogs."

"That's not entirely true," I said. "The fact is, I don't like animals in general. Dogs, cats, rodents – one is no worse than another. Is there something wrong with wanting to get some fresh air? I knew you couldn't say no to taking Fur...Frodo for a nice little afternoon stroll. And I needed some exercise, too."

"Ha!" she answered. "Now I know there's something fishy going on. I've never heard you utter the words 'I need', and 'exercise' in the same sentence, before, unless it was to say, "I don't need exercise!"

LeeAnne smiled and kept her silence until we turned into the parking lot of the park. Signs pointed directions: large, medium dogs to the right, small dogs to the left. There was only one other car in the lot. Not what I'd expected.

We exited the car. Maggie put Frodo on his leash, carried a small bowl for water, and pocketed some small plastic bags.

"Maybe you should carry a Go Bag for that dog, like new mothers for their babies," I joked.

"That might be a good idea. Maybe I could find one to match his little carrier."

"You mean the dog purse you had him in?" I asked. "That's embarrassing. Look at the poor thing, you've taken away all his masculine dignity."

We entered the park through a gate that had posted: Small dogs only. No bigger than fifteen pounds.

LeeAnne laughed. "I don't think his masculinity is in doubt. He's sniffing and marking his territory on every tree and shrub in sight."

I glanced around the park. It was a nice setup, centered in a clearing surrounded by trees. I could hear traffic noise in the distance. Around the perimeter, a chain link fence separated the large dogs from small ones. An exercise area with ramps and hurdles was situated on each side, with water fountains, grassy spaces. There was even a sandy stretch for the mutts to relieve themselves, with receptacles to dispose of those plastic waste bags at either end. Stone benches for resting while your dog ran, completed the décor of the enclosed space.

I looked around. "I assumed there would be more people out on this beautiful day."

"A lot of the people who use the park come early in the morning or later in the evening before and after work," Maggie said.

"And," she added, "I've noticed the majority of them have big dogs. Older people like us have smaller dogs."

"Yeah, I saw the signs at the front. I guess that's so the big dogs don't eat the little ones. I hope the…" I clamped my lips shut.

"You hope what?" Maggie asked.

I'd almost let slip I hoped the James's would be smart enough to enter the small dog side of the park. I thought I'd mentioned I had a small dog. "Uh…I hope no big dogs get loose and chase Frodo," I stammered.

"Not much chance of that," said LeeAnne. "I only saw one other car in the parking lot. It seems pretty quiet in here."

I glanced around. "Yeah. Maybe too quiet."

Chapter 32

Stand-off with the James Gang

At that moment, two people stepped out of the wooded area to our left, moving like characters from a bad B movie. The man, dressed in jeans and a plaid shirt, ran a nervous hand through his disheveled hair that looked as though it hadn't seen a comb lately. He glanced around furtively in all directions like a fox caught in the henhouse and looking for an escape route.

The brassy-haired woman beside him, whose dark roots needed a touch-up, walked with more confidence. Her skirt hiked up too short and her shirt didn't come close to covering her midriff. She eyed the three of us. "Well, well, Mrs. Patterson. You were right. You *were* easy to spot."

"Hello, Evelyn." I nodded to her skittish companion. "Jerry, I presume."

Jerry inched forward a step. Frodo barked and growled, and the man stopped in his tracks. Maggie held tight to Frodo's leash. "Helen, who are these people?"

I pointed to our visitors. "Right. I should make introductions. Jerry and Evelyn James, meet my friends, LeeAnne and Maggie. Oh yeah, the little furry one is Frodo."

"Does he bite?" Jerry stuttered.

"Why? Are you afraid of dogs? If you don't do anything to upset him or make him angry, he probably won't bite." I shrugged my shoulders. "But, who knows? Maggie's only had him for a week. Maybe he's vicious, and that's why he got turned in to the shelter. You shouldn't make any fast moves, just in case."

Evelyn spoke up. "Get over it, Jerry. The broad's trying to scare you."

"Hey, don't call me a broad. Jerry asked me a question and I was honest with him. I really don't know what that dog is capable of."

"Ha!" she said, "I've seen rats bigger than that thing. It doesn't scare me."

I wondered exactly where she came from where rats were as big as small dogs, but my thoughts were interrupted by Evelyn.

"What's your con, lady?"

"Con? What do you mean?"

She popped the wad of gum in her mouth. "Don't play dumb with me. I looked you up. You and your cronies here," she pointed to Maggie and LeeAnne, "fancy yourselves some kind of senior-citizen crime fighting superheroes."

I stood there dazed. "You looked us up? How?"

"On the internet, Helen," LeeAnne said. "You can find anyone or anything on the net."

"Yeah, lady. Now what are you up to?" she sneered.

I merely had a few questions about your boss, I. M. Reddy."

"What about him?" she said as she popped her gum again.

I turned to Jerry who was still eying Frodo suspiciously. "Were you jealous of Mr. Reddy, Jerry?"

"Shut up, lady," Evelyn spat out. "Jerry, don't listen to her, she's trying to get in your head."

Jerry hesitated, so I continued. "Evelyn paid a lot of attention to your boss, didn't she, Jerry? Cooked for him, did his laundry. Took his suits to the cleaners. She paid a lot more attention to him than to you, didn't she?"

Maggie and LeeAnne both stared at me as if I'd jumped on the crazy train.

Evelyn hissed again, "Just shut up, lady!"

Jerry's gaze flicked to her and back to me. He pulled a pistol from behind him and swung it around. "Everybody shut up! I can't think!" he screamed.

LeeAnne and Maggie gasped; Frodo growled.

"Is that the gun you used to kill Mr. Reddy?" I wondered if my voice sounded as shaky as I felt.

He waved the weapon around in the air as though confused about how it got into his hands and who he was going to shoot with it.

His eyes glazed and he pointed the gun at me. "Yeah, I shot the jerk. He used me and Evelyn both."

I momentarily considered correcting his grammar, but decided correcting a crazy guy waving a gun around might not be a good choice.

He ran his free hand through his hair, which did not improve his appearance. This was not a sane man. He pointed the gun in Evelyn's direction. "She ate it all up. 'He needs me', she said. Well, I needed her, too, but she was too busy waitin' on him hand and foot."

He paced back and forth like a caged animal.

Evelyn screamed, "I said to shut up, Stupid!"

Jerry threw his hands up to cover his ears. "I'm not stupid," he shouted back.

Maggie gasped, and LeeAnne spoke in her calming actress voice, "Can everyone calm down a bit? This noise is going to draw attention."

I looked around and wondered who it would draw attention to. There didn't appear to be another soul in the park, unless they were walking their dogs in the woods.

With more bravado than I felt, I asked, "Did you kill Constance Armitage, too?"

He staggered and waved the gun toward Evelyn, again. "Nah. That was her."

Wow! We had both our murderers right here in front of us. I looked at my friends, who had gone pale. How were we going to get out of this mess? Maggie was right. I hadn't thought this through.

"Now look what you've done, you crazy, stupid man. What're we going to do now?" Evelyn shrieked.

Jerry's glazed eyes looked at her, confused.

"You just told these old biddies we committed two murders." She shrugged and pointed our way. "Guess you'll have to kill them."

"All three of us?" LeeAnne whimpered.

"Unless you can come up with a better plan," Evelyn laughed.

With shaking hands, Jerry raised the pistol and took one step toward us. Maggie shuddered. Frodo pulled away from her and charged Jerry as though he was a 200-pound guard dog. He ran around and around, bit Jerry's ankles, and managed to tangle his leash around the terrified man's feet. Jerry screamed, fell to the ground, and his gun went flying.

"Do I have to do everything?" Evelyn fumbled in her purse for a weapon as Captain Metcalf and two deputies walked out of the woods, all with guns drawn.

"Police! Ma'am, drop your purse and put your hands on your head.

"Collins, cuff her. Eddie, retrieve the gentleman's gun."

Jerry James, feet still tangled in Frodo's leash, screamed, "Get this vicious mutt off me!"

The detective, his gun now trained on the terrified man, grinned and called out, "Mrs. Taylor, would you please come rescue your dog from this fella?"

The officers hauled the two away and Detective Metcalf stood in front of us, one hand on his now holstered firearm, his other pointing directly at us. "What in the world were you thinking?" He barked.

At that moment, Elsworth, George, and Bernie sauntered out of the woods. Maggie and LeeAnne ran to be embraced by their fellas, while I still stood there shaking and looking befuddled.

I finally calmed enough to speak. "Why did you show up here?" I asked. I could almost see steam coming out of his ears as I added, "Not that I mind. You and Frodo kind of saved the day. Thank you."

"You're welcome," he grumbled. "Weren't you told to stay out of this investigation?"

Bernie stepped up and took my still-shaking hand. "I can clear up part of your question, Helen. It seems Maggie was convinced you were up to something suspicious. She told El about your little adventure. He talked to George and me and we decided to fill the good detective in."

"Right," Detective Metcalf added. "When the gentlemen brought to my attention all the information you had gathered, I decided it would be wise to check out this little escapade."

Now I was getting furious. "Were you skulking back there in the woods all the time that lunatic was flashing that gun back and forth?"

"Not the whole time, but plenty long enough to hear those two confess to two murders."

He raised his eyebrows and chuckled. "I must admit, it was difficult to keep these three gentlemen," he panned our little group, "from running out here to rescue you ladies before we got the information we needed to nail those two."

"Heaven forbid our safety should get in the way of your confessions," I huffed.

"You can thank your gentlemen friends for sharing the documentation that convinced me you all had some pretty glaring evidence."

I grinned. "Thank you, Detective."

"Mrs. Patterson, this in no way is me giving you ladies free rein to run around willy-nilly and put yourselves in danger. Our department isn't big enough to follow you around and try to keep you out of trouble."

Bernie put his arm around my waist. "We gentlemen will try to do that job for you, Detective."

He laughed and shook Bernie's hand, then did the same to Elsworth and George. "Bring the ladies to my office for interviews tomorrow. Right now, I've got to get these two booked and call Captain Justice in Savannah to come pick up Evelyn James. The Constance Armitage murder was in his jurisdiction. He will most likely have some questions for the ladies, too.

"Now, please take them home. They've had an exciting day."

Bernie and I turned to the rest of our group. Now that the

adrenaline had passed, my legs felt like a couple of wet sponges. LeeAnne was pale and shaking, and Maggie's cheeks had a flush that most likely signaled a spike in her blood pressure.

"Sorry I dragged you two out here. I thought this would be a safe enough place to meet. I figured there would be lots of people around."

"You thought?!" Maggie spat out the words. "Helen, you Didn't think! You dragged us out here because you were obsessed with this case. You didn't take into consideration that the James's might try to kill us. You put us all in danger – and for what? To prove to yourself you're better than the police?"

Tears streamed down her face. Elsworth embraced her and kissed her forehead. "I know you're upset and angry with Helen, my love. But the fact that you told me about this scheme of hers says you, at some level, knew she might be up to something dangerous."

She sniffled and nodded her head in agreement, but still refused to look at me.

George stepped up and took charge. "Okay, folks. Let's head home. Elsworth drove, so he, Maggie, and Frodo, the real hero of the day, can ride together. Leeanne, if you'll allow me, I'll drive the rest of us.

She handed him her keys. Maggie and Elsworth turned to leave. Neither said another word. With a heavy heart I blindly trudged to LeeAnne's car, my eyes filled with tears I was afraid to shed.

Bernie caught my mood. "She'll forgive you. Give her some time."

Somehow this myopic little man was always able to read my thoughts. I took his hand. "I hope so."

Epilog

etective Metcalf and Captain Justice both interviewed us and let us off with a stern warning to stay out of their police business. They were kind enough to fill us in on the motives for the murders, plus some Savannah gossip.

It seemed Jerry, jealous of Reddy, followed him to Loblolly and confronted him about Evelyn. They fought, Reddy pulled a gun and in the struggle, it went off and killed him.

Evelyn, in the meantime, was determined to collect the money owed to Reddy by Constance who had hired him to dig up dirt on ReeAnn and Cindy Walberg. She went to the gala in search of Constance to make sure she paid up. They scuffled in the ladies' room. Evelyn pushed her. Constance somehow grabbed hold of Evelyn's earring as she fell backward. She hit her head on the sink, and Evelyn fled.

Captain Justice said he had heard rumors that David Armitage, Constance and Catherine had been embezzling money from the Armitage fortune. Of course, those couldn't be corroborated because the rich dealt with their own.

One week later, Vincent called to see if we could accompany him again to meet with Reesie and Cindy. Maggie had almost forgiven me – at least she was talking to me again, which was a start.

We coordinated a time and set preparations in order. Vincent showed up promptly at two o'clock. He sported a casual shirt and tie, dress slacks, and a huge black eye.

"Wow," I said. "Float like a butterfly, sting like a bee. What happened to you? And what does the other guy look like?"

His scratched face turned scarlet. "No floating or stinging – except perhaps these gouges on my face." He gave a nervous cough and continued. "I confronted David about pulling information from my phone to harass my daughter. He said he and Constance's sister had thought it up." Vincent's jaws and fists clenched and he went on. "He laughed and said my side piece and my illegitimate child had no right to the Armitage fortune. No one can use those words about Cynthia or my daughter – NO ONE!"

He took a deep breath and almost smiled. "I hit him! Neither of us is much of a pugilist. The fight was more like a couple of pre-pubescents duking it out on the playground. However, certain indiscretions on his, Constance's, and Catherine's parts, have come to light. He is now persona non grata in the Armitage family, and is no longer a problem."

"Oh my," said Maggie.

"How romantic," added LeeAnne.

He pointed to his bruised face. "I'm afraid to have Cynthia see me like this, but ReeAnn insisted I come today, for some reason. Cynthia is going to think I'm nothing more than a street brawler."

"You might be surprised," cooed Maggie.

"Yes, women like men who fight for their honor," added LeeAnne.

"Do you think so? I've tried everything – offered to pay for her to go to nursing school, to buy ReeAnn's school clothes, put them in a nice house…"

I slapped his shoulder. "Those are all 'things'. Despite what you rich people believe, money can't buy happiness. And it most assuredly won't buy Cindy!"

"But I love her. I want her to have the best."

"The best money can buy?" I asked.

"Yes. Of course."

I brought my hand up to slap his shoulder again and he flinched. "You still don't get it," I hollered.

Maggie took my arm and pulled me aside. "Let me try, Helen. You don't need to go all tough guy on the poor man. He's been through enough."

She took Vincent's hand. "What do you think Cindy needs?"

He thought for a minute. "Well, she wants to be a nurse, and she wants ReeAnn to have a safe place and nice things."

I sighed and Maggie held up her hand to silence me.

"No," she said. "Those are wants, not needs."

Vincent looked at each of us, puzzled.

LeeAnne spoke. "Cindy needs someone who will love her for who she is – fun, lovable…"

Vincent cut in. "…impetuous, free-spirited, impulsive. All those attributes about her I fell in love with."

"Yes!" We all answered.

LeeAnne smiled. "Tell her that."

"It's that easy?"

I laughed. "Of course it's not that easy. But it's a start. Now come with us, and we can get you ready to see your daughter."

We led him into the dining room, Reesie ran to him and grabbed his hand. "C'mon, Mr. Armitage, we have a surprise for you!"

He took her hand and smiled. "You may call me Vincent – if your mother approves."

She turned to Cindy, who stood there staring at Vincent's face.

"Mom, is it okay?"

Without removing her gaze from Vincent, she stammered, "Yeah, sure." She grabbed his head and turned it from side to side. "You poor man. What happened to you?"

He looked into her eyes. "It's a long story. I'll tell you later when little ears aren't listening. That is, if you will allow me to take you for coffee after your shift tonight."

She blushed, nodded and cast her eyes to the floor.

Reesie took over the conversation. "Mr. Vincent, Mr. Vincent. Guess what? Our choir won regionals and we get to go to sing against a bunch of other kids in Savannah. Do you want to come hear us?"

She glanced at her mother again. "Can he come with us, Mom? Please?"

"I don't know, ReeAnn. Mr. Armitage is a very busy man… "

"I would love to come hear you sing," he said. He turned to Cindy. "Just tell me when and where, and I promise to be there."

"Okay," Cindy whispered.

She smiled tentatively at Vincent. "I apologize for ReeAnn. She tends to be a little pushy sometimes."

Vincent laughed. "Takes it from her mother. That's a compliment, by the way. I am only now beginning to appreciate that straightforward outlook on life you have always possessed."

Cindy blushed again.

"C'mon, Mom and Mr. Vincent, let me show you the surprise."

She took one of each of their hands and led them to a table decorated with wildflowers and hand-written place cards. "I picked the flowers and made the name thingies myself," she said proudly.

"It's beautiful," Cindy exclaimed.

Vincent agreed.

She propped Ariadne in the chair beside her name tag, told her mom and Vincent to find their places and sit down, please.

"Mrs. Warner, Mrs. Taylor, and Mrs. Patterson helped with the food," she explained. Then she beckoned Maggie, LeeAnne, and me to follow her. She handed us each a tray and we marched back to the table carrying plastic glasses, paper plates, sparkling grape juice, crackers, and, of course, squeeze cheese.

Cindy laughed at the layout, and the smile on Vincent's face matched Reesie's own as she sat down in the last chair.

We approached the family and wished them 'bon appetite'. "If you will excuse us, we'll leave you alone for your party," said Maggie. "The dining room is yours as long as you want to stay."

"Or until 4:30," I added. "That's when the staff starts setting up for our supper."

Everyone laughed and we made our exit.

The couple – or I should say, trio – still had a long way to go. But they might just make it after all.

The fellas awaited us outside the dining room. "How did it go?" George asked.

Maggie didn't even attempt to hide her elation at having finally gotten Vincent and Cindy together. "It was perfect," she gushed.

LeeAnne couldn't hold back a tear or two from escaping down her cheek, either.

"Yeah, yeah. How romantic," I said as I turned to head to my apartment.

Bernie spoke up. "Wait a minute, Helen. I've got something for you."

I stopped in my tracks. Maggie had her hands over her heart

and LeeAnne's eyes sparkled. *Oh no, I thought. What is he doing? Surely this isn't a declaration of love – right here in the hallway.*

I turned and sighed. "What's up?"

He reached in his pocket, pulled out a small box, and handed it to me. I gasped. He smiled, reached in his pocket again and handed identical boxes to Maggie and LeeAnne.

I stood there shaking and bewildered.

LeeAnne opened her box first. "Oh, Bernie, how sweet."

Maggie was next. She opened her box, smiled, and showed it to Elsworth.

"Go on, Helen," she urged. "See what you got."

I lifted the lid, partly relieved I wasn't singled out for some romantic gift, and partly annoyed I had to share Bernie's gifts with my friends. *Get over it, I told myself. Either you want Bernie in your life, or you don't.*

I peeked inside at the small silver rabbit charm, reached over and kissed him on the cheek. "How wonderful! A reminder of our Case of the Lost Rabbit."

"Or, Hare Today, Gone Tomorrow," he grinned.

Yes, I decided. I definitely wanted Bernie Cox in my life.

The End

www.ingramcontent.com/pod-product-compliance
Lightning Source LLC
Chambersburg PA
CBHW071119170626
46809CB00002B/430